They are the Merricks,
two brothers and a sister, restless, daring, proud.
English by birth, they came to Scotland
with their father to occupy McClairen lands.
And there each would find a love as wild and glorious
as the Highland isle they claimed as their own.
Fia, the only daughter, is the ravishing one.
Ashton, the eldest son, is the passionate one.
Raine is the second son. This is his story. . . .

The Reckless One

"MAKE LOVE TO ME," she whispered.

Love. Dear God. Yes, he wanted to make love to her, to love her, to give her some of the physical pleasure he knew this act could bring and in doing so find for himself that deeper *something* he suddenly had cause to believe existed.

Once, a decade ago, she'd saved his life. He wouldn't ever again be the cause of her anguish or her guilt. He couldn't bed her and risk ruining her future. If only she would tell him to stop . . . but she didn't.

"You have the most beautiful hands," she said. "I want to know what artistry they might work on my flesh."

Good intentions faded. His clasp on her chin became a caress. "You don't want this. It isn't going to lead to some blessed union, Favor," he rasped out. "I have nothing. Nothing at all to offer you."

"You have your name," she suggested in a whisper as fearful as it was hesitant.

"Dammit, don't you think I want to feel you under me, around me?" he ground out. "I want to drink your cries, I want to make you scream with pleasure. I want to take you. Now. Here . . ."

Dell Books by Connie Brockway

McClairen's Isle

The
Reckless
One

Connie
Brockway

A DELL BOOK

Published by
Dell Publishing
a division of Random House, Inc.
1540 Broadway
New York, New York 10036

ISBN: 0-440-22627-9

Printed in the United States of America

Published simultaneously in Canada

January 2000

10 9 8 7 6 5 4 3 2 1

OPM

For Susie Kay Law, who sat down next to me seven years ago and thus began this whole adventure. Thank you, my dearest friend.

Chapter 1

DIEPPE, FRANCE
APRIL 1760

A fine drizzle seeped from the low, gunmetal-colored sky above the prison yard. The head jailer, Armand, bounced his cudgel in his palm, his already bad mood exacerbated by having to stand outside in this weather. Well, he promised himself, he wouldn't stand in it any longer than necessary.

"Hold his cursed head down in the water till he passes out if you must," he barked at the two beefy warders straining to force the half-naked man to his knees before a water trough.

They were having little success. The man fought like the devil. He'd always fought like the devil. Ever since he'd been sent here from the prison at Le Havre, after his short-lived escape.

Armand pulled his timepiece from his pocket and

angled the face into the rush light. Five o'clock and it was already dark. Cold too, he thought, noting the vapor lifting from the prisoner's bare skin. *Damn* cold.

"Curse your misbegotten birth, hurry!" he shouted.

Madame would be arriving soon, heralded by a note received less than an hour before telling him to have ready an assortment of "exotic specimens." Spontaneous visits were unlike Madame Noir. Usually she gave Armand ample warning of her intentions—and her needs—so that he could make certain that her arrival did not coincide with that of his superiors. They would not look kindly on Armand and Madame's little arrangement.

But the perverse itch that tormented Madame this day apparently needed immediate scratching. Aristocrats, Armand thought and spat at the slick black cobbles. Who could account for their whims? If she didn't pay so well for her sport, he would have refused to see her. But she did pay.

A sudden burst of activity at the trough drew his attention. The prisoner had heeled back and rammed his elbow into the older guard's gut. The younger guard retaliated with a vicious blow across the prisoner's temple. A gash appeared above his brow, oozing blood. He dropped to his knees.

"*Non*, Pierre, you imbecile!" Armand sprinted forth, swinging his cudgel. "No marks! Drown him if you must but no marks, do you hear?"

"*Oui*, no marks," Pierre grumbled.

"And you, English *bite*," Armand said, grasping a

handful of the prisoner's hair and dragging his head up. "You had best behave."

The Englishman turned his head. Long, dark hair streamed over his forehead and a rough beard covered the lower half of his face making his features barely discernible. Only his eyes gleamed from the shadowed countenance.

"Or else what?" the prisoner sneered. "You'll kill me?" An evil smile flickered and disappeared in the dark face. "I am afraid, friend Armand, that your threats have quite lost their power to intimidate."

Startled, Armand straightened. The prisoner's gaze followed him, defiant, if edged with bleakness.

"And why is that?" Armand asked.

"You can't threaten a dead man with death," he rasped back in French gutter *patois*—the dialect of the prison. "I saw the clean clothes. Did my father send them for my execution? How sentimental of him.

"No matter. You'll not have them clean off my body, Armand," the Englishman vowed. "You'll not make one penny more off my corpse than I can—"

Pierre's fist plowed into his belly, cutting off his words.

Armand grinned. So that is why the Englishman fought so hard. He thought he was on his way to being hanged. He thought they were bathing him so that after he'd been executed they could strip clean clothes from his body rather than ones stinking of jail. They'd fetch a better price that way. Not a bad notion.

It was amusing and Armand, who rarely had the pleasure of denting this particular prisoner's self-con-

tainment, relished the experience. He motioned Pierre
to revive the Englishman.

With a grunt, Pierre heaved him over the rim of the
trough and dunked his head in the cold water. The
Englishman lurched upright, sputtering and cough-
ing—and fighting. Water streamed down his heaving
chest, leaving muddy trails on its filthy surface. Muscles and tendons corded and swelled in his lean body.
Even in the cold air the sweat beaded on the faces of
the two guards straining to subdue him.

Armand watched with concern. The prisoner had
come here as a youth, but the years had turned him
into a man, a man who, in spite of the deprivations of
prison life, still had somehow developed a formidable
physique.

This is what came of mollycoddling "political prisoners" and allowing them meat and blankets and a
room on the upper levels of the prison rather than in
the fetid subterranean chambers where most were
held. But Armand's master insisted that political prisoners be kept alive in anticipation of possible ransoms.

Armand thought it a waste—and possibly dangerous. Should the Englishman ever put bulk on that tall,
broad frame . . . *Mon Dieu*, even three warders would
have a hard time holding him. As it was, soon one of
the guards would lose his temper and start using his
fists on the prisoner's face. Madame disliked marked
faces. Armand waded into the fray, his amusement van-
ishing.

"*Merde!*" he shouted. "You guard your virtue like a
nun!"

"My virtue?" the Englishman panted, his struggles abating.

"*Oui*. She probably won't even choose you now," Armand said contemptuously.

"She?"

"Madame Noir."

The man stopped fighting, yet none of the tension left him. He narrowed his eyes on Armand. "She picked *me*? Specifically?"

"*Non*. She says foreigners. And you, *mon homme*, are one of the only foreigners left. Do not think to make her pass you by again. If you spit at her this time, I swear I will render you useless to any woman ever again."

"He is not useful to women *now*," Pierre added his voice. "Best take whatever Madame offers, *brut*. It might be your only chance to ever have a woman. Though rumor claims Madame is the one who does the 'having.' " He broke into coarse laughter.

The Englishman ignored the provocation. Armand considered him. "*Should* Madame pick you, do not think to escape," he warned. "No man has ever escaped after one of her nights of pleasure."

A glimpse of teeth flashed in the prisoner's dark face. "Me?" He shook his head. "*Non*. I simply wish to take advantage of the situation, as Pierre suggests."

Armand snorted in disbelief. "You didn't feel that way some months ago when she would have taken you."

The smile disappeared. " 'Some months ago' I still held out the hope that my father would ransom me as he did my brother. I still believed—" He broke off abruptly. After a second's silence he shrugged, a smile flashed once more in his dark face.

"I still believed in something," said Raine Merrick.

"She is unnatural!" hissed the English youth chained beside Raine. "I heard what she is. Depraved! She'll not have me!"

The boy flung himself against the manacles holding his arms spread wide against the rough stone wall next to where Raine was likewise chained. He was seventeen, or so he said. The same age Raine had been when he had been brought to France.

"She'll not use me that way!" The lad's defiance broke in a sob.

Raine ignored him, watching the cell door with cold anticipation as he rubbed his jaw against his shoulder. The pleasure of having his face clean-shaven once again was as heady a sensation as any he'd known in the past five years. Of course they hadn't let him shave himself. They would never have trusted him with a razor. Instead, they'd tied him to a chair for the procedure.

Pierre had taken particular delight in waving the dulled blade above Raine's loins but as Raine refused to react the porcine guard soon grew tired of the sport and contented himself with describing to Raine in graphic detail what "Madame's boys" endured at the hands of the veiled lady.

Raine didn't bother to tell Pierre he already knew all about Madame. She was a legend among the prisoners.

It is why, months ago, he'd spat at her feet when she'd arrived to look over her "prospects." He still bore the scars from the beating that little act of rebellion had incurred.

But at that time he'd still been certain that the years he'd already spent in this prison were somehow a mistake and that the two short weeks of freedom he'd had after his escape would soon be returned to him for the rest of his life. Almost a year passed before he'd realized his father would not be sending a ransom and that the prison he'd been sent to was a far harder place to escape than the one from which he'd come.

A desire for revenge had taken hold of Raine. He'd survived in this hellish place driven by a seething need to make his father pay. But this prison had a way of stripping a man of all but his most basic drives. Eventually his pride had withered and died as he focused all his dwindling reserves on the increasingly herculean task of staying alive.

Even the rumor that his father had ransomed Ash could not rouse his sense of injustice. By then he'd seen far worse injustices. No, Raine no longer wanted vengeance; he simply wanted to survive. And that meant escaping or dying in the attempt.

He'd die soon anyway. Few lived as long as he already had, killed by disease or illness, another inmate, or simply the slow inner corrosion that eventually found its physical expression in death.

He had one chance to escape and it depended on Madame Noir's choosing him over the other "candidates" Armand had dredged up. He looked around at the other men. Two were long-time residents: a hatchet-faced middle-aged colonist from the Americas and a slender Prussian dying of consumption. The English youth chained to the wall next to him was new, delicate, and sullen-looking.

Suddenly the door to the cell grated open. Raine peered through the gloom at the dark figure hovering in the outer corridor. His attention sharpened.

Madame Noir.

Chapter 2

Madame Noir had arrived to make a selection for her evening's entertainment.

Raine watched the black-clad figure step through the cell door. Hidden beneath a nearly opaque, ebony veil and layers of midnight-hued silk, she moved with an odd hesitant grace. A black velvet cape covered her shoulders and long black gloves encased the slender hands holding her skirts above the stagnant puddles on the floor.

Armand followed her, his face flushed and his ridged brows lowered in displeasure. Beside him shuffled a huge monolith of a man bundled against the cold, a thick cape draped over his massive shoulders and a woolen scarf wrapped about his thick neck. The eyes beneath the brim of his hat were sharp and piercing.

Silently Raine cursed the fates. Why couldn't she be accompanied by someone like Pierre? Big, but dull-witted and slow.

She turned and spoke to her man, stopping in front of the torches. The backlighting revealed her profile through the heavy veil; a slender throat, a sharp-angled jaw, a patrician nose. The men who returned from a night in her "care" swore she never removed that veil. No one had ever seen her face—even Armand—and no one knew her real name. She always registered under the pseudonym "Madame Noir" at the hotel she used for her entertainments.

She finished her whispered conversation and turned toward the prisoners. With what looked like a conscious gathering of purpose, she came toward them, her attendant shadowing her. She paused before the colonist.

"Too old," she murmured in exquisite, aristocratic French and continued circling the room. She stopped in front of the Prussian. He lifted his wet head and gazed at her with dull, hopeless eyes. "This man will die if he is not made warm," she said.

"Yes," Armand agreed uninterestedly. "A Prussian."

She remained studying the shivering man.

"But I might have a desire for a Prussian someday," she said quite calmly, and moved on.

Immediately Armand barked out an order that the Prussian be taken down, dried off, and fed. In another, one might possibly mistake Madame Noir's comments for compassion, Raine thought cynically. She moved toward the English youth.

Armand scuttled to her side. "He's new, Madame. English. Young. Feel." He chattered like an auctioneer. "Go ahead. I have never known you to be shy."

She lifted the boy's chin. His lower lip trembled.

"Very young." She sounded uncertain. "But English, you say—"

"Please! I come from a noble family. I cannot be used so!" The youth sobbed. "I am not the one you want! I am not the one—"

"*I am.*"

Madame spun around at the sound of Raine's calm voice, her veil swirling about her shoulders and settling like the dark wings of a nighthawk. She cocked her head sideways, increasing her resemblance to a small, sleek bird of prey.

"Monsieur is English?" she asked, interest sharpening her inflection.

"Aye." He watched her carefully. "English. You have a taste for Englishmen, Madame?"

Behind the heavy veil he thought he saw the glimmer of her eyes. He forced himself to stand still and turned his palms up, inviting her inspection. "I'm your man."

"Perhaps."

Armand hurried over. He grabbed a handful of Raine's hair and jerked his head back.

"Here, Madame. Come. Examine. Look. I know Madame is most careful in making her selection."

She came within a few feet. Her heated scent filled his nostrils, unexpectedly stirring his senses. A woman's perfume. Without warning, sensual images from his all-but-forgotten past ambushed him, flooding his mind, filling his thoughts.

Musk and flowers, cleanliness, and dark promise. Womanly and virginal all at once. Straining bodies, sweet aftermath. The sudden sensual memory stunned him with its force.

He closed his eyes, breathing in deeply through his mouth, tasting as well as scenting her. He hadn't been in the same room with a woman in five years, having hidden in barns and cave during his short freedom. Yet could that alone account for the thickening in his loins?

This woman was a bawd, a profligate jade, a byword for pollution, and while he'd once been a randy youth eager for most any sexual sport he'd never added perversion to his extensive list of vices.

Yet the mere scent of her stirred him.

"Touch him," Armand urged.

Did she hesitate before reaching out? Did she note the uncontrollable forward cant of his body in anticipation of her hand? Her gloved fingers brushed his naked skin. He forgot everything else.

His breath caught. He backed away. Not because he abhorred her touch. Just the opposite. Because he wanted it. Her fingertips fluttered down his chest to his belly to where his breeches hung low on his hips. He shivered, willing her hand to slip lower still, waiting for that intimate touch, aching with arousal, heedless of the spectators.

Her gaze dropped to the evidence of his arousal. Abruptly, she snatched her hand back, like a maiden.

"Madame wished a challenge?" Armand was asking. "Here is such a one. Arrogant. Young. Healthy."

"I don't think—"

"Forgive me, Madame." Her servant lumbered forward.

"Yes, Jacques?"

"I believe this one would suit very well."

Raine studied the mountainous Jacques. Since when did a servant advise his mistress on her sexual requisites? She did not reprimand him, however, but only hesitated before gesturing toward the English boy.

"Perhaps him," she said, and it sounded to Raine as though she was asking. "He is—"

"Very young," Jacques finished, his tone cautioning.

Raine ground his teeth in frustration. She had to pick him. She *must*.

"I will be whatever Madame wishes me to be." He forced the words out between his lips, surprised at how easily they came, how facilely he abdicated the last shreds of his pride. "I will do whatever Madame wishes me to do."

He held his breath.

"All right," she finally said. "I'll take him."

Jacques nodded approvingly.

"Very good," Armand said. "I'll send two guards with you."

"Not necessary," Jacques said, handing Armand a

heavy-looking velvet pouch. Raine blessed the man's self-assurance.

"But it is, Monsieur," Armand argued. "I know this man."

Madame made a dismissive movement with her hands. "Has there ever been a problem before?" she asked coldly. "I do not wish spectators at my sport. I desire . . . privacy with him."

"I understand, but Madame, you must see that if this man should escape—"

"Do you dare to press me?"

"*Non*, Madame!" Armand assured her, hauling a thick set of keys from his belt and opening the lock that held Raine manacled to the wall. "Still, I fear this one." He fastened a length of chain between Raine's manacles. "I have the solution: The guards will ride post, on the back of the carriage. You will have privacy. I will have peace of mind. This is sensible, yes?"

Armand jerked Raine forward and handed the end of the chain to Jacques.

"If you insist," Madame said, irritation vibrating from her slender form.

She stalked from the cell, her skirts rustling. Armand hurried after her, barking for the guards. Raine, who'd kept his head bowed throughout the proceedings, glanced up and found Jacques watching him.

The huge man shrugged off his cape, throwing it over Raine's naked shoulders, robbing the act of charity by saying, "I will chain you in the coach across the seat from her. If you hurt her . . . If you so much as blow your filthy breath in her face, I will rip off your head and piss down your neck. *Comprends*?"

Raine's lips curled back. "I assure you, your mistress is safe with me."

"Good. Be civil, be wise, and all shall go well for you. Better than you imagine."

Raine could not keep the derisive sneer from his face. "Your largesse undoes me. I wonder if hers will."

In answer, Jacques shoved Raine between the shoulder blades. He propelled him through the door and down the low corridor toward a flight of stairs leading up to the prison's receiving yard. There, just outside of the gates, waited a closed carriage. The prison guards were already perched on the footmen's steps at the back. Armand stood beside the open door.

Any attempt to flee now would be futile. Choking down his frustration, Raine shuffled across the yard through the open gates. Outside, he stopped, unable to help himself, and lifted his face to the weeping sky. He drew breath outside the prison walls and closed his eyes.

"Go on, son." Jacques's voice was surprisingly mild. "Get in."

Raine hefted his chains and flung them in onto the floor of the carriage. Jacques reached past him, snapping a padlock through the links and locking them to a bolt on the floor. Damn the man's caution!

Unceremoniously Raine climbed into the carriage. Across the carriage, bootheels scrabbled against the floorboards. *She'd* already entered. He peered through the dim interior.

She was almost indiscernible in her black gown and heavy veils, being tucked as she was as far back into the corner as possible.

As though, he realized, she was scared to death of him.

Chapter 3

*I*t was possible Madame Noir regretted her decision to choose him; that titillation had taken a backseat to fear.

But this woman was notorious for her *outré* appetites. The more probable reason for her ostensible fear was that it was all part of some perverse game. A game which, if Raine played it correctly, he might use to his benefit.

If he could convince her to unchain him he would be out of this carriage in seconds, losing himself in Dieppe's twisting alleys. With such thoughts, he crouched low as he entered the carriage, conscious of the part he needed to play.

Mindful of how his shoulders crowded the doorway and blocked the light, Raine slouched down onto the seat opposite her, angling himself in such a way that he did not appear threatening. He could hear her short agitated breaths, feel her tension.

Jacques called out from up top and the horses plunged forward, pitching her across the slick leather seat. Raine flung out a hand to keep her from falling.

"Take your hands off of me," she whispered.

She was not commanding him. She was pleading. As false as he suspected her trepidation to be, her simulated fear worked insidiously on him. His body reacted instinctively to the implicit submissiveness in her appeal. Was she pretending that she was an anxious virgin closeted with a ravening beast? If so, her fantasy marched closer to the truth than she could know.

It had been years since he'd felt such lust.

"Take your hand off me." Her voice quavered. He obliged, releasing her slowly, letting his hands slide down her sleeve. He did nothing to hide the direction of his gaze, allowing it to linger on the agitated rise and fall of her breasts.

Role-playing be damned. He wanted her.

"Madame," he said softly, lifting his arms and spreading open Jacques's cape, displaying his shackled wrists and naked chest, the scars of Pierre's frequent "disciplinary actions" ridging his white prison-hued skin. "As you can see, I am at your disposal, to do with as you please."

She shrank back against the deep, tufted leather seats. "You don't understand," she whispered.

"I do not," he agreed. "You will teach me, though. What *is* your pleasure, *petite* Madame? You touch; I am not allowed to touch? You arouse and then withhold the culmination of the arousal? Is that how you achieve satisfaction? Pray, do your damnedest by me. I am in a lather to be so victimized."

"Quiet!"

"Just tell me the rules of the game, Madame," he said tersely. He was more than willing to pay whatever price freedom demanded. He sank back against the seat, his aroused body flaunted for her perusal. "You have only to look to see how primed I am for whatever sport you chose," he said.

"O Lord." Her whispered epithet embodied the virgin maiden's horror of a lecherous suggestion. 'Sblood, she was a good little actress.

"I am yours." He leaned forward and gently grasped her wrist, drawing her gloved palm forth until it lay flat low on his belly. He drew his breath in on a hiss of undeniable pleasure. "Can you feel my muscles clench with the promise of that which you withhold?"

She tried to snatch her hand back but he kept it there, desperately trying to gauge the nature of his role. How much to ravish; how much to seduce. His very life depended on his ability to judge her reactions. Once, a lifetime ago, he'd been well on his way to being a master of such sensual expertise.

"I was resigned to my celibacy, Madame," he said grimly, "having long since purged myself of the tormenting memories of a woman's soft body, a woman's sweet mouth, a woman's ardent embrace. You've resurrected those, given them substance, teased me with their reality." His voice grew low and fervent. She tried to tug away, but her efforts lacked conviction. She wanted to hear this confession. Bask in it. Damn her.

He grabbed her other wrist and, heedless of her sudden resistance, yanked, tumbling her into his embrace. He hauled her into the lee created by his widespread legs. His arm snaked about her waist, the chains locking him to the floor jangling noisily.

She gasped, her hands trapped between them, pushing at his cold chest. The feel of her gloved fingers stroked his nerve endings. His heart thundered in his chest in equal parts fear and arousal.

"Cry out and I'm dead 'ere I've been of any use to you," he grated out. She was svelte and tensile as a young she-cat, her hips narrow. Even through the thick layers of her skirt he could feel the delicate jut of her pelvic bones brand his inner thighs. Her veil settled over his knees in a drift of black silk.

"Let me service you," he whispered, the line between playacting and reality blurring with the heady feel of her. His patience was wearing thin. She would find herself ravished in fact if he played this game much longer. "Let me touch you. Fondle you. Inflame in you a fire to equal my own," he purred. "Enjoy me."

He rocked lightly against her, striving to keep the anger from his voice. Anger as much with himself as with her, at the body that betrayed both his mind and spirit. "Here. Now," he said. "Let me take you. I cannot wait. Only unchain me," he ground out urgently, "and I will swive you as thoroughly as a spring stallion at his first mare."

"Let me go!" The veiled face jerked back. Raine cursed his impetuousness.

He released her arms immediately. He'd read her incorrectly, decided that coarseness would appeal to what he knew of her appetites. Instead, she'd been appalled. He was not mistaken in that reaction; no one could act *that* well.

He forced his features into a submissive expression, dropping his gaze so that she might not see how it burned. Trembling, she scrambled into the seat opposite him.

"Forgive me," he began in a hard, far from humble tone. But he'd been stretched a bit far, worn a bit thin. By this game. By her. "I should not have allowed my desires to make me so bold." His hot eyes lifted contemptuously to her concealed face. "But then, I thought you liked your captives vulgar and base. 'Tis the rumor in the prison where you purchase your toys."

As soon as the words were spoken he cursed himself again. He hadn't planned on speaking thus. The words had simply come. He sneered at his manacled wrists. He'd thought that over four years in prison had culled the impetuousness from his soul.

He waited for the inevitable; a blow across his face, an imperious call to turn the carriage around.

Amazingly, it did not come. She only squeezed herself farther back against the seat. "Sir. Please. Be still. Be quiet. The guards might hear you. Only wait, I pray you," she urged, "wait!"

"I am your creature, Madame. You have only to command me," he replied flatly. "As you well know."

They drove in silence until the carriage lurched to a halt. Raine peered outside. They were in the yard of a hotel. Beyond the three-story building, Raine could see only an occasional light in the distance. They were near the outskirts of the city. Good.

The carriage door swung open. Jacques stuck his massive head in and fitted a key into the padlock securing Raine's chain. He unlocked it, wrapping the links around his fist and jerking Raine across the carriage.

With a snarl, Raine stumbled out. Pierre stood waiting for him. An anxious-looking middle-aged man emerged from the hotel and assisted Madame Noir's descent. Together they hastened into the hotel.

"I will take him up to the room," Pierre said to Jacques. "Once there, he is your responsibility. You best make sure he is returned by first light tomorrow."

Jacques eyed the bloated French jailer with ill-disguised disgust. "Has Madame ever neglected her part of the bargain?"

"No," Pierre said. "Make sure she does not grow lax in her . . . satiation. This one is wily. Reckless. Come."

Without waiting for a reply, Pierre yanked Raine after him, leading the way to the servants' entrance at the back of the hotel. From there they climbed a flight of stairs, stopping before a linen-paneled door at the top. The door swung open and the innkeeper, bowing and smiling, backed out of the room.

Jacques grabbed Raine's arm and thrust him into the

ornately shabby room, barking at Pierre to remain outside. Raine stumbled to his knees beside a four-poster hung with dull blue satin drapes. Madame Noir hovered on the other side.

"Madame," Jacques said, eyeing Raine and holding a pistol out to her. "I will pay the jailer and his partner and return."

"Must you leave?" she asked, coming around the corner of the bed.

"I do not trust the guard to give his partner his portion and I would not have you interrupted should the jackal come here looking for his share.

"In the meantime, keep this pistol trained on him." Jacques nodded toward Raine. "If he moves, shoot him."

She took the gun, leveling it at Raine. Slowly, he climbed to his feet.

"*I* will kill him if he tries anything," Jacques promised tersely, and then, with a worried glance at Raine, he stomped from the room, slamming the door shut behind him.

Raine stared at the gun. The pistol bore looked as cavernous as the entrance to hell, which, Raine allowed fleetingly, it just might be.

Without a second's more hesitation he acted.

His hand flew out, snatching the barrel and twisting it viciously. With a cry, she released it. He grabbed her wrist, spinning her around and slamming her back against his chest, pinning her free arm to her side.

His forearm jerked her head back, pressing against her throat. It would be a simple matter to break that slender neck. With one hand he manacled her wrist, with the other he held the gun. Carefully, he released the hammer and shoved the pistol into the waistband at the back of his breeches.

"Scream now, Madame, and die now," he whispered into the veiled ear so close to his lips.

In response she began struggling fiercely, her free hand tearing at his wrist. She kicked, but her movement was hampered by the thick layers of skirt. Still, one booted heel found his instep, crunching down and drawing from him a hiss of pain.

He wrenched her head back against his cheek, bringing the concealed face near his mouth. "Cease!"

She whimpered, her struggles abating but not ending. Immediately he became aware of her buttocks pressed against his loins.

He smiled humorlessly at his body's heated attempt to subordinate reason. Since the moment she'd stepped into that damned cell, she'd bewitched him. Perhaps his years in prison had perverted his sexuality because, 'struth, she aroused him more than a thousand fantasies he'd devised to keep him company over the long years.

"Please," she rasped. "Please. Listen to me!"

"No, Madame," he whispered. "You listen. Heed me well. I will never return to that place. Not alive. And you are the means for me to keep that vow. You are *my* prisoner now."

She moaned, her face twisting away from his, the silky veil slipping against his lips. "Please—"

"Shut up," he growled as a sudden realization over-whelmed him.

He needed to kill her.

Without doing so his chances of this gambit succeeding were well nigh nil. Should he actually make it alive out of the hotel he would not last an hour if he had to drag her along with him. He didn't have time to gag and tie her; Jacques could be back at any moment. And if he left her behind, she'd raise an immediate cry. He should kill her: quickly, silently, *now*.

But he couldn't. As much as every instinct for survival demanded it, he could not kill her. In more frustration than anger, his arm tightened around her throat. She began kicking again and he lifted her, hitching her against his hip, filling his arms with the firm, supple woman.

The old devil-may-care humor that had once been the hallmark of his character awoke in response. The rash, heedless boy who'd died, unredeemed and unransomed in a French prison, was resurrected.

No, he couldn't kill her but at least he could claim something from this night. Damned if he wouldn't see the infamous Madame Noir's face.

He grasped a fistful of dense, gauzy material. "Madame, you are revealed," he said.

He wrenched the veil from her head. Hair pins scattered at their feet, their small, sharp staccato a prelude to the silken whisper of her veil fluttering to the floor. Loosened tresses, soft and heavy as damask silk, cascaded over his bare forearm in shimmering waves.

Red-gold. Antique gold, healthy and luxuriant.

Confounded, Raine seized a handful of the silky stuff and jerked her head back.

Fine skin. Creamy and utterly smooth. Blue eyes, dark blue. Near indigo. Frightened. Young. Very young.

Too young.

"Madame," he said, easing his forearm's pressure from her throat, "who the hell are you?"

Chapter 4

The girl—for certainly she was not much more than that—wrenched away, his surprise aiding her escape. She wheeled to face him and her hair came further undone, spilling about her shoulders and tangling with the jet beads decorating her bodice, the black silk a foil for the gleaming gold strands.

Black, too, were her brows. Or so nearly black as to make no difference. The contrast between them and her red-gold hair was startling. Straight, slender and severe, they lowered over the bridge of her nose. Wide, passionately full lips curled back over her pearly teeth, exposing the slight unevenness of the front pair.

"Who are you?" he demanded again.

"I have been trying to tell you!" she said. "But you . . . you idiot! Imbecile! You would not listen.

You must grab and hurt and fight before you even
know what you are doing. Thrice I asked for your patience!" She pointed a gloved finger at him accusingly.
"*Thrice*! Could you not wait? Must you try to kill me?"

"Mademoiselle," he ground out, anger quickly supplanting his astonishment at finding himself harangued
by a small, spitting she-cat, "if I'd wanted you dead,
you'd *be* dead."

In answer to this, his most threatening voice, she
flung up her arms in disgust. "Bah!" she spat. "You
English are all alike. Push! Bully! Reckless. Fine, Monsieur. If you must be reckless be reckless with your own
life, not mine and not Jacques's."

To claim astonishment would have been understat-
ing Raine's reaction. The girl quivered with indigna-
tion. Or, fear. Raine's gaze sharpened. He knew she'd
grown pale because of the color slowly returning to her
cheeks and the breath, which stirred a few strands of
gold, came in pants.

He *had* frightened her. From the very beginning.
What he'd read as a jade's deviant role-playing had
been real. She probably wasn't even cognizant of the
degradation he'd been willing to embrace in order to
escape. Hell, he thought, she probably hadn't understood half of what had gone on during that carriage
ride.

"Pray, speak, Mademoiselle. I'm a captive audience," he said, mindful of the pistol sticking comfort-
ingly into the small of his back.

He crossed his arms over his chest, noting her gaze
drop to his bare skin and skitter away as she blushed.

Dear Lord, she looked like a novitiate, Raine thought, and thus was reminded of another novitiate, a lass whose gaze burned with a far more secular fire than this one's. But Merry's dark beauty had been earthy while this girl—well, she was no beauty.

Those brows, for one thing, too boldly, defiantly straight. And her jaw was too square. And her nose too aggressive. Though, 'struth, she'd gorgeous hair. And a lower lip he'd greatly like to sink his teeth into, it was that rich and full. Her eyes—no one would fault them if they could but be appreciated beneath the dark slashes of those condemning brows.

"Stop staring at me!" she said, scowling even more fiercely.

"I'm not to speak, grab, or bully as well as not *look*? Well, now that you've finished looking *your* fill," he said, noting in satisfaction that her cheeks grew rosy once again, "do you think you might enlighten me as to *what in God's blood is going on*?"

She flew the few feet separating them and reached up, smothering his mouth behind her fingertips, hushing him urgently.

"Quiet, you . . . you blasphemer!" she hissed. Dear God, she even spoke like a convent—

The door slammed open with such force that it bounced against the wall and slammed shut again, giving Raine a glimpse of Jacques's beet-red countenance. Raine grabbed the girl and yanked the pistol from his waistband, pointing it at her head just as the door flew open once more and Jacques surged through it.

"Carefully, *mon ami*," Raine advised. Jacques came

up short, the sight of the pistol barrel a few inches from the girl's temple stopping him as effectively as a brick wall.

"We should have taken the younger one," the girl said.

"Bah!" Jacques spat contemptuously, his gaze trained on the pistol. "That quaking aspen leaf? No one would mistake him for *La Bête*."

"*La Bête?*" Raine echoed. "Who is The Beast?"

The girl's attention swung to him. "You misheard," she said quickly. "Not *La Bête*, Monsieur. *Lambett*. My husband."

She could not have surprised him more had she announced she had a tail. He could not say why. She simply didn't *look* like a wife.

"Monsieur. Lower the pistol," Jacques urged, making a broad, pacifying Gaelic gesture. The plea in his voice in no manner reached his eyes. "I'll shut this door. You lower the gun. We will explain. Everything."

"And if I choose not to lower the gun?"

Jacques's countenance turned dusky. "Then we sit here until it falls from your numb fingers. Because if you try to leave we will simply call the alarm." Apparently, his conciliatory mood had evaporated.

"I could always kill you," Raine suggested.

"If you shoot, the sound of gunfire is its own alarm," Jacques said with no small satisfaction. "So drop the pistol, eh?"

So Jacques disliked being threatened. So had Raine at one time. It was amazing what one could get used to if the need arose.

"I have a better idea," Raine said. "I keep the gun where it is and you tell me everything anyway."

"You *merde*!" Jacques burst out. "You gallows offal! How dare—"

"Jacques!" the girl broke in. "Please! This is getting us nowhere. Explain to him or I will."

Raine studied her. A sheen of perspiration covered her face, shimmered above her luscious lips. A lie from her would be easy to discern.

"An even better idea," Raine said. "*You* explain, Mademoi—Madame Lambett. And you, Jacques, remain very, very quiet. Or I will shoot you and then I will . . ." He smiled tellingly at the girl. "Well, you won't be around to discover that, will you?"

"You were right," Jacques said to the girl, his eyes on Raine. "We should have taken the aspen leaf."

"Now, one last time, explain."

The girl nodded slowly. "As you will, Monsieur. My husband, Richard Lambett, died a month ago from the fever. He was English."

Raine's interest was piqued yet he remained mute.

"I see you have some appreciation of how unlikely such a marriage is . . . was. But the heart is not always so wise, is it?"

"I wouldn't know, would I? Having spent the years in prison most men are bedding wenches." Raine sneered at her sentiment, causing her indigo gaze to drop.

"Oh! *Pardon*, Monsieur. I have been most callous."

Dear Lord, she was apologizing to him for a breach of etiquette. He could not hold back a snort of laughter and just caught her quick sidelong glance of satisfaction. Damned, if she hadn't fashioned that ingenuous statement to disarm him. She was cannier than he would have suspected—a worthy adversary.

"I now know you own an unwise heart," he said. "Unfortunate for you but having little to do with me. And now pray excuse me, Madame, for *my* callousness."

She delivered him a sharp, assessing gaze. Good.

"Continue," he said.

"My husband, he was a diplomat," she said.

"Apparently not a very good one," Raine said. This time the glance came with a scowl. "Pray, correct me if I err, but England and France are still enemies, are they not?"

Behind her Jacques shifted uncomfortably on his feet.

"*Oui*, Monsieur." Her voice was tight, her eyes bright. Ire or pain? He could not tell. "Still, I would not have you speak unkindly of him. Perhaps if we had not fallen in love, if his attentions had remained on political matters—"

"Dear lady, such catholic willingness to accept blame speaks volumes about the Sisters who had you in their care,"—this won a startled glance from the wench. He'd been right; she *was* convent-raised—"but even nuns might balk at blaming a war on a minor diplomat's amorous daydreams."

The scowl became pronounced and Raine quelled an inappropriate desire to laugh. Regardless of the diversion this wordplay afforded, his life was still held in the balance. And unless Raine's eyesight had suffered during his incarceration, big silent Jacques had edged closer while she'd distracted him. Raine swung the gun toward the giant.

"Come, *mon homme*. Practice the patience your lady upbraids me for lacking. Be still, Jacques, or be dead."

Her lush mouth pursed. Yes, she was definitely piqued.

"Enough background. What do you want of me?"

Jacques nodded unhappily. She took a deep breath.

"A half year ago my husband received word that his uncle in Scotland had died leaving him heir to a great estate. He set about trying to make arrangements for me and little Angus to travel to Scotland."

"Little Angus?"

Her gaze dropped demurely. "Our son."

Son. Raine's gaze traveled down her slender figure to her waist. The necklace she wore could encompass it. Still, a corset could account for its narrow span.

"As you might well imagine, securing passage to Scotland for a French lady and her son is a difficult matter. Particularly for a French lady of some preeminence—albeit diminished. I am an orphan, Monsieur, fostered in my aunt's household, the same household where I have been living since my husband's death.

"Happily, after much searching my husband was able to contact a privateer and make arrangements for our travel. We were—we are—to follow the tide out tonight."

"So why," Raine asked, "are you instead here with me, masquerading as a notorious jade, rather than bustling little Angus through Dieppe's shipyard? Not a word, Jacques," he cautioned the other man.

"Because," the girl said with a sudden flash of ire, "my husband died a few months ago and the man we were to meet on the docks expects to deal with a man, an Englishman. He wrote yesterday. In his note he ranted against having agreed to take a woman onto his ship. He says it is bad luck. That his men will rebel. He even goes so far as to suggest that we find other passage but ends his letter by saying he will grudgingly honor his agreement."

Raine waited. She held out her hand, palm open in a gesture of impatience. "Do you not comprehend? I am alone. The passage has already been paid and I have no more money. There is no reason this smuggler, this . . . *pirate* should honor his obligation. I needed an Englishman and Jacques knew where to find one."

"And how is Jacques so savvy?"

"My aunt . . . *she* is Madame Noir. Jacques is her steward. He always had an affection for me, even as a child and when he discovered my difficulty he . . . he presented a solution." For the first time since he'd dragged the veil from her golden head, she looked self-conscious and abashed.

Raine's gaze swung toward Jacques. He didn't look much like an aristocrat's steward, but admittedly Raine had had little experience with that breed and so withheld judgment. "So 'twas your idea to pluck an Englishman from prison to masquerade as Monsieur Lambett."

"*Oui*," Jacques agreed. "I knew the arrangements

Madame Noir made, the pattern, the names of those with whom she dealt. I knew that at so short a notice, the prison was Mademoiselle's only hope of finding an Englishman willing to act as her husband."

Every bit of Raine's instincts for survival urged caution. He didn't like this story. He mistrusted it.

"But"—Raine backed up a few feet, angling toward the door, his pistol still aimed in Jacques's direction—"your plan hinges on finding a *willing* Englishman."

"Monsieur," the girl said, her brows dipping into a V of consternation, "why would you refuse to aid me when you can only benefit from my offer?"

"What exactly is your offer?"

"You go to the docks tonight, pretending to be my husband. You meet with the smuggler captain, then . . ."

"Then?"

"I arrive, we board and sail for Scotland. Once we are on land, we go our separate ways."

"What about little Angus?"

"Angus? He will be with me, of course."

"And once in Scotland you'll walk to this great estate of your husband's?"

"*Non!*" she said impatiently. "Do not be foolish. My husband's people, they await me . . . us." A shadow dimmed the bright night sky of her eyes. She released a barely audible sigh and, catching his eye, smiled wanly. "Little Angus will be the new laird, *n'est-ce pas*? The point upon which all their plans and strategies and hopes hinge."

An odd way of putting it, but Raine supposed that in

some families a son might be looked upon with such concentration of pride and hope. Just because it hadn't been so in his family didn't mean it was a lie.

For the first time, Raine found himself believing her. Not all of it to be sure, but that last part perhaps, because of the sadness in her eyes. She looked as he imagined a fond mother might look upon realizing the burden of expectation being placed upon her child: resigned, troubled, a shade resentful.

"Monsieur, will you not help me? What harm have we done you? You have already enjoyed some hours of freedom, clean clothes, and will soon partake of a warm, hearty meal." She sounded tired, as though the strain had finally caught up with her.

As if on cue, there came a thump on the door. Raine's head slew about, looking for some way to escape. They'd only to call out and he'd be dead.

"Monsieur!" the girl pleaded on a soft whisper.

"Come, son," Jacques urged. "What have you to lose and how much to gain?"

He could return to Scotland. How many nights had he lain on his moldy pallet and plotted his movements after his escape? Now he had the chance to fulfill those plans.

First to Scotland and Wanton's Blush, the castle on McClairen's Isle where his thrice-cursed father lived—but not to see his unnatural sire. No, he would go there secretly to retrieve the jewels his mother had hidden shortly before her untimely death. The jewels he'd seen her stow in the false bottom of an oriental tea chest. The jewels he'd never told anyone about. Not even Ash.

And then, with his stolen birthright hard in his pocket, he'd sail for the New World—and freedom. Real freedom. Freedom from Scotland and McClairen's Isle and Carr and, most of all, his past.

The servant outside the door pounded again. The girl watched him anxiously, wetting the full curve of her lower lip.

And, too, there was something to recommend itself in the notion of spending several nights ensconced on a ship—as Mr. and Mrs. Lambett they might even share a cabin—with this black-browed, oddly attractive girl.

He grinned, releasing the hammer on the pistol and shoving it into his waistband. "Open the door, Jacques," he said quite calmly. "I'd as soon eat before we head for the docks."

Chapter 5

True to the girl's word, the servant at the door carried a tray loaded with food: crusty loaves of fresh baked bread; meat pies with wisps of fragrant, herb-scented steam rising from the slits in their lard crusts; a cold shoulder of mutton and a mound of hot, syrup-coated apple slices.

Whatever doubts Raine had about the pair's candor, clearly they courted his cooperation. For the first time in years he filled himself to satiation, paying half attention to the girl as she outlined her plan. She gave him the lines he was to say, the manner in which he was to approach the "smuggler captain," the times and place of the meeting. The other half of his attention pursued his alternatives.

But try as he might, he could not come up with any

plan that promised as much as the one the girl proposed—*if* it was true. Besides, if he walked out of the room he doubted he would get far. His last experience had taught him the necessity of plans and allies.

He had no allies; he didn't even know what lay beyond the next hill. And even if he did escape, to what? Without papers or money, he would be forced to wander until he was recaptured or had managed to accrue some wealth—if he didn't end his life in some wretched tavern brawl first.

He wanted more than that. His years of incarceration had dared him to consider whether his life could have some value. He'd found he wanted more than that future he'd been pursuing before France: a dingy echo of his sire's brilliant sins.

He glanced at the girl across the table from him. She'd recaptured her golden hair in a knot at the nape of her neck—a pity, as her free-flowing tresses were rare lovely. Tension marked the corners of her mouth as she endeavored to convince him to accede to her plan.

Raine suspected begging did not come easy to her. God would mark a woman with such uncompromising brows only as fair warning to the opposite sex. Raine gave a fleeting thought to her dead husband. She would have any husband on his knees, this one.

Jacques, chewing through a hunk of grizzled meat, remained silent. Wise man to let the girl do his procuring. The light of the tallow candle cupped her cheek in a warm glow. When was the last time Raine had touched anything as soft as her cheek looked to be?

He refilled his cup, trying to vanquish the spell she cast and pick out how much of what she told him was true. Not that it mattered. If all he needed to do was appear on the docks and speak in genteel accents to some English pirate, and by doing so broker a passage to Scotland . . . Well, was it not worth the risk of trusting this pair?

Though Dieppe's docks were crowded, the *Le Rex Rouge Inne* was unusually deserted. But then, Raine thought, peering through the carriage window at the tavern where he was to meet the smuggler, he knew little of life in these dockyards. Dieppe was a fresh-born harbor town.

A gust of wind found its way into the carriage and beneath his newly acquired coat. More from long-forgotten habit than need, he drew the thick wool folds shut. Beside him the girl shivered, her cobalt gaze fixed outside. Since he'd agreed to her scheme she'd been quiet and preoccupied.

On the driver's seat above, Jacques waited for a signal from the smuggler. As soon as he received it he would alert Raine, who would then proceed to the tavern to complete negotiations for their passage. He jingled the three gold Louies in his pocket, money he'd extorted from Jacques by claiming—not without some validity—that he might have to sweeten the pot should the smuggler prove recalcitrant.

If all went accordingly, Madame Lambett would wait within the carriage until an agreement had been made; then she and Jacques would fetch little Angus from wherever she'd secreted him. Fond mother that she was, she hadn't wanted to bring her son to the docks before it was absolutely necessary. The thought of little Angus awoke Raine's curiosity about the young woman's dead husband. "How did he die?"

She turned her head. In the dim light of the carriage her eyes looked nearly black. "Monsieur?"

"Your husband, how did he die?"

"Oh. An infection of the lungs." She averted her face once more.

"You were much attached to him?" he asked.

She remained mute.

She did not want to speak to him. He could not much resent her decision. She knew nothing of him other than that he was English and she'd found him in a prison. She hadn't even asked his name. Of course, she needn't fear for her safety what with Jacques only a heartbeat away.

The thought of the giant servant damped the spark of ardor still plaguing Raine—but did not altogether drown it. He could not forget the feel of her trapped between his thighs, her hands against his naked skin, her body molded to his. Even now, while his mind unraveled the next few minutes into a hundred possible ends, his body was still preoccupied with hers.

The minutes ticked by, the interior of the carriage grew warm with their shared heat. From outside came the clatter of an occasional passing vehicle, the sharp clink of shod hooves on cobbled streets, men's voices, distant and muted.

"Why were you so crude, so rough with me?" The stiff leather seat creaked as the girl shifted.

Her sudden query surprised him. He'd been relaxed, simply enjoying her scent, her warmth, and the sight of her. She repeated her question grudgingly, her gaze anchored firmly outside. "Why were you so crude?"

"The woman you impersonated *is* crude," he said, perplexed. Surely she knew the sort of woman her aunt was, especially since she had used her proclivities so effectively to obtain his release.

"But you touched me even when I made clear that I did not want it."

He was unsure of what she wanted and so remained silent, waiting.

"Yet you speak well, in the accents of the aristocracy. Are you? Are you well-born? Is your crime against the well-born?"

"Madame, is it not a bit late to be asking for a letter of introduction?" Raine asked, amused by her accusing tone.

"Why were you in prison?" she blurted out, this time accompanying the question with an anxious glance. "Did you . . . did you assault some woman? An aristocratic lady?"

She thought him a rapist? Ah well, the mistake had been made before. Still, at one time, he would have been affronted. He would have politely damned her to hell and proceeded to spend the night proving his irresistibility to the opposite sex.

But yes, he supposed she would think that, given how he'd nearly forced himself on her earlier. He rubbed his cheek consideringly and for the first time in years he wondered what a mirror would reveal. He smiled and she misread his reaction, shrinking back against the cushions.

"No," he said to ease her fear, "I have never taken a woman against her will."

"Then"—she hesitated—"then why were you in prison?"

" 'Political reasons,' a phrase I give you leave to interpret into meaning someone hoped to profit by my incarceration."

"I don't understand."

"And you an ambassador's wife?" he taunted lightly; but she'd turned that disconcerting gaze upon him again and he answered with a small sigh, amazed at her seeming youth and perturbed by it.

"What did you do?"

"What didn't I do?" he muttered, and then, "I was imprisoned because I could be and I was *kept* imprisoned because of some French bureaucrat's fantasy that someday someone might ransom me." He leaned closer and was rewarded by her faint, heady fragrance. " 'Twixt we two, however, I can assure you that no one other than yourself would ever have found a reason to set me free. My thanks."

He smiled again, this time without rancor, suddenly heedful that, indeed, were it not for this woman he would not be sitting in a warm carriage, clean and clad, astonished by his unexpected freedom and fearful he might yet lose it.

But instead of reassuring her, his smile seemed to

make her even more anxious. The corners of her mouth dipped unhappily and her fingers worried each other in her lap. "You hated being caged."

He laughed this time, in spite of himself, and heard Jacques shift atop the carriage in response.

"Rest easy, friend Jacques," Raine called out in a low voice, "your mistress would play the wit. I simply appreciate her sallies."

He studied the girl. She looked fresh and vulnerable and, he allowed, a bit piqued that he'd laughed at her. Jacques was right to worry about her. Raine had once known a hundred men who would have feasted on such innocence as hers. They'd once been his boon companions.

"Aye, Madame. I hated it. But never so much as now."

"Why is that?" She moved forward, her curiosity momentarily making her forget her fear. The carriage window framed her head and shoulders, the light outside glinting off her hair and spinning a bright nimbus about her silhouette. She would, indeed, be unsafe traveling unescorted. She was, he thought distantly, unsafe with him.

"Because I'd forgotten what freedom was like," he said, "and now I remember and the comparison is . . . keen."

Backlit as she was, it was impossible to read her expression.

"Why did your family not—"

"My turn," he cut across her query. Ash was gone, Fia probably bartered off to the wealthiest suitor by now, and he did not want to think of Carr. He had no interest in his sire, nor any desire to ever again behold him. Though he supposed it might prove inevitable once he'd reached Wanton's Blush.

Wanton's Blush.

Once again his future held choices, options, and prospects beyond the simple ambition not to be killed in the next prison brawl. The realization rushed in on him with heady force.

"Monsieur?"

He blinked like a man coming into the sun after too long in the dark, overwhelmingly aware of the debt he owed this young woman. Even if, as he suspected, there was more to this girl's scheme than she was letting on, at least tonight possibility existed where yesterday there had been none.

"I owe you a debt," he said.

"Please, Monsieur. You owe me nothing. You are aiding me." She dipped her head, studying her gloved hands. A long tendril slipped over her shoulder. She looked fresh, soft, and tantalizingly vernal with a youth he'd never experienced himself. "I am in *your* debt," she murmured.

Now, to ask the heavens for *that* boon would take even more audacity than even he had ever owned. But she'd made the declaration and he had never denied being an opportunist. "It would seem we are mutually indebted, eh *ma petite* Madame?" He paused. "Can I . . . May I touch your hair?"

It hadn't been what he'd meant to say and he heard in the stumbling hesitation of his voice a yearning controlled only by some remnant of pride. *Oafish bore*, he berated himself, *blathering fool. How polished, how urbane. 'May I touch your hair. . . .'*

Yet he awaited her answer.

He saw the slight dip of her chin, the barest of assents. Slowly he reached out, as careful of alarming her as if she'd been a Highland colt seeing a man for the first time. She held herself just as still, just as cautiously. His fingers hovered above the gleaming tresses, moved. Felt.

Silk. Cold silk. So polished as to seem crisp, so slickery cold. He rubbed the lock between thumb and forefinger, closing his eyes, intently cataloguing its texture and richness. His fingers worked higher, moving up, identifying the point where the strands lost their metallic coolness and grew warm with proximity to her skin. He opened his hand wide, letting the strands flow between his fingers, crushing the silky mass in his fist and releasing it and the faint fragrance of soap. He sighed.

"How old are you, Monsieur?" he heard her ask wonderingly. He opened his eyes.

"I am a few years into my third decade, Madame."

"So young? *Mon Dieu*," she breathed. "How many years were you in prison?"

"What matter—"

"How many?" she insisted.

"Four."

"You were just a youth . . ." He barely heard her and the horror in her voice made him uncomfortable. Disconcerted he looked away and then immediately back again because he'd not feasted his eyes on a woman like her in years.

"It is unfair," she murmured. "This is not right."

Once more her naivete goaded awake the long-dormant devil within, a misplaced part of himself that could still be amused by such things as a girl's innocence. " 'Right,' *ma petite*? What has *right* to do with my fate . . . or yours?"

His hand was still in her hair. Slowly, his eyes never leaving hers, he wound a handful about his fist. She resisted, but not adamantly. With each light tug, the stiffness of her body melted like warm wax before a brassier. Her lips—as full of voluptuous promise as her brows were of stern disapproval—parted slightly in astonishment. He saw the glint of her white teeth, a flicker of surprise in her eyes. Sweet clove-scented breath fanned his—

"There he is!" The small, driver's hatch flew open and Jacques looked down at them.

The girl jerked back, wincing as she came to the end of her tethered tresses. Raine freed her. Damn Jacques.

"Remember, speak only English," Jacques hissed. "Wait until he is very near. He won't want you to draw attention to him and I daresay his French is abominable."

He snapped the trapdoor shut. Raine looked at the girl. The odd light had leached the color from her skin.

"A kiss for luck, *ma petite*?"

Her eyes grew round. "*Non*, Monsieur! I am but recently a—"

"—and I am but recently free." He clasped the back

of her head and pulled her forward, crushing her petal-soft mouth beneath his. For just one heady instant her mouth was pliant and then she fought, pushing him away.

"Get on with it," Jacques called down.

Raine angled his head in a courtly bow, reached past her, and opened the carriage door. "Madame, your debt is paid." He jumped down to the street and without bothering to look back crossed toward *Le Rex Rouge*.

A tall man stood under a lantern hanging beside the door. He held his voluminous cape close to his body, warding off the stiffening wind. His expression was eager, his body tense.

Raine slowed his pace, glancing about. Three men stood huddled together at the corner the building, rubbing their hands together above the sullen glow of a small brassier. At the end of the street, a driver slumped atop a closed landau, his ill-matched pair shifting in their traces. It was too quiet.

The tall man stepped beneath the lantern. He'd a pale, cruel face.

"Lambett?" he called out.

"Yes," Raine answered. He halted. Jacques had warned him to be discreet, yet the smuggler called his name loudly across a nearly deserted cul-de-sac.

At the corner, one of the men lifted his head. Down the road the chaise door opened. The tall man nodded with evident pleasure, extending his hand, moving rapidly forward, his pale face—

Pale.

No seafarer had a face so pale.

He'd been set up. He heard the woman's voice call out behind him. "It's a trap! Run!"

The advice was unnecessary. He was already running.

The girl watched the tall figure of the nameless young man sprint past the soldiers tumbling from the carriage and be swallowed by the night. From his position atop the carriage "Jacques," also known as Jamie Craigg and more currently "La Bête," cursed roundly, whipping up the horses and heading for the docks.

Once he got over his anger, Jacques would see she'd not only done the right thing, but the best thing. Soon the soldiers from the docks would join their fellows in chasing down the man they thought was *La Bête*, the most notorious smuggler to ever make mock of the French authorities. For the first time in a fortnight the docks would be relatively free of troops. The real *La Bête* could thus, in relative safety, load important cargo before heading back to his native Scotland.

The "cargo" touched her fingertips to her bruised lips. She had never been kissed before. Never known an unrelated man's touch. His had been the first. A tall, hard Englishman with sherry-colored eyes, sprung from a fetid jail. He would not have liked his fate had she really been Madame Noir, of that she was certain. Then why did she feel so guilty?

The honesty the Sisters at Sacré Coeur had demanded of her provided a quick answer. She was no better than Madame Noir. She'd simply put the young man to a different use.

She bowed her head and offered a short prayer that he find his way to freedom. Yet, even as she finished her prayer and crossed herself, guilty at having used another being so wretchedly, she knew she would not have done one thing differently. She did not act on her own behalf now.

She drew back from the window, snapping the curtain shut as though by doing so she could shut out the Englishman's image. What she did, she did for her clan, to rectify the decade-old wrong she'd caused them.

She was the only who *could* rectify it.

She'd been reared on that knowledge, molded and shaped by it. Even in the French convent where she'd been sent so many years earlier, the letters from Muira Dougal had kept her obligation ever before her. Now, finally, the time had come for her to act.

Favor McClairen was going home.

Chapter 6

*I*t took an hour to row out to the ship. The half dozen men in the long boat strained silently against the oars. At the helm, Jamie guided their way, threading the heavily laden boat through black water like Charon bringing the newly departed across the river Styx.

Except she wasn't dying, Favor reminded herself. She was going home. She should be ecstatic. They'd made it when all odds were against them.

For days the entire north coast had been covered with not only soldiers but guards and laborers, merchants and seamen, all seeking the notorious smuggler, *La Bête*—or more to the point seeking the unheard-of sum being offered for his capture. Apparently Jamie had made fools of the French authorities once too often.

After a few days in his company she understood how he'd managed that not inconsiderable deed. 'Twas Jamie who'd determined that their best odds in evading capture lay in hiding in plain sight. He'd anchored his ship in a port, not in one of the tiny inlets smugglers generally favored.

Still, while most of the authorities' efforts had been concentrated on coastal areas, they hadn't altogether neglected the harbor towns. It had been necessary to arrange a diversion that would give them time to load their contraband—as well as Favor. Again, Jamie came up with a plan. But for it to work they'd needed an Englishman—an Englishman they could leave behind. But where and how to find a willing dupe?

Amazingly, it was Sacré Coeur's Most Reverend Mother who provided the answer.

Now, perhaps the Abbess had information from other sources, but it was certainly interesting that her brother, Father Dominic, was also Madame Noir's confessor. For whatever reasons the Abbess was uncommonly well versed in that notorious lady's habits and for this Favor was grateful.

The plan had been simple. One of the convent's milkmaids dropped a word into a French lieutenant's ear regarding the Abbess's anticipated windfall of fine Scottish wool blankets on a certain night at a certain locale. In the meantime Favor went to the local prison disguised as Madame Noir to select an Englishman who might readily be mistaken for the infamous English smuggler.

Everything had gone as arranged.

Except for the Englishman's eyes. And that he'd sworn he would never return to prison again. And that in asking her permission to touch her hair he'd looked quite as naked as Favor had ever felt.

The rowboat bumped lightly against the side of the ship's barnacle-covered side. Favor frowned. She had nothing to feel so guilty about. Once the guards realized they didn't have *La Bête*, the Englishman would simply be sent back to prison where he'd have ended up if she had been Madame Noir.

Hushed voices called out from above and Jamie answered in kind. A second later a rope ladder dropped down and two men leaned over the side of the ship. She took hold of their hands and they hauled her onboard. A second later Jamie, panting and swearing, hoisted his girth up and over the gunnel, followed shortly by his men.

"Get her to the cabin," he ordered in a heavy Scottish accent, jerking his head in Favor's direction. "Hoist anchor and put yer backs to settin' sail. We're fer home, laddies."

A rumble of approval met this announcement. Curious glances followed her as a balding man took her elbow and steered her through a doorway into a small cabin. Before she could turn, the door closed behind her.

She looked around. A narrow cot was nailed to one wall, likewise a table on the opposite wall. On this stood a chipped washbasin. Gratefully, she dipped the end of her kerchief into the frigid water and dabbed at her face.

Outside the door she heard a woman's voice. Apprehension followed her surprise. It could only be Muira Dougal, the woman whose iron will and driving determination had shaped Favor's last nine years. No one had told Favor Muira would be onboard. She hadn't prepared herself to meet the woman who'd . . . Favor floundered for a word that could adequately describe the degree to which this woman had influenced her life. All of it done from hundreds of miles away, mostly through letters.

In some very real ways, Muira Dougal had invented Favor McClairen. Certainly the child who'd arrived on this foreign soil no longer existed.

"How did it go?" Favor heard her asking Jamie.

"Well enough, Mistress," Jamie Craigg answered deferentially. "The guard at the prison didn't blink twice when the girl said she was Madame Noir."

"Is she any good then? Will she succeed in what she must do?"

Jamie paused before continuing. "Aye. She'll do. Though I'll say this"—a deep chuckle rumbled out—"if a man was in on the joke, so to speak, he would see right enough that the lass dinna understand the woman she played."

"Well, Jamie Craigg"—Muira's voice dropped in pitch, became biting and hard—"I'm glad you're so amused. But this isn't a joke. It's our last chance to regain what was stolen from us and if you no longer hold that a sacred endeavor, there are those of us that still do."

"Forgive me, Mistress," Jamie said gruffly. "I just found the lass—enchanting is all."

"Enchanting?" the woman echoed thoughtfully. "Good. She'll need to be enchanting, and more, for her purpose. What happened next?"

Favor pressed her ear to the door, straining to hear Jamie's reply. ". . . wary and hard, as hard a man as I'd not like to cross. But she had him eating out of her hand soon enough and sending him into the arms of the French as docile as a lambkins."

Favor's throat knotted with guilt.

"But then, just as he's about made it to the lieutenant's side, the lass calls out a warning. The Englishman dashes one way and we dash the other."

The door to the cabin suddenly swung open and Favor scuttled back. An elderly woman stood before her, her lantern raised. Favor squinted at the bright light, trying to see past its glare.

"Listening at doors, Miss?" the woman asked.

"If it aids my cause," Favor answered calmly.

"Ach!" A wide grin split the face of the thin woman. She turned her head toward Jamie, who filled the door frame behind her. "Bold!"

The bright light dangled a moment longer in front of Favor's face. Finally, irritated by it, she forced herself to face it squarely. "Would you kindly take that thing out of my face, Madame?"

A low chuckle greeted her imperious tone. The old woman lowered the lantern to her side. "Speaks like a McClairen wench. Uncrowned royalty is what the McClairens always thought themselves."

Muira's smile faded. "That's good, lass. You'll need all that queenly bearing and more. But tell me, come nightfall does a haughty manner keep the vision of Merrick murdering your kin at bay? No." She answered her own question fiercely. "Only an act of recompense will do that."

Favor backed away, caught off guard by the old woman's bald-faced reference to the night Favor had all but destroyed her own clan. She chided herself for her naivete. She'd thought Muira might offer her a word of welcome. She should have known better. She'd had a decade's worth of letters to instruct her differently.

The old woman studied her impassively and Favor returned the examination. Muira Dougal, née Mc-Clairen, had the sort of face seen on ancient Greek coins, genderless and refined, arrogant and haunted. Her eyes were heavily hooded, the narrow face hung with crepelike flesh. Her thin mouth was uncompromising. Only the bright blue eyes blazed as though lit by a fire from within.

For a full five minutes the two women faced each other, neither willing to break the silence. Even Jamie seemed loath to interfere in their silent discourse. He shuffled uneasily on his feet, glancing anxiously from one to the other. On the one side stood the woman who had for nearly a decade, single-handedly bound the far-flung McClairen clan together. On the other side stood the girl whose brother was that same clan's long-missing laird, in essence an uncrowned king, the girl that Muira Dougal intended to sacrifice in order to return the McClairens to their full glory.

"Yer nineteen years old." Muira finally said, her tone giving nothing away.

"*Oui*, Madame," Favor answered.

"Jamie says you improvised your escape here. Called out a warning to the English bastard you'd duped. Is this so?"

"*Oui.*"

"From here on there'll be no more improvising. None at all. Is that understood?" The woman's hand darted out like a striking snake and grasped Favor's chin.

"*Oui*, Madame. *D'accord.*"

"Agree? I did not ask you to agree. I asked if you understood."

Favor felt herself flush. "*Oui.*"

"And there will be no more French," Muira muttered distractedly. "*She* had only a smattering of French. Remember that." She looked over to Jamie. "You knew her. What do you think?"

The big man cocked his head. "I don't see much of the McClairen in her, that's a fact. They be a black-headed breed, like yerself. All of them taller than she by some measure. Regal, yes, but gay. This one is handsome enough but fierce-looking."

"Hair can be dyed, brows can be plucked," Muira murmured. "A resemblance can be created out of gestures and habits, a way of standing, a turn of speech."

She twisted Favor's chin, pulling her face this way and that in the light. "There's not much here to work with, I grant you, but it's there in the angle of her jaw and the purity of her skin. Her nose is all McClairen. And when I add the rest . . ."

Resentment made Favor pull away from the cold, dry fingers. She disliked being spoken of as though she were unformed clay waiting the potter's hand. She already had a set of features, individual and her own. 'Twasn't much, true, but when one could not call her future her own, even so little was precious. Though she did have Thomas. The thought of her long-unseen brother brought an attendant wave of worry.

"Thomas is gone?" she asked.

"Aye, lass," Jamie answered.

"Good," she said, but she could not keep the wistful note from her voice. She hadn't even been aware her brother was alive until a few years before when his letters had begun arriving at the convent. Thomas McClairen, bondage servant, sea captain, Marquis of Donne and laird of the McClairen.

She hadn't seen him since he and their older brother John had been taken to London to await trial for treason. He'd been sentenced, deported, and sold into bondage for his part in the uprising of '45. Their older, thus more "dangerous," brother, John, had been hanged, drawn, and quartered. John had been sixteen.

"He'll be gone a fair length?" she finally asked.

"Long enough for us to accomplish what we must," Muira answered.

Favor nodded. Thomas would be a dangerous man to defy and impossible to deceive. He'd spent his years of servitude on the deck of a ship, his master being the captain-owner of a small shipping business. He'd won his master's respect and later his trust. After his bond had been satisfied, Thomas had bought a share in his former master's shipping business and become captain of his own vessel.

He'd prospered and looked to prosper even more but his sight was set on a different goal. He'd returned to Scotland seeking the downfall of the man who'd betrayed the McClairens and stolen their birthright: Lord Carr.

To accomplish this he'd taken "Donne" as his surname, it being one of the McClairen lairds' old, long-forgotten French titles. In London he'd established himself as a disreputable ne'er-do-well and attached himself to a group of young devils who habitually made a pilgrimage to Wanton's Blush, once the McClairens' castle, now a hellhole of gaming and debauchery. There he'd befriended—to whatever degree such a creature as Carr was capable of friendship—Carr himself, all the while looking for the perfect manner in which to, in one fell stroke, destroy Carr and all he owned or held dear.

All this Thomas wrote to Favor in letters, in dribs and drabs. Favor pieced the hints together, discerning Thomas's goals in what he said and what he omitted. But something had gone wrong with Thomas's plan. His last letter to Favor had said only that his resolve had been shaken and he needed to regain it somewhere far from Scotland. Which was good for Favor's purposes.

Thomas knew naught of Muira's plan. If he caught

wind of it he would do everything in his power to keep Favor from becoming involved. But she was involved. Muira had written hundreds of pages to her elucidating just how very involved she was.

Because Favor was responsible for her clan's near extermination.

And if the good Abbess at Sacré Coeur had eventually convinced Favor that God had forgiven her, she knew very well that the same could not be said of her clan.

Favor pulled her thoughts away from her dark musings. She looked up, finding Muira's cool, appraising gaze fastened on her. How could she have thought that woman would have a kind word for her? Muira held her responsible for the death of every person she'd ever loved and more, of the death of her heritage.

Favor's return to Scotland was no prodigal's homecoming, no happy end to a decade-long exile.

It was penance.

Chapter 7

The Northeast coast of Scotland
McClairen's Isle
Six months later

Lord Carr looked down from the tower window at the bleak courtyard of Wanton's Blush. A storm was coming in. A stiff wind smote the rocky island with backhanded fury, ripping what leaves were left from the branches of oak and rowan and hurling them across the square. Overhead, dark mauve-veined clouds rolled ominously westward. If one turned around and looked out the east windows, one would see huge waves shattering themselves on the jagged rocks surrounding the island.

If one were to look out the east windows. Which Carr would not. Had not, in fact, in years if at all avoidable. Not that his present view pleased him any too much.

Like a cheap whore too long in the trade, Wanton's

Blush was showing her coarse antecedents. All the accoutrements Carr had so painstakingly plied upon her homely surface could no longer hide what she was: a Scottish drab.

The redbrick he'd ordered to cover her façade had crumbled in places, the gaping pox marks exposing the gray hand-hewn rock beneath. The courtyard he'd had paved with shimmering pink granite had heaved, pushed from below by tough Scottish turf that sprouted like hairs on a hag's chin.

The corrosion had seeped inside, too. Oh, not drastically—and not yet too apparently—but the signs were there. The expensive plaster moldings had cracked in several rooms. Chipped marble mantelpieces went unrepaired. Water stains darkened the walls of the south wing. Nothing too remarkable but telling.

Carr had acquired Wanton's Blush for the price of some information. In his youth he'd come to Scotland for an extended vacation, thinking to stay until his creditors in London forgot the immense sums he owed them. He'd accepted that he was bound for a lengthy visit. There he'd met Janet McClairen, the doted-upon cousin of this very castle's one-time owner, Ian.

She, being rich and smitten with him, and he, having nothing much else to do, married. They'd lived here, under Ian's benign auspices until Carr had decided he was tired of the *décor*. So, when the opportunity had arisen with the ill-fated Jacobite rebellion of '45, he'd relayed pertinent information about its leaders to Lord Cumberland. After the rebellion had been squelched and Ian and his kin either executed or deported, the grateful Cumberland had seen that Wanton's Blush and its lands went to Carr. Then, Carr had changed the *décor*.

He'd made Wanton's Blush over, sparing no expense in converting her into a showpiece. A U-shaped fortress built on the highest outer curve of the island, the main body stood perpendicular to the sea. Two wings sprouted from towers at the north and south corners, protecting the wide interior courtyard from the constant winds. Italianate gardens had once bedecked the terraces Carr had cut beneath the courtyard but the years had watched the slow encroachment of the native weeds. And since none of Carr's guests were wont to spend their waking hours idling there—their waking hours being primarily nocturnal—he did not fight too hard for those Italianate conceits.

The problem was, Carr admitted without regret, Wanton's Blush no longer interested him. It had served its purpose—indeed, *still* served its purpose: enticing from afar the wealthiest and most notorious gamblers of England's most distinguished families.

Carr was no fool. He still poured enough money into the cursed place to tempt jaded palates. Wanton's Blush still boasted the best wine cellar in Scotland, the best chef in England, and still contained a premier collection of artwork and artifacts, treasures he would take with him when he left here and returned triumphant to the scene of his former humiliation. The old venom seeped to the surface.

After Janet had died, Carr had set about accumulating enough wealth to pay off his dunners and set himself up as befitted his station. It had been slow going. Too slow. So he'd married another heiress whose wealth hadn't been nearly as grand as she'd intimated to him, the bitch. She'd met with an accident, as had his third wife.

By then he'd had the wealth he needed, but King George, grown sanctimonious in his dotage, had long since taken umbrage with Carr's unfortunate habit of losing wives. He'd not only made it clear that Carr would not be welcomed back in London, nor in any society that the king—damn him—controlled, but he'd written him an edict: If any female ever again died while under Carr's care, Carr would pay for it with his own head.

And so, Carr had sat up here in this northern nowhere for twenty-five years. Twenty-five years in unofficial exile—first self-imposed, later imposed by a king's will.

But soon all that would be over, Carr thought, drumming his fingers. Wheels were turning. The wooing of some, the blackmailing of others, flattery, coaxing, threatening . . . all his exertions were on the cusp of bearing fruit. Soon. A few months and he would once more reign in London's exalted society.

But first, he thought, turning from the window, he needed to attend to a few immediate matters, a bit of housekeeping before he quit Wanton's Blush once and for all.

He crossed the room, approaching a shriven, unkempt figure hunched over a littered table. He wondered if the old witch knew the reason the sea-facing windows were draped. Probably. She seemed to know everything. Not that he cared overly much. What could one old Gypsy do to such as him? Except be of use.

"Well, what do you see, Pala?" Carr asked, examining the nails of his hand.

The woman shifted, her layers of discolored shawls and patched skirts swirling out and settling over her feet. A seamed and leathery face peered up at him from between a curtain of lank gray hair.

"Well?" he prompted.

She stabbed one filthy finger at the little pile of ivory knobs scattered across the table's mahogany surface. "She loved you. No man owned so much love as you had from her."

A little thrill, all the more exotic for being so very rare, ran up Carr's spine. Pala was referring to Janet, his first wife, the only woman he'd ever truly loved. For a second, Janet's face danced before him: a black silken fall of hair, pale skin, dark amber-colored eyes. She smiled, an off-balance smile, utterly charming. Her eyes glowed with unhappy affection, unhappy because loving him had never made Janet happy.

"Yes," he said to himself. "She did."

"She loves you still."

The Gypsy's voice abruptly dispelled his sentimental mood.

"She loves you even from the grave." The Gypsy's sly accents curled through the air, wheedling and testing.

Calmly Carr sauntered over and looked down at the table where Pala had spread her divining tools.

"Oh, yes. I'm certain she does." His lips curled into a semblance of a smile. "Is *that* why she's haunting me? Her and her thrice-cursed clan? Because she *loves* me so much!"

He slammed his fist down on the table and the intricate configuration of bones burst apart, skittering across the surface and falling to the floor.

Pala speared him with a venomous glare and dropped to her knees. She scooped up the knucklebones and cradled them against her sunken chest, crooning indecipherable gibberish under her breath. "You have broken one!" she said accusingly.

"Yes?" His brows lifted with mild annoyance. His composure had returned. "What of it? You could buy the hands from a dozen corpses with the money I've given you."

"Pala never asks for money."

Carr smiled. At times the old Gipsy could be amusing. "Of course not. I forget your exact words but the gist of it was that such an act might sully the purity of your discourse with the spirits. Yet you've never refused my 'gifts.' Correct me if I'm wrong."

Pala crouched lower. Her mouth was sulky.

"How much do you imagine my 'gifts' have amounted to since I found you lurking in my stables two years ago?"

"I am not lurking," she protested feebly. "I . . . I follow the spirits. They tell me you are in danger. I come to warn you. Did I not warn you of the mad dog?"

Carr regarded her through hooded eyes.

"You know this true!" Pala insisted, jerking her head up and down. "For you, I read the portents, I listen to the spirits whisper, I see what has gone before and I see what will come. Has Pala not been of use to Your Grace many, many times?"

"A few," Carr allowed, pulling a chair out from beneath the table and dropping down into it. Pala *had* warned him about the rabid dog. Just as she'd seen the foundering of a smuggler's ship and the rich trove that washed ashore from it. And certainly she knew more about him than any other living person, far more than anyone could without supernatural aid.

He stretched out his legs and laced his fingers across his flat belly. The feel of the silk-embroidered waistcoat soothed him.

"Please, most gracious sir." Pala's voice dropped to an unctuous mewl. "I read the bones for your guests, too. They like."

"You've been an effective little diversion, I'll grant you that," Carr murmured. "It is hard enough to lure Lord Sandwich away from his cursed Hellfire Club and harder still to keep him here with his rich and largely insensate companions. You sometimes manage to do that, what with your augury and omens. How much real, I wonder? How much fraud?"

He leaned forward, fixing Pala with a meaningful stare. "Don't ever take me for a fool, Pala. Don't ever be so unwise. Or greedy."

The Gypsy's gaze slipped away from his. She dropped her bones into a leather pouch, drawing the thong about her neck and tucking it into her bodice. "I don't lie to you. I tell you only what the spirits tell me. What the bones say. If they lie . . ."

She shrugged and Carr smiled at her sophistry. The old witch was a woman after his own heart. If the bones lied, how could it be her fault? She was simply a messenger.

"You know why I trust you, Pala?" he asked. "Aside from the fact that if you were to ever prove untrustworthy you know I would kill you, that is?"

The cheap necklaces about her thin throat rattled as she cautiously shook her head.

"It is precisely because your messages from the spirit world reek more often of gin than brimstone. An infallible witch? An honest one?" He laughed. "Those qualities don't exist among noblemen so how could they exist in the likes of you?

"No, Pala, it is precisely because you fail and cheat and whine that I listen. You are treacherous and cowardly. Only the dead could prompt someone like you into risking her neck by claiming she hears them." He settled back once more. "It isn't so long ago that witches were burned. But you know that, don't you?"

Pala hunkered in the center of the room, like a rabbit baited for a fox.

"Now then, I know you heard something, saw something, or even smelled something among those bones of yours. Something to do with Janet. What was it? And no more drivel about her undying love." A little prick of something like regret rose within him. He ignored it. The dead returned for one reason only: to annoy the living. "In point of fact she did die. Now what . . . did . . . you . . . see?"

A sudden blast of wind rattled the glass in the windows as a low moan issued from the chimney.

"I cannot help what I hear," Pala finally whispered. "You ask and ask, you know when I lie. I *not* lie. She loves you. Even now, even after what you did. She forgives."

"Oh." He stood up and was about to walk away when he heard her speak, her voice flat and soft, marked by the lack of inflection in which she issued all her most accurate portents.

"She desires . . ."

"Yes?"

"To be reunited with you."

Carr snorted, disappointed. More maudlin sentiment. He'd over seventy guests in residence this day. Since Pala did not appear to have any suggestion on how to rid the castle of the haunts, he'd best go attend the living.

"She wants to be with you."

"Well, I'm afraid the dear girl will have to wait a bit, won't she?"

His smile faded as he saw the intensity with which

Pala stared at him. He was not mistaken. He'd engendered it in enough men to be wholly familiar with its every aspect. Pala was afraid.

"There is more," he prompted. "What do you know!"

"She is *not* waiting. She comes back. To forgive. To protect from them. As she always did."

Them. The McClairens. Alive, Janet had shielded him from their unproven certainty that he'd betrayed them, refusing to believe he would do such a thing. At least, at first. By the time she'd died, so too had most of her clan. Later, thanks to the fortuitous whoring of his son Raine, he'd had the excuse he needed to kill off any remnant of that cursed clan.

In truth it had been no great surprise when the McClairens had begun creeping from their graves, seeking in death the retribution they'd been denied in life— though they'd certainly bided their time in coming back.

Janet . . . now Janet was a different story. Yet here was Pala claiming Janet was only now returning. It made no sense; Janet had been haunting him for years.

"In what form will she haunt me? When will she come back?"

"Now."

"I don't understand."

"She is no spirit no more. She has found a vessel. Here. At Wanton's Blush."

"What do you mean?"

"She is reborn in another. One who is not aware she

shares her body with another soul. But you will know. You will recognize her."

His heart hammered painfully in his chest as he moved forward, grabbing the old woman's arm and hauling her to her feet. "If you are lying I will tear your heart from your chest myself and force it down your throat."

"I not lie!" Pala cried. "She loves you. She wants to be once more with you!"

Carr flung the old woman away, running a trembling hand through his peruke, shoving the wig back on his head.

Janet returned, he thought numbly.

He had to find her.

The door to the tower room slammed open. Pala, her skirts bunched high, scuttled out and disappeared down the steep tower staircase. Carr followed a moment later, his expression distracted. Blindly he followed the winding stairs downward and through a low arched door. He turned sharply and collided with a stooped female figure.

A thick black veil concealed the left side of her face leaving the right side uncovered, exposing a twisted mouth, deformed jaw, and one sunken eye obscured by a drooping, nerveless lid. Carr recoiled. It was hideous.

The creature shrank against the wall, her twisted body trembling.

"Who in God's name are you?" Carr demanded.

"Gunna, Yer Grace," the old woman mumbled in

thick Highland accents, lifting the corner of her veil across her mouth.

"Damn, another witch! Whatever are you doing in my house?"

"I do fer yer daughter, sir. Miss Fia. Have done fer years." The woman shuffled sideways like a land crab. It was repulsive.

" 'Swounds!" Carr swore softly under his breath, looking away. He remembered now. Fia had an inordinate and inexplicable fondness for this creature—Gunna, was it?—and she, in turn, seemed to be the one person who had some influence on his increasingly intractable daughter.

"What the hell are you doing here, hag?" he demanded.

"Followin' yer bidding, Yer Grace," the old woman mumbled.

"How so? By spying on me?" he demanded.

"No! No, Yer Grace! Ye said as how whenever I'm not tending Miss Fia I should keep meself to the east and upper rooms where the sight of me wouldna offend ye or yer guests. So here I be, Yer Grace."

Carr looked about and blanched. Surely enough, the window behind Gunna framed a view of the churning North Sea. Somehow, what with his distraction, he'd taken a wrong turn and ended here, overlooking the very cliffs from which Janet had fallen to her death.

A little thread of apprehension tightened his back muscles and set his scalp tingling. It was as if Janet herself had led him here.

"Yer Grace?" he heard Gunna ask.

He quelled the shudder taking hold of his limbs and fixed his attention on her cowering figure. His pride would never allow him to reveal anything even remotely akin to dread to so wretched a creature.

He brushed past her, sneering as he went, "For a man who loves beauty why do I suddenly find myself surrounded by hags?"

Chapter 8

There were close to a hundred guests overflowing the front salon. Carr fixed a well-practiced smile to his face, practicality having reestablished itself. The damned haunts he could deal with. It had been the notion that Janet could actually return. . . . Nonsense! An ignorant woman's ravings.

He waded into the crowd, greeting people as he went. No matter that he did not know a good half of them by either name or face, nor that they appeared at his door as the hangers-on of those who'd received *bona fide* invitations. The more wastrels, the better.

He poured himself a glass of port, downed the contents in one draw and poured another, eschewing the pale tea he drank most evenings. He eyed the crowd with a connoisseur's appreciation. No huge-stakes men here tonight. Mostly middling wagerers. A number of gulls, a cheat or two.

"Your Grace!"

Carr lifted a brow in acknowledgment of the tall, extremely thin man threading his way toward him. It was James Wells, Lord Tunbridge, distant cousin to the future king, George III. Tunbridge was said to be educating the crown prince in royal—and royally carnal—sports. An agreeable situation, seeing how Tunbridge was in his power.

"I would have a word with you, sir," Tunbridge said breathlessly. "I . . . It's important. Very important."

"Really?" Carr asked. "To whom?"

"Why, to me." A light sheen sprouted on Tunbridge's high forehead.

Deuce take it, the man wanted something. Carr was not in the mood. "Later, Tunbridge. My guests—"

"Your guests will wait, Lord Carr," Tunbridge said, his voice hardening. "Please. I have been of great service to you these past few years, as well you know, and now I would ask but a few minutes of your time."

"You're making demands, Tunbridge?" Carr asked mildly. "How very annoying for me and how very dangerous for you."

Tunbridge flushed but raised his chin. He was going to be plaguesomely persistent.

"Very well," Carr capitulated, taking Tunbridge's arm and drawing him through the open doors that led out into the courtyard.

Outside, the sun had relinquished the sky and the wind had died down. A thin fog drifted up the low, flinty apron that sloped away from the castle. The noise from the party within melded with the elemental rumble of the sea.

"Now, what is it, Tunbridge?" Carr faced the tall man.

"Your daughter, sir."

"What of Fia?" Carr asked with awakening interest. Of late his gorgeous young daughter was an unpredictable creature, one minute an unruly jade and hoydenish flirt, the next, a Sphinx, inscrutable and cold.

Her attitude toward him had certainly changed in the last year. Once she'd been his familiar, seeking his company and amusing him with her sardonic wit. But now she'd turned her gifts against him, and honed them, too.

What had Fia done now? Publicly denigrated the fool's manhood?

"Before you choke on whatever it is you have to say, Tunbridge, I feel obliged to tell you that I have no intention of fighting any duels over anything Fia may have said or done," Carr said. He held up his hand, silencing Tunbridge when he would have interrupted. "No. Listen. If you have a quarrel with the girl that only blood-letting can satisfy, I suggest you find one of her swains to champion her. I shan't."

"No! Of course . . . why . . . I mean . . . no! No!" Tunbridge grew bright red.

For reportedly being one of London's most celebrated duelists, Carr thought impatiently, Tunbridge certainly lacked dash. "Out with it, man! What the devil are you trying to say?"

"I . . . I don't want to *kill* Miss Fia. I wish to *marry* her!"

Carr stared at him a full minute before throwing back his head and laughing. He laughed until his side hurt and tears leaked from the corners of his eyes. He laughed until he could laugh no more and when he'd finally finished, he sniffed and withdrew a lace kerchief from his wrist and dabbed at his eyes and nose, occasionally hiccuping up another little chortle.

"Oh, thank you! I had need of a divertissement. I vow, Tunbridge, I would never have taken you for a wit."

Only then did he see that Tunbridge was not laughing. The color had leached from his face, leaving bloodless lips forming a thin line. Tunbridge had been serious.

When Carr realized this, he also remembered anew that Tunbridge—whose dueling career had been severely curtailed when Carr's son Ash impaled Tunbridge's hand on a stiletto—was still accredited to be more than passing proficient with a rapier. Still, Carr really wasn't in the mood.

"I will give you the benefit of the doubt, sir," Tunbridge ground out, "and assume that you misunderstood my intent, that being to take Miss Fia to wife."

"No, I didn't misunderstand you," Carr said, tucking his kerchief back in his sleeve. "And the answer is no."

"Why not?" Tunbridge demanded. "My lineage is impeccable, I am a baron, but most tellingly I am in the royal family's confidence.

"You, sir, ought to appreciate the extent of my influence on His Majesty as I have used that influence this past year and more in persuading him to revoke his decree that exiled you to Scotland. I have almost convinced His Majesty that your habit of losing rich young wives is, indeed, an unfortunate tragedy and nothing more sinister. I can just as easily convince him otherwise."

For a full minute the two men studied each other in silence, Carr with bored indifference, Tunbridge quivering with outrage. Finally, Carr sighed. "Are you quite through, Tunbridge? Fine. A moment of instruction 'ere we proceed to your suit."

Tunbridge blinked, startled.

"The trick to blackmailing, Tunbridge," Carr lectured calmly, "is that one must be willing—and able—to carry out whatever threats one uses to pressure one's victim into complying with one's purposes.

"Take, for instance, yourself. I know you'll do your best for me because should I fail to return to London—and that very, very soon—you realize that I will have no choice but to console myself with my latest acquisition, that being Campion Castle. How long has it been in your family, Tunbridge? Two? Three hundred years?"

Tunbridge's quivering ceased. His face had fallen into the slack proportions that Carr was beginning to recognize as being as habitual as they were unfortunate.

"Not only that," Carr continued mildly, "but I ashamedly admit that I will then likely enjoy imagining your own situation in a deportation vessel, having finally been brought to justice for the business with that Cheapside whore so many years ago."

"But I was drunk!"

"Ah!" Carr wagged his index finger playfully. "But I was not."

Tunbridge blanched further.

"Now, I have been reasonable this time because finding another toadie with your particular connections so late in the game would prove tiresome. It can be done, of course, and should it prove necessary, will be. Bear that in mind, Tunbridge, the next time you feel the urge to try your hand at extortion." Carr cocked his head. "Do we understand each other?"

Mutely, Tunbridge nodded.

"Good. Now, pray tell me, what is all this about Fia?"

Like a puppet whose strings had been severed, Tunbridge's shoulders slumped. His face betrayed his potent unhappiness. "She is a siren! I swear it. She drives me to distraction."

"Yes." Carr nodded. "I hear she's good at that sort of thing."

"She's bewitched me, I tell you. She's a succubus!" Tunbridge continued, his voice desperate. " 'Tis the only way to account for this obsession she has roused in me."

"Now, wouldn't that be a lovely rumor to start on the eve of her presentation?" Carr muttered irritably. He might have to deal with Tunbridge after all if he continued this sort of gibberish. A "siren" was fascinating; a "succubus" was disturbing.

Tunbridge held out one hand in supplication. "I must have her. I must."

"Don't be ridiculous."

"But why not?" Tunbridge asked pitiably. He looked utterly bewildered and in pain. Carr silently applauded Fia's skill. "I am rich. I am well connected. Whyever not?"

"Because I *already* control you," Carr explained. "Marrying Fia to you would be redundant. No. Fia will marry someone who does not bow beneath any of the other influences I can bring to bear." His smile relayed a certain pride. "Because Fia is the ultimate inducement."

"But . . . but *I want her*!" Tunbridge complained, having abandoned all attempts at manly forbearance.

Carr clapped him companionably on the shoulder. "Come, man. Grow a spine. Besides, Fia would use you up and spit you out within a fortnight. Begads! The chit is but sixteen! Why, she's just using her milk teeth on you. Imagine what she will be at twenty. Thir—"

The faint sound of a Highland pipe drifted out of the fog, cutting Carr's words short. He lifted his head sharply. "Did you hear that?"

"Hear what?" Tunbridge asked indifferently. "What would you say should Fia declare she wished to marry me?"

"She doesn't." Carr squinted into the soft shimmer of the twilight-kissed fog. A dark figure moved therein.

He was certain of it. A dark *masculine* figure clad in a belted plaid. "Do you see anything out there?"

"Why won't she?"

Carr spared Tunbridge one dismissive glance before once again scanning the mist. "Why *would* she?"

Apparently, the answer to this pointed query finally convinced Tunbridge of the futility of his petition. With a deep sigh he slunk away. Carr barely noticed. His eyes were turned toward the drifting fog. His ears strained to hear the McClairens' sepulchral pipes. Nothing.

Damned haunts. Had the dead nothing better to occupy their time than with children's games of hide-and-seek? With a curse, Carr quit the terrace and followed the dew-glistened granite steps down into the garden. He strode purposefully along the footpath between the topiaries, bizarre and fantastical shapes clipped from living yew and boxwood. The fog swirled about his legs, the damp seeping through his white silk stockings and staining the pale blue satin covering the heels of his shoes.

At the end of the garden, where yet another set of pink granite steps led to a still lower terrace, Carr paused and peered out. Below him bracken and gorse had infiltrated the once regimented beds of roses and rare botanicals. The shadows had thickened down there. Night had found purchase. The fog was denser, the air colder.

"Come out, you cursed McClairen spirits! I am here! Haunt me!"

No reply met his shouted challenge. No ghostly

form materialized. No pipe trilled from the darkness. Nothing.

Every time he'd had an . . . experience it was the same; a furtive movement from the corner of his eye; a gust of chill wind where no wind could be; a drumbeat in the middle of the night that could have been his heartbeat but wasn't.

It was driving him— *No!* It was not driving him anything. It was distracting. An annoyance. That was all.

"What's this?" he shouted to the gloom beneath. "Do the dead still fear the living? Do Scots flee the British even in death? Cowardly phantoms!"

The very silence seemed to mock him. With a hiss of rage he swung around and retraced his route, keenly aware of eyes upon him, of ghostly smiles jeering. He'd begun stalking up the stairs to the terrace when his eye caught a splotch of muted color tangled amid the mist and rose vines beside him. A scarf? Odd he hadn't noted it before, but then, his attention had been on other things.

One of his female guests must have been using the gardens for an assignation. Damned cold weather for an assignation. He leaned over and picked it up. He'd started forth once more when he chanced to glance down. Abruptly he stopped, riveted by the sight.

In his hands he held a frail length of heavy silk, its once bold colors dulled and faded by time or wear or a decade of being drowned beneath the sea. One side was raw and frayed though the other edges were neatly rolled and stitched. Someone had rent it in violence.

He closed his eyes. Opened them. It had not disappeared. Or mutated into some other piece of cloth. He crushed it in his fist. He recognized it.

This was Janet's *arisaid*, a woman's version of a plaid. The McClairen plaid. He could not mistake it. She'd worn it the day she'd died. It had been he who'd ripped it, infuriated that she would dare consider wearing it to his ball. One piece she'd wrapped around Fia. This was the other half.

He'd not seen it since he'd watched it floating beside Janet's body at the base of McClairen's Isle.

Where he'd thrown her.

Chapter 9

"Carr didn't even look for Jamie and his pipe," Muira cackled. She sat at the dressing table in the bedchamber Carr had reserved for Favor Donne's chaperone.

As Favor watched, Muira dipped a cotton wad into a jar of grease and began rubbing the ochre-tinted paint from her face. "Not that he'd have found him. He may have lived in the castle over twenty years but he doesn't know half her secrets, one being as how a body whispering on the parapet beneath the south tower will sound like he's standing in the gardens below the courtyard."

"You're very sure of what Carr knows and what he doesn't know," Favor said.

"I should be. I've been listening to his raves and curses for two years and I've been watching him for a dozen before that. Aye. I know Carr's black soul as well as my own," Muira said. She tossed the stained cotton into the fire and began rolling the clothes she'd shed into a small bundle that she would later store in the locked chest at the foot of her bed.

Favor looked around the room, wondering what secrets it held. Happily, her own room was unconnected. She disliked the idea of Muira having unimpeded access to her.

"If only I could remember some detail about Janet that only Carr would have noticed," Muira muttered, her eyes narrowed in concentration on her image in the mirror.

"Well, you'd best come up with something soon," Favor said. "We've been guests at the castle two weeks and so far he hasn't taken any more note of me than a scullery cat. Aside from dancing naked in the firelight, I don't know what else I can do to attract his attention."

Muira flashed her an annoyed glance. She finished plumping out her cheeks with a bit of cotton wadding and quickly dusted her face with fine white powder, taking special care with her brows and lashes. That done she twisted her white hair into a bun atop her head.

No one who saw her now, looking so pudding-faced and pale, would recognize her as "Pala," the dark, wiry Gypsy whom Carr had found in his stables nearly two years earlier.

"I've spent two years filling Carr's head with hints and omens about Janet's return," Muira said. "If you fail to make Carr believe you are she, it's because you *want* to fail."

She regarded Favor thoughtfully as she stuffed her bodice with woolen bolsters. "Is that it? Are you wondering what would come of you if you could call your future your own?" Her brogue thickened with her growing contempt. "Yer still thinkin' on that English prison scarecrow, aren't ye?"

"No." Favor denied the charge.

"Aye." Muira nodded. "Jamie says as soon as he returned from France, just before we come here, ye asked him if he'd ever heard what become of the man."

"I know you'll not believe this but I asked because I feel—"

"Guilty." Muira spat out the word. "So you say. So you've said this past half year. Well, it seems to me your fine conscience has developed a large appetite. Now me, I'd think that any lass responsible for the deaths of most all her clansmen wouldna have room for any more guilt."

"You'd be surprised at the things of which I'm capable," Favor stonily returned. The old woman's methods of persuasion were never subtle but certainly one could not gainsay their effectiveness. Since she'd brought Favor from France she had lost no opportunity to remind Favor of what she owed her clan. They'd each learned a great deal about the other.

Favor had learned to hide her vulnerabilities. Muira had learned that the biddable puppet she'd hoped to manipulate was an independent young woman not easily managed. It had been a lesson the old woman disliked and one that had pitted the two women in constant conflict.

"Or," Muira said now, "are you wondering whether or not your blooming sweet youth really does need to be sacrificed after all?"

Favor faced her silently.

"Well, darlin' lassie, all those men that died because of you were blooming with youth, too. And they all deserved bonny brides and plump bairns and warm hearths. My husband, my brother, and my three sons among them."

"I know." Favor did, too. She'd sneaked out to the stables the night they'd arrived at the castle and found Jamie, who was masquerading as Thomas Donne's driver. She asked him to intervene in the battle of wills between her and Muira. Instead Jamie had told Favor about how on the night of the massacre Muira had lost every one of her family yet still found the strength to rescue the wounded and tend them back to health.

But Favor, guided by the Abbess's sweet reasoning, also knew that she was only in part responsible for the tragedy that had occurred that night. It had taken the Abbess years to make Favor believe that. Yet daily, what with Muira carefully tending it, she felt her old guilt growing back.

"We did not hide here, risking the last of our men's lives smuggling French brandy, just to keep you happy in that fine French convent of yours. We did it because we had plans for you, plans you have a blood debt to carry out."

"I have never denied it." Dear God, no. Not she.

The weight of the McClairens' expectations had at times near crushed her, but she hadn't bowed before it. She would not break now. No one wanted to pay off that debt more than Favor.

"We did not work and plan and sacrifice for all these years so that you could ruin everything now, at this last stage."

"I won't ruin anything."

"If all goes right—and that's in your hands—the isle and her castle will soon once more belong to the McClairen. Is that not what you want?" Muira demanded.

"Yes."

"Then mind me well, you must not *act* like Janet McClairen, you must *be* Janet McClairen. Do you ken?"

"I've tried," Favor said, unable to hide her frustration. "My face aches with my efforts but Carr doesn't seem to notice."

"Then try harder!" the old woman said grimly.

Favor did not back away. She did what she did for her own reasons, to put her guilt finally and completely behind her. "Time's running short and you've not been able to supply me with the key to Janet McClairen. Perhaps your memories are faulty, your recall not as keen as you think. Perhaps you can't teach what you don't know."

Abruptly, Muira chuckled. "You doubt my thespian skills, child? Don't. Have I not convinced Carr I'm a sweet old lady?"

She blinked myopically, her mouth curving in a benign smile. In a trice she'd become every inch the vague, elderly relative she pretended to be. Favor watched with grudging admiration.

They'd arrived six months ago and taken up residence in Thomas Donne's empty manor house. Soon after, Muira had forwarded Lord Carr a letter ostensibly written by Thomas Donne, introducing her as Mrs. Douglas, his aunt, and his little sister Favor's chaperone.

As Muira had predicted, Carr couldn't resist adding a wealthy, ill-protected heiress to his guest list. An invitation had been immediately forthcoming and a few days later Muira had trailed Favor up the steps to Wanton's Blush shedding lace kerchiefs and whispered "oh, mys." They'd been at Wanton's Blush on and off as guests ever since.

Muira's smile disappeared. "You're right on one mark, though. Time is running short. You need to find Carr alone tonight. But that'll never happen if he sees me at yer side.

"Damn the man, I think he has yet enough sense to be afraid of your brother. He doesn't want to chance having me report anything amiss in his conduct toward you." The notion tickled her and she chuckled.

"I'll go down soon," Muira said thoughtfully, "I'll drink a wee bit, and a wee bit ostentatiously at that. You come down in an hour. By that time I'll seem to have fallen asleep. You'll be able to catch Carr alone without him worrying on the repercussions."

She stood up, drew on her gloves and picked up a fan. Moving to the door, she paused briefly. "Tonight it must be. 'Pala' promised Carr his dead wife would be returning for him. I saw his expression. He's rabid to see her."

Muira shook her head, fascinated. "Even though he flung her from the cliffs, he still pines for her. He honestly believes he loves her. And that she loves him." She gave a brief, rueful laugh. "Our plan is perfect. Once he finds her again, he'll never let her go."

Her expression hardened. "Only then will you have paid yer debt. After he weds you, and McClairen's Isle belongs to the McClairens once more."

An hour later, Favor McClairen rose from where she'd remained seated since Muira's departure. She carefully arranged the fall of her wine-red taffeta skirts, adjusted the treble ruffles of black lace that fell from her sleeves and exited her room.

Her face betrayed no emotion—and indeed, there was none to betray. She felt like a member of the audience witnessing a play from the balcony seats.

She would convince Carr she was his dead wife come back to life. She would marry Carr. She would then disappear, returning to France where he would never dare seek her. And then she would wait for however long it took for Carr to die and then the castle would be back in McClairen hands. For this was Scotland where a woman inherits her dead husband's estate.

And if between the first and the last something (consummation) occurred (or was forced), which she would personally find unpalatable (*abhorrent*), she would still, at long last, mark "paid" to the debt she owed—

A black-haired wraith flickered and vanished in the corner of her eye. Startled, Favor spun to face the creature and only then realized that she'd seen her own reflection in a mirror hanging on the wall.

She gazed unblinkingly at the creature—beyond pale, spectral white skin, empty black eyes, soulless as a selkie.

She studied the mirror seeing white flesh, high cheekbones, small bowed lips, a slender throat, and thin arching brows. All of it an illusion, the product of an artist's tricks of embellishment, accentuation, and de-emphasis. Powder laced with the finest, iridescent lead created her white skin. Carefully applied salve made her lips look thinner than nature had ordained them, and a bit of rouge accented her cheekbones.

More rouge, beneath the jaw, created the impression of a long neck and Muira's tweezers had produced those thin, arching brows. A drop of belladonna dilated her pupils to such an extent that they nearly eclipsed the blue of her irises, making her eyes appear less blue.

Finally, thrice weekly Muira pulverized bits of roots and berries and dyed Favor's tresses black. A dead color, Favor thought privately, so deep an ebony, lacking any of the sheen of health.

At least in repose, Favor was as close to looking like Janet McClairen as Muira and her paint and potions could make her. For the rest, she needed to rely on the memories of those who'd known that long-dead lady to augment her resemblance. Experimentally, she flicked open her fan. Briskly—because Janet McClairen did nothing languidly—she covered her lips, lowered her eyelids and glanced sidelong. Too coy. She tried again—

"I say, Miss Donne, you won't be so cruel as to use up all those blisteringly come-hither looks on your own reflection, would you? I mean, you will save at least one for me?"

Favor spun around. Lord Orville stood with one shoulder rammed against the wall. His voice was slurred, his mouth puckered scoldingly. Favor backed away.

On her first evening at Wanton's Blush, Lord Orville had cornered her in a vacant room. Without preamble he'd grabbed her and kissed her with lip-splitting brutality. Even now her belly rebelled at the memory of his cool, wet lips. She'd tried to get away but he'd been too strong. She hadn't dared scream. Carr might send her away for being prudish, or worse, form an aversion to her maidenly sensibilities.

Only the timely arrival of Orville's giggling wife being hotly pursued by a disheveled footman had distracted Orville long enough for Favor to break free of his embrace and flee. Since then she'd managed to avoid him.

Her luck apparently had run out.

"Cat got your tongue?" Orville drawled. "Lucky cat."

Sophistication, she adjured herself. It was her only hope. Orville would have no idea how to handle a woman whose worldliness surpassed his own. She forced her breath to an even tempo. Snapped the ivory fan closed.

"Lord Orville"—she rose on her tiptoes and pretended to peer behind him—"is that your wife I see disappearing up the stairs with one of the stable boys?"

He sneered. "What of it? May she have her fill of him—or rather"—he laughed without amusement—"may the lad have his fill of her. Everyone else does."

He pushed himself from the wall, his lip curling back. "I'd much rather have my fill of you, Miss Donne. Bite by bite."

He strolled toward her, tapping his long white chin. "I'd be tasting something rare, something few other men had sampled. Oh, don't look surprised, my dear. I've asked after you, you see. We all have."

"How tedious of you," Favor said, forcing herself to stand still. "I can't imagine why since I've shown not a whit of similar interest in you."

"*Tch. Tch.* Such a rude little Scot. Aren't you curious about what I've discovered?"

"No."

His smile grew. "I know your older brother is some sort of dispossessed Scottish thingie—dispossessed because he chose to go off to the Americas rather than stumble 'round the Highlands with the rest of his Jacobite-loving kin. Seems eminently sensible to me but apparently your clansmen thought it showed a certain lack of fealty."

He was watching her carefully, seeing whether his words caused pain. It flashed through her thoughts that perhaps Orville was one of Lord Cumberland's agents sent to the Highlands to rout further insurrections.

If so, he would get no joy from her. She knew by heart the tale of her brother's supposed cowardliness and dispossession. She should. Thomas had created it. It allowed him to move freely among these English usurpers—despised by them as a traitor to his people at the same time as they embraced him for being a *roué* willing to spend money.

"I'm afraid he's not greatly regarded by his kilt-wearing brethren. But don't look so sad, Miss Donne. I hear his wealth greatly succors him. And you."

Favor continued regarding her reflection, a vain woman bored with the conversation of a tiresome man.

"Do his old clan affiliates threaten him? Is that why he left Scotland so abruptly?"

Favor leaned closer to the mirror and rearranged a black curl on her temple before answering. "Hm? Thomas? Lud, no, nothing like it. As far as I know, my dear brother is in America." She gave him a vacuous smile. "Now, if you'll excuse me—"

She'd almost made it past him before he stepped in front of her. Her smile slipped. "Sir?"

"How is it he left his little sister behind?"

"Perhaps because he's visiting his plantation and his little sister has an aversion to sweat; and sweat, so I'm assured, is abundant on a plantation. Though," she said, her gaze traveling over Orville's damp brow and glistening upper lip, "we don't seem to lack for it here, either."

Orville flushed. "You're a saucy wench, Miss Donne."

"But not nearly spicy enough for a sophisticated palate such as yours." She cursed the pleading note she heard in her voice.

Orville heard it, too. Immediately his confidence returned. "I'll be the judge of that." He leaned forward, his sour breath sluicing over her mouth.

The courage supporting Favor abruptly gave out. She wheeled, grabbing up the hoops beneath her billowing skirts, and ran. For a moment all she heard was the hiss of rustling taffeta, the staccato of her own heels, and the far-off sound of voices growing even more distant as she fled.

Then she heard Orville give chase.

She raced past her own chambers. They could offer no safe haven. She would never be able to fetch the key and lock the door in time. Her only chance lay in evading him.

"How delightful!" he called. "I adore games!"

She made it to the servants' staircase and ducked beneath the low lintel, feet clattering on the worn stone steps, slipping as she went, her skirts choking the narrow, winding passageway. She burst from the door at the bottom and fled on. Through another door, down another set of stairs, always the sound of his footsteps behind. Through more doors, to another dim passage.

She had no idea where she was. She'd been culled like a yearling deer from the herd, driven to the far reaches of the castle, to the dark, uninhabited parts.

Her lungs burned, her skirts dragged like dead weights from her hands. She stopped, panting, looking about. She could run no more. Desperately she lunged for the nearest door handle and pushed. Reluctantly the door gave way.

She scrambled into the room, turned and eased the door shut, pressing her back to it. She waited, her heart hammering, searching for another way out.

There was none.

She was in a bedchamber, long unused and neglected. Ghostly sheets draped all the furnishings except the huge bed in the center. Its filmy curtains hung torn and shredded from the canopy like the night rail of an ill-used bride. Boxes and chests lined one wall. A thick stack of paintings leaned against another.

A hushed atmosphere of suspension permeated the room, as though only timid ghosts kept company here, holding their spectral breath, waiting for her to leave. She strained her ears to hear Orville's footsteps. Nothing.

She counted to one hundred before moving cautiously across the room, her wide skirts sweeping a broad swath in the dust. She stopped at the tall bank of windows on the opposite wall and pulled back the gauzy drapery. Her breath caught in her throat.

The evening sky bloomed above a seething cobalt-colored sea. In a gothic excess, day lay bleeding its brilliance on night's black shoulders. She had never seen such a sunset. "My Lord," she gasped.

"Milady."

Her heart checked. Before she'd turned around,

Orville was on her. He grabbed her around the waist, hauling her off her feet. He shoved her hard, face first against the window. His mouth fell on the back of her neck, sucking greedily.

She cried out, kicking and sobbing in terror. He laughed. The sound extinguished her fear, cold water on a fire.

She was Favor McClairen. She was not some vile Englishman's doxy. She was not *any* Englishman's victim. Not *anyone's* victim. She reached over her shoul ders and clawed at his face, satisfaction flooding through her as she felt his flesh rend beneath her nails.

"Bitch!" He grabbed one wrist and twisted viciously, slamming it against the window frame with numbing force. He grasped her other hand and treated it the same.

"Scottish whore!" he hissed into her ear. "I'll mark you for that and damned be your bastard brother! We'll see—

His words were cut off in a strangled sound of surprise. Abruptly Favor found herself free. She sank bonelessly to the floor, twisting to see what had happened.

The room was darker now, nearly black. Two figures struggled in its center, pitched in an ill-matched contest. One was tall and broad, his fists spearing through the air with blinding speed and devastating effect. In seconds, he'd landed a series of brutal blows. He stopped abruptly and straightened as the slighter figure teetered and crumpled into a heap on the floor.

The stranger turned his head in her direction. He

hesitated but then came toward her, she thought to offer her his hand.

She lifted her face, shaken and grateful, and gave him a tremulous smile. "Thank you, sir. I . . . I can't begin to express my gratitude. I . . . thank you so very much."

He neglected to hold out his hand. She frowned, perplexed by this lack of manners after he'd just championed her so completely. He took another step, bringing him into the last rays of daylight coming through the window. She suddenly understood his reluctance to touch her.

She'd last seen him being swarmed by the French soldiers she'd set on him.

Her Englishman.

Chapter 10

The tall man's eyes narrowed on Favor. In a rush of relief she realized that he couldn't possibly recognize her disguised as she—

"Are you thanking me for my current services or the ones you made such good use of in Dieppe?" he asked.

So much for anonymity.

His voice was rough-smooth, his gaze shuttered, the light refracting off the clear, wild honey of his irises. Only the slight curl of his upper lip indicated his current disposition. It was not a pleasant one.

"It *is* you," he said. "What sort of perfidy had you planned for that poor sot?" He jerked his chin in the direction of the motionless Orville. "Damned if I oughtn't dust him off and apologize, for any man entangled with you, Milady Treachery, deserves at the very least his fellow man's pity and most probably his aid."

Favor only half-attended this biting denunciation. She was too busy staring. Lud, he was big. Far taller and wider than she remembered. He wore tight black breeches that had seen better days and the white lawn shirt he wore was untied and loose, revealing his muscular bronzed chest.

He was darker than she recalled, too. The angularly rough features were tanned now, the square jaw blue-black with an incipient beard. His rumpled sable-colored hair fell in loose curls about a strong, broad throat.

But there was some other difference. Something elemental. Something important.

She tilted her head, trying to identify it. She had it. The man who had been shackled spread-eagle to that prison wall had been desperate, pushed to the crisis point. This man owned himself completely.

It put him at a distinct advantage. Now she was the one controlled by fate and others' fortunes. She disliked the reversal in their positions.

He'd moved closer to her, agile and light-footed for so large a man. She shrank against the wall, suddenly realizing that one danger had supplanted another. Her heels beat a tattoo as she struggled to rise. He reached down, grabbed her upper arm, and lifted her to her feet.

She attempted to dart past him but his hand flashed up, circling her throat in a warm, tight grip, keeping her where she stood. She forced herself to meet his gaze. With one large thumb, he tilted her chin back. Her pulse thudded heavily against his palm.

"Well," he murmured, his gaze slipping over her cheeks and mouth and throat like a caress, "what say you, Madame Noir, or Widow Lambett, or whoever the hell you are?"

"Favor," she said. "Favor Mc—Favor Donne."

He went utterly still, his gaze scoured her features. "Damn you, what trick is this?" He dropped his hand to her upper arm, this time his grip not merely restraining but hurtful. "I don't know what game you're playing now, but I will have the truth."

She winced. His teeth snapped together. "The truth before I . . . the truth!"

" 'Tis the truth, I swear it!" she cried. "My brother is Lord Thomas Donne. He owns the manor house five miles inland on the north highway. You've but to ask anyone here to receive that same answer. I am Favor Donne."

He eyed her derisively. "And what is a nobleman's sister doing in France, masquerading as a licentious bawd?"

She hesitated a heartbeat, searching for a likely explanation. He shook her. "Out with it!"

"My brother . . . He is also *La Bête*, the smuggler," she whispered. " 'Twas he the French sought in Dieppe. 'Twas he I protected by giving you over to the soldiers in his stead."

He thrust his face closer to hers. His eyes no longer looked cool, but torrid. He looked older than he had in

France—harder, too. Certainly more dangerous. Silently she prayed that he would believe her.

"I swear it," she rasped.

Slowly, his grip loosened, became less punishing.

"Damn," he finally said but he seemed to be replying to some internal avowal, and not to anything she'd done. "You haven't answered my question yet. What were *you* doing in Dieppe, little falcon? And why the new plummage?"

"What?" she asked in confusion.

"Your fierce brows are gone and you've dyed your hair. Why?"

"Because"—she cast about for a plausible answer—"because the English gentlemen are partial to dark hair."

"I never heard it was so."

"And where would you have heard *anything* about the current modes?" she asked, praying he wouldn't punish her impertinence. "Or did you have the *Gentleman's Quarterly* delivered to your cell?"

Appreciation flickered through his expression. "*Touché.*"

"And what are *you* doing here?" she asked haughtily, pressing her momentary advantage. Had he found out her identity and followed her here to extract some sort of revenge? The concept sent a shiver through her. Let that be a lesson to her never to heed the urgings of a guilty conscience. She should have let the French soldiers take him.

"Oh, no, pretty peregrine." He shook his head. "A decent attempt at diversion, but I'm no callow youth to be distracted by a lush mouth uttering haughty demands. We were discussing *you*.

"Why were you in Dieppe? 'Twas it your job to mind the smuggling ship's rudder?" he asked sarcastically.

"Of course not!" she said quickly, examining and discarding evasions with lightning speed. "I was with relatives who'd had the care of me for years. It was safer for me in France than here. Because of Tom." She glanced up, gauging his reaction. Impossible to tell. "You know about Tom, of course."

"Do I?" He abruptly released her, and stood back, crossing his arms over his broad chest. She backed away, rubbing the marks he'd left on her upper arm. His gaze touched dispassionately on the reddened area.

"Tom left the country just after Culloden. Followed by the price the rest of the clan chieftains had put on his head."

"Why?"

She lowered her eyelashes, bit her lip in feigned humiliation. "He was at Culloden but he was just a boy. He saw how outnumbered and outarmed the Highlanders were. Tom"—she paused for effect—"Tom has never been much for a fight. The sight of blood curls his toes. He left the moor when the fighting began."

His sudden laughter made her eyes snap open. She scowled. He was grinning at her hugely, his white teeth flashing in the semidarkness. "God preserve me, you could convince a cat to bark, you little liar."

"Have you no delicacy?" she demanded, brazening it out. "I've just confessed my brother's disgrace."

"That being that he ran away from the battlefield because he's an aversion to blood?" He shook his head. "You'll have to do better than that, love, especially if you're going to chase that fable with one about the same cowardly brother becoming a notorious smuggler. Unless of course, '*La Bête*' hides belowdeck whenever there's a spot of bloodshed."

"Don't be ridiculous," she snapped, chagrin supplanting fear.

"No need, as you're being ridiculous enough for both of us."

"I don't care if you do believe me—"

"Oh, you'd better," he broke in quietly, returning her fear to her.

She swallowed. "Thomas orchestrates the smuggling so that there will *be* no blood-letting. Last year the French started closing in on him. They offered a reward for any information leading to his arrest.

"It was only a matter of time before someone told the authorities about me. We would not bring trouble to those who'd fostered me for so long. So, Tom devised a plan whereby I could escape. It needed a decoy."

"Me. And here I'd thought I owed the inestimable Jacques a visit. Where is your gargantuan friend?"

"He's here and his name is Jamie and he's my . . . my brother's driver."

"How delightful to have so multitalented a driver."

"He had nothing to do with your . . . situation. He simply followed orders," she said, envisioning Jamie and this huge, lean man closed in mortal combat.

"Don't worry, sweetling, I won't hurt your tame bull."

She breathed a sigh of relief. His expression flattened. "But tell me, where is your clever brother? I'm all agog to make his acquaintance."

"He's abroad."

"Avoiding more unpleasant things? So why are you here without him?"

If she stuck close to the truth perhaps she could convince him to leave her alone, to go away and do . . . what *was* he doing here? "My brother may appear to be a wealthy man, but he's not. *We're* not. And neither is our clan. In fact, my whole family is quite, quite poor."

"Yes?" he prodded.

"I'm here to . . . to repair the clan's fortune." She skirted closer to the truth than she would have liked.

"Fortune? Do you mean by that you are casting nets in the matrimonial waters, Miss Donne? Here?" His voice revealed his skepticism. "At Wanton's Blush? Well, I give you high marks for originality. Not many a blushing debutante would think to come here to seek a mate."

"Where else would such as I go? A Scottish nobody without lands, family, or connections to recommend myself?" she demanded hotly, for he'd pressed too close to a truth she'd never allowed herself to inspect. Even if she could call her future her own, where would someone like her find a "happily-ever-after"?

"Only at Wanton's Blush could someone like me find a suitor who would not look too closely at my antecedents or, even if he did discover them, care who they were. As long as I am richly gowned, bedecked and bejeweled, here I am accepted as the eligible heiress I appear to be."

"You mean the smuggling business isn't all it's cracked up to be? And here I thought it one of the more profitable occupations open to an ambitious young man."

"Nay," she said harshly. " 'Tisn't. Not nearly profitable enough to repair a fortune stolen by English ba—"

"Be careful, Miss Donne," he interjected dryly. "Your future husband may just be one of those English *ba's*."

"I understand that," she answered tightly. "But you see, I don't have any choice. Your English didn't leave any Scottish men to choose from—rich, poor, or anywhere in between. They killed them all."

She had the impression her words had struck a chord and that he was growing sympathetic to her tale.

"Aye. That has the ring of truth to it," he said after a moment. "But then, I have a certain history with your bell-toned lies."

She'd been wrong. He cared nothing for her people's slaughter. "Ridicule me all you like," she snapped.

"Tuck your lower lip in, sweetling, 'tis too tempting by half pouting thus. But I'm sure you know that full well."

She stamped her foot in annoyance and then stared

at the offending limb in consternation. She hadn't stamped her foot since she was a child.

"What a fine tale and what a fine heroine you make, Favor, me love," he said in a light, mocking tone. "So brave and passionate. How noble of you to sacrifice yourself for your clan." His expression flattened. "If only I could believe in that nobility. But you were very willing to exploit me."

"I'd do the same again today. You were already condemned. What did you have to lose? Besides"—she stared defiantly at him—"you escaped, did you not? Well, then you got more than the bargain called for."

"Oh, no," he murmured, "I didn't get *any* of what the bargain called for."

He stepped forward, intent, predatory, his concentration focused to a rapier sharpness. She stepped back. Her shoulders collided with the wall. He smiled, one side of his mouth turning up and carving a deep line beneath his high, broad cheekbone. A wicked smile, that. A devil's smile.

He lifted his hand toward her face. She flinched but he only reached past her, placed his palm flat against the wall next to her head and leaned in. His stance emphasized his much greater height. He eclipsed her with his breadth. His gaze drifted down her face and throat and lingered where her breasts swelled in agitation above the low, square décolletage.

"I'd been purchased from jail to provide sport for you."

"Not for me!" she denied. "For Madame Noir."

"Who you pretended to be," he reasoned, his voice

low and seductive. He angled his head and inhaled, his mouth inches above her flesh. She shrank down; there was nowhere left to retreat. The wall behind her bare shoulders was cool. Every inch of her skin seemed suddenly heated.

"You shouldn't have dyed your hair," he mused. He picked up a lock, his knuckles brushing her collarbone. Sensation danced over her skin in response. He rubbed the tress lightly between thumb and forefinger, testing the texture. "It was prettier before. Plundered gold. Now it's funereal, like a dead raven's eye."

"Flatterer," she whispered.

His gaze shot up to meet hers. His dimple deepened in surprised humor, then dissolved. The wide mouth relaxed, became pensive. His brows dipped, as if in puzzlement.

"Who would have ever thought you . . . of all the women in the world . . . *you*," he whispered in a voice so low she barely heard him.

Watching him studying her body made her feel ripe and lush, liquid and uncomfortable. She couldn't have looked away if she'd tried.

"Please."

"Please what? Please myself? What would that take, do you imagine?" he asked. "I had a kiss from you once and I still remember your taste. Isn't that odd?" He lay the artificially darkened tress on her shoulder, arranging the curl with patient care. "Isn't it?"

"Yes."

"I'd been in jail for four years, you know," he said. "Four years is a long time to remember those carnal pleasures I was just learning to appreciate when I was captured. After I escaped—with your aid—it took me a few days to realize I was safe. But then . . . then I sought out those pleasures—when it didn't mean risking my life."

His face hardened. "And do you know what? Do you want to know something very odd?" His face was very close, his mouth looked very soft, the only soft thing in that hard visage. "Do you?"

She nodded, mesmerized by his low hypnotic voice, the heat of his hand playing just above her collarbone.

"Even in the blistering heat of the most powerful climax, I still tasted *you*."

She tried to hold back her gasp. Failed. Earned another one-sided smile.

"What's this? A blush, little peregrine? Too raw? By God, I believe I've embarrassed the wench." He gave a humorless laugh. "And to think I mistook you for Madame Noir. I really had lost the knack of reading a woman."

"She was my relative," she said.

"Allow a modicum of respect for my intelligence. I doubt you've ever even met the lady—No!" He lay a callused fingertip against her lower lip. "Your mouth begins to form a lie before it's even half thought. Spare us both yet another of your fictions." Hesitantly, as though compelled, he grazed his fingertip back and forth along her lower lip.

"I can't help what you believe or disbelieve," she answered, a sense of panic unlike any she'd ever experienced rising in tandem with the electric feeling suffusing her mouth, her cheeks and throat, her breasts and thighs.

"Damn me, lady hawk, is there any truth in you at all?"

Her voice wouldn't work. She stared in mute appeal.

"Christ's blood," he murmured with that wicked, Satan-inspired darkness flooding his voice, "I can't decide if God is punishing me or you. Let's find out, shall we?"

He closed the short distance between their mouths. His lips touched hers with deliberate delicacy, clung. Her eyelids drifted shut.

Warm breath. Velvet mouth, firm and testing. Just a kiss, just the softest brush of his lips and yet her knees weakened and her head spun. He moved closer. She sensed it, felt his breadth surround her, above her . . . Threatening? Protecting? By the Virgin, she couldn't tell.

Her head fell back against the wall. His fingertips branded one side of her throat with gossamer fire, skated down and across the top of her breasts, found the edge of her décolletage and slipped along it, moving with lingering deftness beneath—

A jolt of molten sensation electrified her. Her eyes flew open, her startled gaze leaping to meet his unreadable one.

"Let me go," she pleaded. "Please. I am not rich and I have no name with which others might seek to align themselves. All I own is my virtue. Please don't take that from me."

Was his breathing staggered? She couldn't say. Her

own thoughts were in too great a turmoil to heed another's state, her own breath too ragged.

"Let me go," she repeated. "Please! I don't even know your name."

" 'Tis Ra—Rafe," he said, but his hand dropped to his side and he moved back. "Though I've had far more intimate discourse with women who've had far less knowledge of me than that."

"How dare you speak to me like this?" The words broke from her rising panic. "I'm not one of your women of the streets taking money to lift my skirts."

"Oh, rest assured, I did not find all of them on the streets," he said. "And I had no money to offer."

Fire swept over her chest and throat and burned in her cheeks. "So that's what this is about."

She had known this game she and the rest of the McClairens played would extract an ever-stiffening price. She had not foreseen this, though.

"What's that?" he asked, a smile loitering in his dark gaze.

"You've sought me in order to penalize me for my actions in Dieppe. To take your revenge in . . . in having me against my will," she ended brokenly.

When she finished, he snorted in disgust. "Rest easy. Your virtue is not at risk. Odd as it must seem to you, I would like to hold on to the notion—no doubt a self-deluding one—that I might find pleasure with a woman without resorting to rape."

At her wide-eyed amazement, he broke out laughing, shaking his head. "And as for your idea that after four long years in a hellish hole I had naught better to

do with my newfound freedom than hunt you down in
order to toss you on your backside . . . By all the
saints, Madame, your conceit outstrips even my own!"

Put thus, it did seem improbable. Only someone
unhinged would set himself on such a course. She felt
another blush rise to her cheeks.

"What are you doing here, then?" she asked.

He regarded her thoughtfully a second before answering. "Have you ever heard of McClairen's Trust?"

"Aye," she answered. Every McClairen knew the
legend of the lost jewels. "It's a parure of rubies and
diamonds; a necklace, earbobs, brooch, and circlet.
'Twas said to be a gift that Queen Mary gave a Mc-
Clairen lady in gratitude for her aid in discovering
Darnley's treachery."

"Aye," he said. "That's the one."

She frowned. " 'Twas lost. Probably sold to finance
yet another glorious return."

"Ah! A cynic and a Scot?" He laughed. "Who'd
have thought the two could coexist in one body. As for
the Trust, some say that the McClairens hid it at Wanton's Blush and here it remains."

"And *that's* why you're here? I don't believe you."

"Have you a better explanation? Besides the irresist-
ible lure of breaching your own maidenhead, of course.
Assuming that you aren't lying and it's unbroken yet."

"Knave!" she said, more from embarrassment at his
reminder of her foolishness than at his crudity.

His gaze mocked her. "I've been here a week already. 'Tis been an easy enough venture thus far. Carr
keeps most of the east rooms empty, using them as a

warehouse. So here is where my search has begun." He swept his arm over the room.

"The McClairen Trust is naught but a child's night-time story," she said gruffly. "If there were any rubies and diamonds they've long since disappeared. I am surprised you know the tale, though. It's only a local legend. How *do* you know about it?"

"I had a cellmate named Ashton Merrick. He told me."

Her eyes widened. Of course. 'Twas common knowledge that Carr's sons had been captured by some Scots seeking revenge against Carr. They'd sold them to the French as political prisoners and the French kept them for ransom. Just as everyone knew Carr had refused to pay for their return until last year—or so she was told—when Ash Merrick had briefly reappeared.

Mayhap Rafe had met Raine Merrick, the source of all her grief. Mayhap this man even knew something of that thrice-damned rapist's fate. "Ashton Merrick had a brother," she said.

"Aye."

"Did he share your cell, too?"

"No. Raine Merrick was kept in a different city. A different prison. I doubt he even knows if Ashton lives or is dead. I don't."

Favor closed her eyes. "God keep Raine Merrick from that knowledge if it were to provide him a dram of comfort," she muttered.

"You hate this Raine Merrick?" he asked.

She didn't want to discuss that black-souled demon. Not now. Not ever.

Behind them Orville stirred, groaned, and rolled over. She needed to leave. Once more she drew on the Abbess's wisdom: Act a queen and you don't need a crown. She squared her shoulders.

"Orville will shortly awake. Unless you plan to murder him—which," she hastily continued on seeing the thoughtful manner in which Rafe regarded Orville, "will only cause a search of the premises—I suggest you leave here.

"Now, my thanks for your aid. In return, I promise I shall not tell anyone of your presence here." She started past him but he stepped in front of her.

"Oh, no," he said. "I haven't given you leave to go yet. I have been thinking."

Alarm danced up her spine. His expression had grown wolfish. She mustn't let him see her fear. She raised one perfectly arched brow. "Thinking? Ah. I trust this is not a novel experience?"

His mouth quirked appreciatively. "I don't want anyone to know about me. It's been a bit venturesome having to steal food from the kitchen at night. And if I don't find my jewels in this wing, I'll have to search the occupied parts of the castle. I'll need to blend in to do that. That means I'll need clothes. Nice clothes."

"So?"

"So, you will bring me both food and clothes. Unless, that is, you want your host, Lord Carr, to find out that his heiress and her brother are not so flush as he'd assumed."

"You wouldn't dare tell him. You couldn't afford to confront him. He'd have you hanged as a thief."

"I don't need to confront him at all. I have only to write a letter."

"That's blackmail!"

"Yes," he replied easily. "I know. But though it doesn't look to be nearly so interesting a revenge as the one you envisioned, it will have to do."

Chapter 11

Raine leaned against the doorjamb, enjoying the sight of the young woman's rigid spine above the tantalizing sway of her hips as she swept down the hall and disappeared into the gloom. He'd seen her crossing the courtyard a few days before. Something had been familiar in her stride, in the set of her shoulders, and the way she held her head. For a moment, in profile, she'd resembled someone from his past but then she'd turned and the sense of long-ago familiarity had been supplanted by a much more recent one. But it wasn't until he'd seen her closely that he'd realized that the black-haired girl fleeing an amorous pursuer was the same golden-tressed widow who'd so thoroughly duped him in Dieppe.

She'd dyed her hair and plucked the fierce slashing

brows—which, oddly enough, he rather regretted—
and disguised the full sensuous curve of her mouth under a thin painted line. She'd even done something to
her eyes, causing the pupils to devour their iridescent
blue—a grave error in his estimation should she indeed
be seeking a mate.

Had she gone to such lengths to, as she claimed,
make herself more appetizing to the English gentleman's palate? Perhaps. She would never be a classic
beauty, her sharp-angled face lacking that oval symme-
try such demanded. But there was some element that
drew the attention, a certain comeliness, some quality
that made a man want to watch her mouth move as she
spoke, to touch the high outer curve of her cheek.

Raine pushed off the wall, turning and strolling back
into the room. Miss Favor should be on her knees right
now, thanking God that the past years had taught him
restraint. Not a great deal of restraint, but enough that
he'd asked her name before tossing her on that rickety
bed and finding out just how attentively the holy Sisters had guarded their charge's virtue.

Aye, Favor McClairen was lucky. Her name had
stopped him. But in his impetuous youth . . . or
should he find out she'd lied again . . .

He sighed. Unfortunately, there was no doubt she
was Favor McClairen—whether or not she and her
brother chose to call themselves Donne. He'd recognized her. She was no longer a child, but the obstinate
set of her chin was the same, as was the fierceness in
her eyes.

His smile faded. He glanced down at the unhappy

Orville, currently attempting to rise to his hands and knees. Raine dusted off his hands and considered Favor's advice. She was probably right. The last thing he needed was to have Favor's suitor searching for him.

Orville raised his head, peering blearily about. With a grimace—after all Orville hadn't been doing anything Raine himself hadn't considered—Raine rapped him sharply on the jaw. Orville's eyes promptly rolled back and his head hit the floor with a thud.

With a grunt, Raine hefted him over his shoulder and straightened. He headed down the corridor in the opposite direction the wench had gone. He needed to think.

Perhaps Favor really was seeking to repair her clan's fortunes by making a spectacular match. Certainly he, better than most, knew how desperately those fortunes needed repairing. After his father had betrayed the McClairens to the Crown, he'd been rewarded with every bit of property and wealth the clan had once owned. But that hadn't been enough for Carr. He'd made sure no McClairen would reclaim a ha'penny of it by the simple expedience of murdering them all.

Raine dodged the memory of the instrumental part he'd played in his father's plan. He opened a door leading to the occupied section of the castle, poked his head out, and, seeing no one in either direction, dumped Orville. Orville moaned and Raine shut the door.

He followed the tower's narrow winding staircase up to the next level, needing no lantern to illumine his way. He knew Wanton's Blush well, every secret passageway and concealed niche, every hidden room and priest's hole. More times than he could remember he'd hidden here to escape his father, thanking a usually indifferent Creator for the superstition that kept Carr from these rooms.

At the top floor, Raine headed for the small bedchamber he'd been using as his headquarters since his arrival. There he struck a tinderbox and lit the lantern on the table inside the door. Wearily he snagged a bottle of Carr's finest port from a tabletop and kicked a dusty armchair toward the single window overlooking the sea. He sank down on it.

He uncorked the bottle with his teeth, took a deep draught, and wiped the back of his hand across his mouth. He paused at the rough feel of his beard. He needed a shave. His gaze fell to his white shirt, slightly stained in spite of his having washed it thrice since his arrival. He smiled at such delicacy. If nothing else, his years of incarceration in that sty had imbued in him a deep and abiding passion for cleanliness.

He leaned his head back, letting his long legs sprawl out before him. As soon as he found his mother's jewels he'd buy himself a hundred new shirts and as many breeches. He'd never again wear a soiled stockinet cloth or sweat-stained waistcoat again. Mayhap he'd become an eccentric and breathe only through a scented silk kerchief.

When he found his mother's jewels? Today it seemed the more likely question was *if* he found them. As far as he knew he was one of the only people to have ever seen the fabled jewels.

'Twas shortly before her death. He'd been nine years old and on a mission to steal a sugar lump. He'd arrived at the kitchen door to find his mother already there. Knowing her views on small boys who pilfered sweets, he'd ducked into the larder.

As he'd watched, an angry-looking redheaded fellow had entered. Afraid of being caught spying, Raine had hunkered down. Though he hadn't heard much, it was clear the stranger was trying to compel his mother to some act and just as clear she was not to be compelled.

Finally, the stranger left and his mother soon thereafter, her lovely face a mask of worry. Desiring only to comfort her, Raine had slipped out of the kitchen and followed. But rather than head for her private chambers, she'd hastened to the small office she used to receive the local merchants and instruct the household staff. Before Raine could catch up with her, she'd shut the door behind her.

Worried, Raine had peeped through the keyhole. He'd seen her bend over a battered oriental tea chest and begin manipulating the wooden tiles on its surface. Suddenly a shallow drawer had popped up from its center.

Reverently, his mother had withdrawn a heavy gold object from the drawer. It was large, shaped roughly like a dragon, or a lion, and fitted with big, rudely cut stones. She handled it only a second before placing it back in the hidden compartment.

Raine, uncertain of what the object was, nonetheless

knew it was something his mother wanted kept concealed. He'd never told anyone about it. Not even Ash. Certainly not his father.

Only later, when he'd begun to hear rumored tales of something called the McClairen Trust, had he realized what he'd seen. By then his mother was dead. Having no great love for her people, and even less for his father, he'd kept mum.

During his years in prison he'd thought often of that homely brooch. It became his lodestar. He'd spent hours plotting exactly how he would liberate it, where he would go with it, how he would sell it and to whom, what price he would ask. He built his entire future around its retrieval, not at all sure he would ever live to experience it.

Now he had the opportunity to realize those dreams.

If he could only find the bloody chest.

Getting into Wanton's Blush without his father's knowledge had been no problem. Raine had simply joined the line of servants awaiting their masters' carriages. He'd grabbed a trunk from the ground, heaved it to his shoulder and followed a footman into the castle and up the servants' staircase. There he'd dropped his burden and taken an abrupt detour to his mother's room, assuming he'd be in and out of Wanton's Blush in less than an hour.

There his plan had gone suddenly awry. Nothing was as he'd remembered it. Worse still, not one item of his mother's remained.

Raine took another swallow of port, recorked the

wine bottle, and set it carefully beside his chair. He'd been searching the castle ever since.

The upper stories of the east façade, in general disuse four years before, were now totally abandoned, given completely over to storage. And what storage! If nothing else, the last week had given Raine a newfound appreciation of the demon driving his father. He'd never seen such a testimony to one man's avarice. The place was honeycombed with crates and trunks and furnishings, stuffed with a fantastic mixture of valuables and litter.

Nothing had been thrown. A man could spend half a lifetime sifting through the wreckage and ruin, the treasures and tripe accumulated by a dozen generations, searching for that one small oriental chest.

Not that he had any choice. He had no money, no skills, no past, no future. He couldn't—or rather wouldn't—approach his father. Carr believed his youngest son to be rotting in a French prison and as far as Raine was concerned he could just continue to believe so. He would have been there yet had it not been for her.

Raine laced his fingers across his belly and let his chin rest against his breastbone, pondering. Things had become complicated.

Favor McClairen.

He smiled. He was beginning to think God was not indifferent after all, but simply sat upon His celestial throne patiently awaiting the opportunity to perpetrate pranks upon mankind. Nothing else could account for the fact that she, of all the women in the world, should have been his unintentional liberator.

Interesting that she was using her real Christian name. He understood her need to keep the McClairen part mum; Carr would have her flogged from the place should he know. So obviously she didn't expect the name "Favor" to be recognized. And truthfully, he allowed, who would remember that the scrawny girl who'd saved his life nine years earlier had been named "Favor"? Certainly no one in Carr's household would have asked after that child's name. Except for himself—and that months later, after his wounds had healed and the girl had disappeared.

He closed his eyes, the taste of the excellent port not quite enough to purge her own delicate flavor from his lips. Had her name been Sal or Peg or Anne he might well have done exactly what she'd accused him of planning and tossed her on the bed.

But she was wrong on one score. It wouldn't have been for revenge.

He'd been deceived and used so many times that her small betrayal didn't even make an appearance on his most-notable list. Amusing, really, that she obviously felt the sting of guilt so keenly. His congratulations to the holy Sisters.

No, he would have taken her because he wanted her.

The lust and longing he'd kept at bay ever since she'd left him abruptly broke free with devastating results. He inhaled deeply, his muscles tensing. He hadn't meant to tell her how she'd haunted him, how images of her had primed him for sex more than willing flesh and clever mouths. He hadn't meant to arm her with that particular knowledge.

But then, she was still babe enough not to even realize the weapon he'd handed her.

He frowned. How did one account for her implausible mixture of innocence and savvy? That ingenuous, direct gaze and the accomplished lies? It was a puzzle and, more, it was stimulating. Nearly as arousing as her sweet little body.

He felt again the texture of her velvety breasts, the supple yield of her body, and replayed that simple kiss.

He wanted more.

But then, damnation, her name *was* Favor McClairen, a girl who'd every right to hate him and wish him dead. The one girl in the world whom he was obligated to aid in every way he could.

The girl whose life he'd ruined.

Chapter 12

"Drag him up to the gate!"

The ropes binding his wrists snapped taut, jerking him off his feet. He landed face first in the hoarfrost, the shards scraping his chin and forehead. He hadn't the strength to even turn his head.

"Up, ye English bastard! Up, ye puling fucker!" A hard bootheel slammed into his side, breaking what had been cracked. He groaned. It was all he could do. Hands grabbed his arms, jerking him to his feet. He swayed. More hands seized him, half-dragging, half-carrying him to the arching postern before an ancient tower. There they stood him, weaving and half-conscious, beneath the teeth of the raised iron gate. Elbows and fists jostled and shoved; angry voices rang in his ears; the stink of sweating bodies and the reek of green reed torches clogged his nostrils.

A thin, metallic taste drenched his mouth. Blood congealed on his lips and dribbled from his chin. Blood clouded one eye and blood stained his shirt.

"McClairen!" They were shouting now, voices raised in triumph. "McClairen! Come out to us!"

High above him he heard a weak female voice answer, "What is this? Who do you seek?"

A hand in the middle of his back catapulted him forward and he staggered to his knees. Behind him a harsh voice answered, "We come seeking the McClairen!"

He squinted, saw a gaunt middle-aged figure in rags, such fury in that face as to rob it not only of its gender but of all humanity. Hers had been the first staff to break across his shoulders.

"There is no McClairen clan," the voice above answered, fainter this time.

"Nay, lady, you are wrong!" a man's voice answered, "for we be that clan. The English might chase us from our homes and burn us in our crofts. They might harry us like cunny but we've survived. We are McClairen's people, and we've brought the laird an English rapist to teach Scottish justice."

"What? How's this? Who is that boy?" the lady asked, her tremulous voice rising, seeming to mirror Raine's own fear.

"Carr's evil seed who sowed his own germ 'neath the skirts of a nun's habit!" the woman in rags screamed. "A McClairen lass, she were!"

"Dear God, is that Carr's son?"

"Aye. Carr who betrayed and deceived us, who had our pipes and plaids stripped from us, who stole our lands and

killed not one but three wives! Well, no more! This we will not suffer! We will have justice!"

The crowd roared in approval.

"Send us our laird so that we might be proud once more!"

"Ye fools!" the woman cried out, despair so ripe in her voice that for an instant it recalled Raine to his senses. *"Ye've murdered . . . my sons!"*

"McClairen! McClairen!" The chant began behind him, picked up tempo and volume, became a din drowning out even the ringing in his ears.

He tried to lift his head and tell them the truth: He hadn't raped Merry. Aye, they'd found them together, Merry naked and him nearly so, but it wasn't rape. She'd made her accusation because she'd been afraid of them, of what they would do if they discovered she'd willingly given herself to Carr's son.

He would tell them. Tell them, too, that he hadn't been the first to lift her novitiate's robes. He opened his mouth. The words would not come.

He knew too well what would befall Merry at their hands if he spoke. Merry would confess. She would be raped then, by every man there. Raped until she most likely died from the abuse.

A fist came out of nowhere, striking his battered side. The world spun, the angry faces dissolving and expanding in a whirl of flame-stained light and shadow.

Besides, he thought dimly, I'm half dead already. How much more could it hurt?

A noose was thrown over his head, the scratchy hemp

quickly greased with his blood. More hands. Another shove. Again he tripped; again he was hauled upright.

"No!"

A new voice. Young. Very young. A child's voice, raised pure and distinct above the guttural roar of the crowd.

"No, ye mustn't!"

A murmur began in the crowd.

" 'Tis the McClairen's daughter."

"The laird's wee lassie."

"McClairen's gel."

He felt a shift of attention thrum through the mob, a ripple of movement as something passed among them. He squinted, peering woozily about. He didn't understand what was happening, half expected to be snatched off his feet at any second and hanged from the gate's tines.

"No, I tell ye! Ye canna kill him. My mother, yer laird's own lady, begs ye to free him."

"The child's daft. Tragedy has chased her reason from her. Go up to her mother, Colin, and find out the truth." A stout young man shoved past Raine, heading into the tower.

"I am not mad! Me mother begs ye to spare this lad. My brothers' lives depend on it."

An unhappy rumble coursed through the crowd.

"Where is yer ma then, bairn?" someone asked.

"Dead!" A voice boomed from the tower window above. "The lady's bled to death!"

The lass burst out a choking sob. And Raine pitied the child, for it was clear she'd made a deathbed promise to her mother and clear she could not keep it. Children take such things hard.

Yet, she tried. " 'Twas more than she could bear, birthing me stillborn brother and then seeing how ye here are sure to cost her the lives of her other sons. She sent me with her dying breath to stop ye. Have ye no honor fer the dead?"

But all the crowd heard was that a McClairen lady had died in this all but tumbled tower where their laird had taken refuge while their enemy prospered in what should have been her home. And their enemy's son was in their power.

"Dead? Ye hear? The McClairen's lady is dead! Haul back on the rope! Draw him high! Make him kick!"

Suddenly Raine felt a small form hurtle into him, thin arms wrap about his torso, a face bury itself in his blood-soaked shirt. Voices broke out around them, shocked and hushed.

"I'll not let ye kill him," she vowed fiercely. "My brothers sit in a London prison and me da rides even now to seek the king's mercy. If ye kill this 'un, ye kill my brothers as surely as if ye wield the ax yerselves!"

He could barely stand with the girl's wee body clinging so desperately to him and his hands tied tight behind his back. The crowd milled uncertainly, their bloodlust temporarily suspended by the sight of the small lass in her white night rail clinging tenaciously to the tall, bowed form of the battered boy.

He tried a smile, failed, and whispered into the kitten-soft head beneath his chin, "Stand back, lassie. They'll not let me live this night through and your brothers are dead already. There's no mercy in London for Highlanders."

"The bastard speaks true!" the gaunt Scotswoman proclaimed. "Stand back, girl. Ye don't ken what he is, what is happening. Stand away!"

The child's arms wrapped tighter about his waist, her whole small body cleaving to his like a barnacle on a hull. "Nay! I promised my mother."

"Take her away."

But no one was willing to lay hands on the McClairen's last living child. Thus they stood for what seemed to Raine an interminable time, fixed in place like characters in a tableau vivant, awaiting death.

Death did not disappoint.

It rode in with the sound of hoofbeats resonating through the frozen ground, a lurid glow streaming toward them on the black highway.

"Redcoats!"

With something like exultance the crowd turned from Raine, snatching up pike and cudgel, outlawed sword and staff. They erupted into motion, streaming forth to meet the advancing troops. Raine stared, only vaguely conscious of the girl reaching up and pulling the noose from his throat.

And then the soldiers were on them. Horses cleaved the black night with lethal hooves, swords slashed flesh, and cudgels battered bone. Piercing scream, grunted effort, and everywhere grease and sweat-stained faces, taut with strain and rigid with virulence.

He blinked away the blood from his eyes and stared down at the girl. She trembled, shook so violently that he could hear her teeth rattling as she stared in wide-eyed horror at the massacre.

It was over quickly. So damn quickly. One minute the night churned in apocalyptic struggle, the next it was nearly silent. All about them Scotsmen lay dead and dying. A few soldiers strode among them, finishing off the survivors.

"*Is he alive?*"

Raine lifted his head, trying to find the source of that familiar voice, his father asking his status with immeasurable indifference. But then, who'd have even thought his father would have ridden to his aid?

"*Yes.*" Another familiar voice, rough with concern. Ashton, his brother, ever trying to stand between Raine and his own reckless nature. "*He's over there.*"

"*Oh.*" A moment's silence. "*And what is that next to him?*"

"*McClairen's daughter,*" Raine heard one of the soldiers answer.

"*Oh?*" Carr asked, his brightening tone evincing the interest he'd lacked on discovering Raine lived. "*How do you know?*"

"*There's a Scotswoman here cursing the little girl. Said if it hadn't been for her they'd have hanged Raine Merrick and been gone by the time we'd arrived.*"

Beside Raine the girl's head snapped up. "*No,*" she whispered.

"*Should I kill her?*"

"*The girl or the Scottish witch?*" his father replied. "*No. Don't bother. The woman looks too old to be breeding any more McClairens. Let her go. As for the girl . . . I suspect that one must consider her a subject of the Crown? And, in a way, now under my care?*"

"*Aye,*" the soldier answered in a confused voice.

"*As I thought.*" Carr sighed. He emerged from the darkness, maneuvering his mount carefully amid the bodies strewn over the frozen ground. He stopped, his attention fully on the child beside Raine, ignoring his son utterly.

"Don't touch her," Raine croaked.

Carr glanced at him. "I assure you, I have no intention of soiling myself by touching her and as for your tone, my boy . . . well, you have provided me with the excuse I needed to rid my lands of any remaining McClairens. Indeed, thanks to you, Raine, there are no more McClairens left." A slight keen issued from the girl and Carr's gaze dropped to the small figure huddled at Raine's feet. "And thanks to you, too, my dear."

He kneed his horse closer, puzzlement drawing his brows together. "Why did you save my worthless son?"

The girl's head came up, her eyes shimmering with tears in the torchlight. "Naught fer love of you, sir, but to save my brothers' lives."

Raine's father stared a second and then he threw back his golden head and laughed. All about them the soldiers, who'd been picking through the dead Scots' clothing like jackals among carcasses, lifted their heads and gave Carr their wary attention.

Raine swayed, nausea rising from his belly. He knew why Carr laughed. There could only be one reason. He closed his eyes, for he couldn't bear to see her face when he told her.

"But my dear, didn't anyone tell you? Didn't you know?"

"Know what?" the child whispered.

"Why, that at this very moment John McClairen's head decorates a pike above the North Gate."

Raine's eyes were closed, but he could not plug his ears. Only a child can voice such anguish, only a child who'd, in

*one single night, lost mother, brother, and the clan she'd
helped destroy.*

Because of him.

Raine jerked awake. He was covered in sweat, as
though his body, even now, all these years later, must
repudiate the events of that night. He eased back
against the seat, staring out at the sea.

Whether Favor McClairen was here hunting a husband as she claimed or was here for any other reason,
he would aid her and never threaten her again or cause
her fear.

He'd never had much experience with honor, nor
had he ever cared to become acquainted with such a
lofty concept. But for Favor McClairen he was willing
to learn.

Chapter 13

Carr sat motionless while his new valet finished shaving his hair in preparation for the new wig. The little man—Randall? Rankle?—slid the peruke in place and offered Carr a silver-foil cone. Carr held it to his face as powder descended about him in a fragrant cloud, covering the wig with a fine white coat. Rankle waited a few minutes for the dust to settle and then carefully removed the cape protecting Carr's clothing.

"Your Lordship looks most impressive," he said.

Carr flicked a little clod of powder from his sleeve. "Rankle," he asked curiously, "did you just comment on my appearance? You did, didn't you? Begad, what is this world coming to when servants offer unsolicited opinions on the appearance of their betters? I should thrash you for such impertinence but as that would probably undo the best of your tiresome ministrations, I shall resist the temptation. This time."

Really, first his magnanimity toward Tunbridge, now his valet. He was becoming positively mawkish.

He stood up and held his arms out from his sides waiting patiently while the valet scurried to pull them through the sleeves of his new waistcoat. Violet brocade, an extremely flattering color.

"Henceforth," Carr continued as Rankle adjusted the collar, "Henceforth, bear in mind that I am fully aware that I look impressive. Indeed, I am interested in your sartorial evaluation of my person only should I *fail* to look impressive."

"I'm sorry, sir!" That was the thing about new valets—it took such a deuced long time to break them in, Carr thought with a sigh as he reached down for his gloves and brought them in a blinding stroke across Rankle's face. The crystal beading on the cuff cut the little man's cheek. He raised his hand to the wound, staring at Carr in astonishment. A flicker of what looked like—by God!—anger flashed in his eyes. Impossible. Creatures such as Rankle did not get angry. They fled.

"I didn't ask if you were sorry. I was informing you of my opinion. And you interrupted me. Now, Rankle, should I ever look less than impressive you shall be dismissed. I imagine finding a position in these heathen parts without a letter of recommendation might be a trifle difficult."

The little valet flinched.

"Now, go away," Carr said. "I have decided not to

attend this evening's dinner. Have my daughter informed." The valet bowed and hurried off.

Carr approached a wall covered in green velvet and tugged on an embroidered bell pull. The material flew apart, billowing out and settling in banks on either side of an exquisite life-sized portrait. He stepped back, studying it tenderly.

"Janet, my dear, why now?"

He hadn't needed the old Gypsy, Pala, to tell him what he knew in his blood, what he'd sensed every night for a dozen years; that Janet was here, watching him. He was used to it. It neither disturbed nor even greatly interested him. The uses one could find for a ghost, after all, were limited.

But this new notion Pala had voiced, that a spirit could infiltrate another's body and in some sense live again, that Janet had done so, in order to come to him in the flesh once more—If she had found new housing for her spirit, he needed to discover it before he left this cursed castle once and for all.

She'd obviously left her scarf in order to convey some sort of message. But what? Had there been rebuke in that gesture?

Carr opened the lid of a chest that stood beneath the picture. It contained some gold, a few jewels, and remnants of the offending *arisaid*.

The night Janet had died he'd been hosting the first party Wanton's Blush had known since its renovation. The most important people in society had made the treacherous trip from London to attend. Among their number had been the king's personal secretary. The trouble, alas, had begun when he'd gone seeking his beautiful wife shortly before their guests were due to come down to dinner.

He found her—along with their brats—on the cliffs. Apparently she'd finally tumbled on to the fact of his involvement in her clan's . . . difficulties. In a fit of pique, she'd sworn to wear her family plaid to his party as a show of allegiance, knowing full well that the wearing of plaids was strictly prohibited by law. And with the king's secretary there!

She had sealed her own fate.

"In all honesty, Janet," he murmured to her likeness, "wasn't it a shade coincidental that you awoke to my 'duplicity' the day I hosted what could have been the most important party of my life?

"Yes." He nodded. "You might as well have jumped off that damn cliff yourself instead of forcing me to throw you over. You did it to ruin my party, didn't you? But I foiled your little plan, didn't I, my dear?"

Idly, he fingered the silk *arisaid*.

"What did you mean by leaving this for me to find, Janet? For you never were one for subtlety. Tiresomely straightforward, if truth be known. So what's this about?"

Thoughtfully, he dangled the torn half of scarf in front of the portrait. Perhaps, if she hadn't died that night he might not have felt compelled to marry those other heiresses; he might not have facilitated their demises and subsequently been banished.

She really did have a lot to answer for.

Perhaps Janet recognized her culpability. "Did you

leave me this by way of an apology? A sort of 'Here, you take the damn thing. It's caused enough grief.'"

The explanation pleased him. "It makes sense. I mean, a scarf isn't exactly the sort of thing one leaves behind as a means of striking terror into a body. I mean, it's a scarf, for God's sake, not a gory eyeball or a pulsing heart, or some such rot."

"Dear me, Father, please advise me should you ever try your hand at striking terror into someone. I shall absent myself immediately," a smooth feminine voice said from behind him. Carr spun about.

Fia stood framed in the doorway, her hands folded primly at the waist of an extraordinarily indecent dress. Another young woman would have looked like an expensive bawd in such a gown. On Fia one barely noted the midnight-blue satin.

Father and daughter regarded each other in silence. Beneath its thin layer of bright makeup Fia's face was perfectly composed. He'd seen an oriental doll once, a porcelain depiction of a theatrical character. It had been fine, detailed craftsmanship, finer than any he'd ever seen. But something about a doll depicting what was in essence a living doll had been unsettling, like seeing a reflection in a reflection. Looking at his daughter gave him exactly the same sensation.

"How long have you been there, spying on me?" he demanded.

She lifted one wing-shaped brow. "I wouldn't spy on you, Carr. Haven't you ever heard the old nursery adage 'He who listens at keyholes hears no good of himself'?"

Her tone was oblique, her brilliantly colored blue eyes, unrevealing. Where once she'd shared every thought with him, now she'd entombed herself in her composure, giving him nothing.

"What do you want?"

"That little man. Rankle. He said you would not be dining. I thought perhaps you'd taken ill. I came to see." Her tone did not imply concern, but impersonal curiosity. "Forgive my inquisitiveness, but does she answer you?" She raised her gaze to Janet's likeness.

Carr snapped the concealing draperies closed. "Speaking in front of a picture is not the same as speaking to a picture, Fia."

"Isn't it? Thank you for explaining the subtlety."

Not a ripple of expression flawed her smooth, ravishing young face. Just as well. His two sons had been hot-headed, emotional children; both had ultimately proven enormous wastes of his time.

Fia was different. Fia was, like himself, a predator. She would never let maudlin sentimentality cloud her judgment, nor pedestrian principles dull her purpose—that purpose being to see that she made the most brilliant matrimonial match English society—'sblood. *European* society!—had ever seen, thus aligning her father ultimately and irrevocably with power, prestige, and money. So much money he would never again need to waste a moment of his life thinking of it.

"What is that in your hand?" Fia asked.

"A piece of scarf Janet wore the day she died."

"Don't tell me her ghost left it for you?" Fia laughed and then reading his expression with horrifying accuracy, said quietly. "Begad, I do believe I've hit on it." She reached out, brushing her fingertips quickly over the silk and just as quickly withdrawing her hand.

"You know," Fia said coolly, "I should very much like to see my mother's ghost. Should you ever have occasion to chat with the transparent dame, kindly point her tattered parts my way when you're done."

"Are you mocking me?" he asked in his deadliest voice.

She considered him calmly. "Perhaps."

Insufferable, yet he dared not slap her and the reason provoked him far more than any words she could have uttered. He did not strike her because he was no longer precisely sure of what she was capable. Certainly revenge. Possibly more.

"Get downstairs," he commanded her, and waited, hating the uncertainty he felt. She'd never directly disobeyed him before. But someday soon she would. He needed to get her wed before then. "My guests ought not to be left unattended."

"You're right. They'll need a pied piper to lead them in their debauchery."

"I'll be down shortly."

"I hope so." Fia began to turn away. "There's a lady there who feels your absence keenly. She was quite distressed when she heard you were not dining."

Carr's interest quickened. Could it be her? Janet? "Lady?" he asked. "What did this lady look like?"

Fia watched him interestedly. "Elderly. Not yet antique but decidedly venerable."

Horrible apprehension filled him. Janet had died in

the full bloom of womanhood. The idea that she might choose to inhabit a body any less lovely than her previous one would never have occurred to him. She couldn't do that to him!

"Who is the lady?"

"Mrs. Diggle? Douglas? A mild-mannered, apologetic old cat. Not your usual guest."

"Douglas," Carr corrected her, his anxiety abating. He knew the lady. Anyone less like Janet would be hard to imagine. "No, she isn't in the mode of my usual guest. But her nephew certainly is and it's for his sake that she and her charge are here."

"Oh?" Fia intoned uninterestedly.

"Yes. He spent the spring here. You remember him," Carr said slyly, seeing an opportunity to reward Fia for her mockery. "Thomas Donne."

Fia had never confessed her infatuation for the tall Scotsman. She hadn't needed to. Every omission, every glance, every stilted conversation Carr overheard her have with Donne told the story of a young girl's first overwhelming passion. Just as her sudden and absolute silence on all matters regarding him told another sort of tale altogether.

Carr was rewarded. Her pupils contracted slightly, her nostrils turned a paler shade about the delicate rims. It was a nearly imperceptible reaction, if one wasn't looking for it.

"Of course," she said briskly. "I remember them now."

"Mrs. Douglas is chaperoning Donne's little sister, a Miss . . . Miss Favor, I believe." He scoured his memory for a face to put to the name and came up with a vague recollection of a comely, well-dressed wench, surprised he remembered that much. He paid little heed to virgins, even wealthy ones. What, after all, was the use? He couldn't marry again and since Favor Donne did not gamble and since he couldn't get at her money any other way, he hadn't bothered with her.

"What is she like?" Carr asked, twisting the knife a little. "Does she look like her brother?"

"I don't recall him that well," Fia said smoothly. "Miss Favor is small. Handsome. Black hair, aggressive eyes, a dark little warrior.

"Now that I think of it, I recall overhearing her asking one of the other guests after you, too."

Handsome? Black hair? And she'd asked after him.

"You know, Fia," he said, "I believe I have changed my mind. I believe I will go down to dine after all."

Chapter 14

*H*igh above the grand ballroom, hidden in a cleverly disguised gallery cut between the arching buttresses, Raine looked down at the spectacle below. The crowd churned like broken bits of brightly colored glass stirred in a giant bowl. The smell of bodies, ripe with heat and perfume, rose in sultry waves. Their din was as incessant as the surf beating at McClairen's Isle's rocks.

Though his vantage point allowed him only an occasional glimpse of an upturned face, he ultimately discovered the two figures that interested him. He spotted Carr first, resplendent in purple, standing as straight as ever, his gestures elegant and languid.

As a child Raine had despaired of ever achieving even a portion of his father's aplomb. Carr had ridiculed his attempts, advising him not to waste his efforts on so hopeless a cause. And when it had become clear that nothing Raine could ever do would raise him in his father's estimation, he'd sought other ways to win his attention. He could not begin to recall all the damage he'd done in that man's name: harassment of the locals, destruction, drunken fights, and mad carousal. All done to prick, discomfit him, embarrass; to somehow provoke a response—any response—from him.

Raine smiled ruefully. Five years earlier such memories would have awoken bitterness. But then, five years earlier Carr had been important to him. Since then Raine had had his priorities forcibly rearranged. He no longer cared about Carr, not even enough to hate him.

He studied his father with detachment. Still handsome, still rigidly straight and graceful. His gestures were just as smooth as ever, his expression as bland and polished. But even from this distance Raine could make out a slight slackening of the once tautly fitting flesh on his face, a looseness under the square jaw and the beginning of pouches under the fine eyes. Even Carr's will hadn't been able to keep the toll of years at bay.

Raine's gaze traveled through the crowd until he found Favor. Yards of vibrant jonquil yellow swathed her upright figure, the light-killing blackness of her dyed hair as coal dust against her white bosom. She moved unswervingly through the crowd, as though she traveled a narrow corridor without doors or windows but only one egress and that far ahead.

Hardly provocative behavior, yet she didn't lack for

attention. A definite pattern was emerging among Carr's male guests. A small train of them had fallen into procession behind Favor. It was subtle, of course; the idiots weren't actually queuing up, but undeniably Favor was gathering a retinue.

He understood the attraction. There was something about her. Something more than a desirable figure—though, by God, she did have that. And, he conceded, a not unhandsome face. Something about her challenged a man or provoked or inspired or—

Inspired?

He'd been imprisoned too long. 'Twas the only way to account for this interest in Favor McClairen. Because she'd saved his life he'd imbued her with qualities she more than likely didn't possess.

If Favor inspired him at all it was with lust, he decided. And it was damned maddening that the woman whose skirt he wanted to toss up was named McClairen. It complicated things. It caused obligation to contend with animal desire.

Obligation would win. After all, for him to owe a debt to another person, particularly one he was in a position to honor, was a unique experience for him. Lust was not.

Once more he focused his attention on Favor. The dowdy female beside her must be her chaperone. At first glance he could not imagine a less effective-looking dragon to defend this particular damsel. But a short observation proved him wrong. Few of the men following Favor made it to her side. Apparently she allowed access only to those who met some standard set by either the old biddy or Favor herself. What would that be?

Whatever the gauge, Raine thought wryly, for a certainty his name would never have made the approved list. But then, he didn't need to chase after Favor McClairen. She was coming to him in—he pulled out his timepiece—about ten hours.

"Here's your food," Favor said sullenly. She flung the tied napkin at Rafe, envisioning the greasy contents making an agreeable splotch on his white shirt.

She hadn't counted on the rogue's having such keen reflexes. He spun away from the window he'd been looking through and snagged the bundle from the air. His shirt was opened, exposing his lean torso. A pistol, tucked beneath the waist of tight black breeches, caused hardly a dent in a flat belly dark with fur. The sleeves of his shirt had been rolled up over broad, tanned forearms.

Her gaze plummeted to the ground, utterly nonplussed by an immediate tactile memory of that warm flesh beneath her hand. This was not Dieppe. He was no longer chained to a wall and she was no longer pretending to be a—whatever Madame Noir was.

More's the pity, an inner voice mocked.

"Why, how civilized!" Rafe said. "With such manners, Miss Donne, I'm certain your brother's doorway must soon be choked with suitors."

"Humph," she said, but could not entirely quell a smile in response to his banter. How odd he was acting, how . . . friendly. She was immediately on her guard.

He clamped a palm theatrically to his chest. "I swear when your mouth twitches like that it sets my heart to racing. Assuredly, whoever instructed you to hoard your smiles knew their power. For should you ever actually grin, I am sure no man could be held accountable for his actions. Certainly I could not testify as to what I would be capable of doing."

She burst out laughing, surprised and amazed. Whatever she'd expected from her blackmailer, it had not been charm or merry foolishness. She'd assumed she would deposit his food in the middle of an empty room and leave. She'd never expected him to be waiting for her.

He smiled back, displaying a full set of even white teeth and surprising her yet again, for his smile filled his eyes with warmth and humor. It was a potently attractive smile, a devastatingly attractive smile, devil-may-care and winning. A man with a smile like that didn't need elegant features and that recognition sobered her.

He sensed her withdrawal, his smile became one-sided and wry. "Ah, forgive me my jest. For a moment I forgot our relative positions and the history that had led us here."

"That being you as blackmailer and me as victim?"

The dimple in his lean cheek cut deeper. "And here I'd cast myself as the injured party. How could I have so misinterpreted our roles? Mayhap it had something to do with you throwing me to the wolves in Dieppe?"

She flushed. Vindicated, he turned his attention to the napkin. He planted a huge boot on the windowsill, using his broad thigh as a table on which he unknotted the linen and spread it open. He bent his head over the package, the movement causing his shirt to gape away from his chest, revealing hard contours she all too clearly remembered. They were even more contoured now. Presumably they would be even harder.

"Beefsteak!"

She jumped. He glanced up, his honey-colored eyes guileless.

"Bless the English for their unholy love of dining on beef. Didn't bring me a set of cutlery, did you, sweetheart?"

"Don't call me 'sweetheart.' And no, I did not. I considered it," she replied dryly, "but rather worried that someone might object to me nipping off with the silver. Believe me, I drew enough odd looks when I dumped my dinner in my lap."

He burst out laughing. "You didn't!"

"I did. How else was I to get your food? I couldn't very well show up at the kitchen door with a sack and a request that it be filled with table scraps. And I most certainly couldn't send a servant. Your presence would be discovered within an hour. Once a servant smells a secret he won't rest until he's ferreted it out."

"Well versed in the ways of servants, are we?" He tore off a piece of meat and popped it in his mouth. His eyes slid half-shut in sybaritic pleasure. He chewed slowly, savoring the process, swallowed and sighed.

Deliberately, he licked the burgundy-laced gravy from each finger.

She'd never seen anyone enjoy food so thoroughly. It was fascinating.

He had long fingers, lean and strong-looking. Soft, dark hairs sprinkled lightly across their backs, growing more thickly above his wide, supple-looking wrists. Very masculine, his hands.

He looked up and caught her watching him. He winked. "Four years of moldy cheese and stale bread soaked in water," he explained without the slightest hint of rancor. "I will never again take the joy of eating lightly. Care for a bit?"

"No." She sounded doubtful. She tried again. "No!"

"Please yourself." He shrugged and popped the next bit into his mouth. "Cake!"

His delighted cry broke her reverie. She scuttled back, as though her thoughts were physical things she could retreat from. He didn't notice, being too busy devouring the cake she'd brought— and ruined when she'd hurled it at him. He had beautiful—

Whyever was she thinking these things? She was daft! He was her enemy!

But was he? That sly, internal voice queried. Or wasn't she, if truth be told, his? Or had been.

Since Dieppe, he had done nothing to cause her any harm. He may have frightened her but even that might have been manufactured more from her own guilty conscience than his actions. In fact, he'd rescued her from Orville.

Her eyes narrowed suspiciously. Yet, as he'd already pointed out, he could still denounce her.

She should tell Carr about Rafe. Immediately. And when he, in turn, revealed her she would affect astonishment and pity. Everyone would think he was a ranting madman, especially since by his own words he was hunting for a fairy-tale cache of jewels. It was a good plan. She should implement it.

She *would* have implemented it by now except . . . except he hadn't done her any harm and she'd done him wrong aplenty.

"Should I be expecting a brace of bruising footmen any moment?" Having finished the cake, he dusted the crumbs from his threadbare breeches. "Or have you decided to take pity on me after all?"

His words too closely followed her duplicitous thoughts. She felt contemptible. She disliked feeling contemptible. She reacted badly to it.

"I brought you food, didn't I?" she asked.

"They always fed the prisoners a bit better before taking them out to be drawn and quartered."

He'd startled her yet again. How could he make light of such a thing?

"I haven't told anyone about you."

"Including the old puss?"

"Excuse me?"

"Your chaperone."

Muira. No, she hadn't ever considered telling Muira about Rafe. The old woman would probably have had Jamie hunt him down and slit his throat. Nothing must interfere with Muira's grand scheme. "You mean my aunt. No. She doesn't know about you."

He smiled again. "My thanks."

Her gaze flickered away and back. He grinned more broadly, as though he knew the course of her wayward and wholly unacceptable thoughts and lowered his leg from the sill. "That was good."

He reached his long arms above his head, rotating at the hip as he slowly stretched from one side to the other, his shirt ends swinging like the foundering sails on a tall ship. She felt the warmth stealing up her throat and turned away so he would not be driven to make any ridiculous assumptions about her blush.

"How goes the hunt for McClairen's Trust?" she asked.

"It goes."

She looked about. Most of the boxes and trunks had been opened since yesterday. He'd rifled through the pictures standing against the wall, too. A portrait of a black-haired lady stood at the head of the stack, face out. It hadn't been there before.

She was beautiful, dressed in silvery blue, the frothy gown slipping from her shoulders. She had a tender smile and a stubborn jaw. Her eyes were bold and her expression pleased.

"How goes the husband hunt?"

His words recalled her not only to her immediate surroundings but to her other obligations. How she loathed her part in Muira's plan. For an hour there she'd forgotten. Perhaps that had been the real reason she hadn't informed against Rafe. He'd provided a distraction, made her forget the eerie mixture of cool speculation and feverish intensity in Carr's expression last night.

"Well?" he repeated.

"It goes."

"Any likely candidates?"

"Perhaps."

Carr had brought her punch. She'd thanked him but further words had died in her throat. The man had killed her people, then laughed as he'd told her that her brother's head decorated a London pike. He hadn't seemed to miss her conversation.

He'd stared fixedly at her, a little scowl furrowing that blasphemously noble-looking brow. It had taken all her self-control not to recoil. Which did not, she supposed, bode well for their proposed marriage bed.

She'd seen Muira out of the corner of her eye. Beneath the soft mask of feeble amiability she'd been gloating. Near rapturous. Favor had left the room soon after, Muira bustling after her, commending her on her coquetry in an exultant whisper. On reaching her room, she'd locked the door against Muira.

Perhaps in coming here she was "locking the door" again. Even with the danger and risk Rafe posed, at least it was a danger of her own choosing, a risk only to herself, taken independent of the McClairens and Carr and Muira. Here it was just him. And her.

"You're not considering Orville for a potential mate, are you?"

"Orville?" Favor repeated.

"Your smile was hardly pleasant. I thought perhaps

you'd determined Orville had the deepest available pockets and for all his lack of charm would serve your purpose."

She didn't consider telling him the name of her projected spouse. Rafe might be a distraction for her, but she knew next to nothing about him. She would take no risk with Muira's plans. Besides, he'd only laugh at her. Or worse, pity her or even—*damn* that inner voice!—be disgusted with her.

"No. Not Orville. He's married. I haven't really decided on anyone yet."

"Oh?" He moved closer to her. He was very, very tall. She had to lean her head back to meet his eyes. "Then I suppose you'll be in a lather to get back to the mart and queue up the prospects."

She snorted in an utterly unladylike manner. "Hardly." The word came spilling out before she could stop it, giving far too much away.

One heavy brow climbed above a toffee-brown eye. "Good."

"And why is that?" she asked.

"Because," he said, "I've decided that food and clothing—the latter of which, by the way, I don't see— are too little to demand by way of reparation. Especially from someone who was anticipating rape."

Her heartbeat kicked into a gallop. Her mouth went dry.

"What do you want?" she croaked.

"You'll see," he said, his sensual gaze gliding over her face and body. "But first, you'll have to take off those clothes."

Chapter 15

Sweat covered Favor's bare arms and neck. The fine hairs at her temple coiled into damp tendrils and clung in little black commas to her throat and collarbone. She licked her lips, sampling the salty mist. Her limbs felt weak and logy. Muscles she hadn't even known she owned ached with overuse.

She looked in the mirror, barely recognizing the well-tumbled-looking, relaxed wench staring back. Her makeup had long since gone. Her skin glowed.

"Oh," she whispered guiltily, "that was grand!"

"What did you say?"

She turned from the mirror, smiling innocently at Rafe. He'd stopped rummaging through the huge crate he'd hefted to the top of a breakfront. "Nothing."

It would never do to admit that helping him search

for McClairen's Trust had been more reward than punishment. She'd shed her beautiful gown and donned the old smock he'd unearthed from some box, trying to hide her elation. She'd spent too much time in front of too many mirrors trying to be Janet McClairen. The relief of her release from that role made her giddy.

It had been wonderful. She'd rummaged, poked, and rifled through cabinets and wardrobes, drawers and chests, under beds and through rolls of bunting and stacks of linens. She hadn't found the Trust or the ornamental box he claimed legend said it resided in—though she'd never heard that part of the legend before.

She *had* found little mysteries and precious keepsakes: a child's ebullient account of his life written a hundred years before; a broken scimitar reverently wrapped in a faded Moorish flag; a woman's crystal flacon that still carried the faint scent of roses. They captivated her with their unspoken histories. McClairen histories.

Her history.

She remembered few of her mother's stories and none of her father's. She barely recalled him at all. He'd returned from London soon after the massacre, his plea for mercy refused; her brothers' fates sealed. He'd returned and been met with the news of his wife's death and his people's slaughter. He'd been dead within the year.

Muira had written to her about her ancestors; long lists of names and dry recitations of battles won and lands conquered. But *these* things, Favor gently touched a child's pearl ring, they related intimate stories. For the first time her ancestors had become real.

What fond mother had tucked this leather slingshot into this drawer? Had someone died wielding this scimitar or had it been broken symbolically? This flacon may have been a great aunt's, this diary her grandfather's.

Rafe didn't object to her dawdling—even when she spread a pack of tattered playing cards upon the floor and pored over it until she'd discovered that the knave of hearts was missing. He'd remained silent, systematically going through each piece of furniture and chest along one wall.

Only occasionally she'd crow with delight over some oddity and look up to find him watching her with an unreadable expression. She didn't know what to make of him. These past few hours, he'd seemed nothing more than a young man filled with enthusiasm for their task. It was as if in this room both of them had found some part of the innocent pleasures of a childhood neither had owned.

"Well, this is the last thing large enough to hold a two-foot-square box," she said, tapping on the lid of a traveling trunk. It was just as well. The sun would set in an hour or so. If she wanted to escape an interrogation by Muira, she'd have to be back in her room dressed for evening by the time the old lady knocked on the door.

Rafe didn't answer so she raised the heavy lid. Inside lay carefully folded satin clothing, copper and plum colored, studded with gems and metallic threads, glinting like the scales of an exotic fish beneath long-desiccated lavender sprigs.

"What is it?" Rafe asked, peering over her shoulder.

"I don't know," she replied, keeping her face averted. He smelled of dust and heat and male exertion, a potent scent, distinct and earthy. She dared not turn. He still wore his shirt open.

"Begad, at least one of those Highland heathens was a dandy." His laughter tickled her ear.

"What is it?" she asked, gingerly lifting the gleaming material.

"I believe it's a gentleman's coat in the Persian style. Quite the mode in the last French court."

"It's fantastic!" she exclaimed, shaking lose the folds and holding the garment up by the shoulders. "What is the purpose of these loops of ribbon, do you imagine?" She glanced over her shoulder.

He stood very close behind her. A long streak of grime marked his exposed pectoral like a brand. His labors had sheathed his dark skin in a silky dampness, accentuating each contour and ridge in the slanting light. A white scar on his belly disappeared under the waistband of breeches, which rode low on his hips.

"Decorative." He reached over her shoulder and flicked his finger against a jeweled bauble. "Damn, it's only glass."

"Oh, and you're an expert on gems?" she asked dryly.

He grinned cheekily, his sidelong glance too knowing by half. "You'd be surprised at what areas I excel in."

She rather doubted that.

She looked away, unwilling to be caught and held by his gaze. It had already happened several times too often that afternoon. It was like drowning in a warm pool of honey.

She quashed the errant thought. The longer she spent in his company, the more easily such thoughts came. 'Twould never do. They were . . . well, if not exactly sworn enemies, hardly friends. After all, she was here under duress, not because she wanted to be here. Even if she *did* enjoy being here, he didn't know that.

She was getting damned—she bobbed her head and mumbled a *mea culpa* for her profanity—confused.

"What are you doing?" he asked curiously.

"Thinking."

"About?"

"How . . . how perfect this would be for the masque."

"What masque?"

"Friday evening, a week hence," she answered, glad to escape her uncomfortable thoughts. She peered into the trunk. More garments lay exposed. Buff breeches, garters of pink rosettes and buckles sparkling with crystals. "We're all to dress in costume and conceal our faces."

His expression smoothed to indifference. "Ah. There's good hunting," he said. "Just make sure the bait isn't taken before the trap is sprung."

"Pardon me?"

His smile was suave. "It's a perfect opportunity for a spot of dalliance. How did you so charmingly put it? 'All I own is my virtue'? I'm simply advising you to retain it so that come your wedding night you can . . . deliver the goods. A masque offers a unique opportunity for men—and women—to sample that which they have no intention of purchasing."

She felt as though he'd slapped her. From easy camaraderie, he'd plunged them back into Wanton's Blush's sordid world. She could not think to reply. Her hands fell to her sides, carrying with them the copper-colored coat.

"Here now," he said, "that expression of censure will never do, Miss Donne. As a prime piece in this particular marriage mart you are here to be approved, not to condemn your fellow guests for taking advantage of that which they came expressly to enjoy."

"And what is that?" she asked stiffly.

"An amoral, conscienceless society."

"You overstate the case."

His laughter contained no humor. "Perhaps you choose not to see what is abundantly clear."

"How do you know so much about it?" she challenged him.

"Everyone knows about Wanton's Blush, Miss Donne," he replied. Pity softened his tone. "Didn't you?"

"Of course." Carelessly she tossed the gentleman's coat back into the trunk. "Whatever odd notions you have about me, you exceed yourself. You know nothing about me. Even less than I know about you."

"Which is exactly what?" he asked.

"That you are a thief. You are a blackmailer. You are here to steal jewels and you have forced me to be your accomplice." Her gaze dared him to deny the charge. He didn't.

"I take it our truce is off," he said glibly.

"Yes. I got your food. I helped you search this room. I have done enough for you. I bid you *adieu*, Monsieur." She wheeled about, sailing past him and to the door with stately indifference.

"Brava." *Clap. Clap. Clap.* He was applauding!

The scoundrel! The wretch! She swallowed an angry retort, refusing to acknowledge his audacity. She took hold of the door handle and pulled. It remained stubbornly shut. Damn! She closed her eyes, mumbled a prayerful apology, grasped the handle in both hands and yanked. Nothing.

"Damn! Damn! *Damn!*"

"Miss Donne?"

Frustration vied with mortification. Frustration won. She seized the handle, shaking the brass handle violently.

"Miss Donne?"

"What!" She swung around.

His arms overflowed with emerald velvet, yards and yards of the stuff. "You forgot your dress."

She bit down hard on her lip, refusing to give vent to the string of epithets piling up behind her clenched teeth. She stalked back across the room, snatched her gown from him, turned, marched back to the door, seized the handle in both hands, and, setting her heels for leverage—

"You might want to try pushing the door rather than pulling it."

Striving for some shred of dignity, she pushed. Silently, the door swung open.

"Tomorrow we'll search the room next to this one."

She wouldn't reply.

"Also, though the beef was good, I wouldn't mind some fowl. Try not to mash up the cake next time."

He *couldn't* make her respond.

"And do remember my clothes. I should hate for my aroma to offend you tomorrow and I intend to keep working this evening."

"I'm not coming tomorrow," she bit out.

"Now, that"—his voice, all afternoon so easy and unruffled, now flooded with darkness—"would be a mistake."

"Miss Donne." Carr stood back from the chair he held out, waiting for her to take her seat. For him to have not only taken her in to dinner but then to seat her so high at the table was beyond irregular. Speculative murmurs rippled beneath the squawk of drink-infused conversation. Favor slid into the seat, refusing to acknowledge the glares of those who would point out that by doing so she usurped a marchioness, a pair of baronesses, and at least half a dozen ladies.

"Miss Donne."

Favor looked up and found herself facing Fia Merrick across the table. The girl looked faintly amused. But as far as Favor could tell, Lady Fia always looked faintly amused, her black wing-shaped brows forever canted at an ironic angle, the ice blue of her gaze perpetually glittering with secret wisdom.

"Lady Fia," she returned politely. What could this enigmatic and aloof girl want of her? Though at least three years her junior, in some ways Fia seemed older than any woman in the room.

"Lord Tunbridge begs an introduction." Long, slender fingers moved fractionally, stirring the air in a little ballet of grace, indicating a hitherto unnoticed gentleman. "Miss Favor Donne, may I present Lord Tunbridge. Lord Tunbridge, Miss Donne."

He nodded, his hooded gaze assessing her closely. "Miss Donne, my pleasure."

Tall and cadaverously thin, the unpadded skin of his face cleaved tightly to a well-shaped skull. He looked angry and hungry. His white hands moved restlessly among the silverware, fidgeting and aligning the pieces.

Favor mentally skewered her right cheek with a dimple, emulating Janet McClairen's one-sided smile. "Thank you, sir."

"Tunbridge is a great friend of Carr's," Fia said smoothly. "Aren't you, Lord Tunbridge?"

Beside Favor, Carr remained silent, clearly comfortable in the role of spectator.

"But not so great a friend as he would like to be," Fia said. Briefly, affecting sympathy, she touched Tunbridge's hand, lingering just a shade longer than simple sympathy would merit. Tunbridge speared her with a ravening glance, which she adroitly avoided.

"They appear to have had a falling out, however," Fia continued. "These things sometimes happen among intimates, Miss Donne. Particularly ones with so long a history as Lord Tunbridge and my father. We must apply ourselves to smoothing things o'er between them. It is our duty as women, being the pacific creatures that we are. Don't you agree?"

The girl's lines were designed to give Favor an opportunity to perform her role. Yet she found herself resisting. The afternoon had given her a taste for freedom. How ironic that a thief and a blackmailer should have provided her with a momentary escape from her fate—a fate she herself had chosen, she reminded herself sternly.

Fia was still calmly awaiting her answer.

Favor still had a debt to repay.

"I am sorry to contradict you, Lady Fia, but I have never considered myself particularly pacific. Perhaps it is your nature to forget a wrong. It is not mine."

Beside her she heard Carr's faint but discernable inhalation. The veins on the back of his hands stood out like ropes. *En garde*.

"So you believe in a biblical variety of justice?" Fia asked.

Favor picked up her wineglass, twirling the ruby liquid, studying it. She needed to frame a telling response, something that would draw Carr. But he stank of perfume and the heat from his body clung to him like an oily mist and he'd laughed when he'd told her about her brother John.

"Miss Donne?"

Janet. They were trying to convince Carr that Janet wanted him back. It was their plan—*her* plan. She'd agreed to be Janet and Janet wanted Carr back.

"Forgive me," she said, smiling Janet's smile. "I confess I was fretting over how honest I dare be. I would hate to risk whatever portion of regard"—she divided her gaze flirtatiously between Carr and Tunbridge—"I might have won. The truth is that I am a creature given to my own comfort, both physical and otherwise.

"In addressing a wrong done me I would seek relief—if justice alone would provide that, then justice would serve me. If recompense eased me, then I would seek compensation. If I felt robbed, I would demand back what had been taken from me." She fluttered her lashes coyly. "I suspect you find that quite shallow and self-serving?"

"I find it bracingly honest," Tunbridge declared. "How refreshing to meet a lady who provides so succinct an outline for her behavior. Who informs a gentleman of her character rather than deceiving him."

Favor felt sorry for the man. He so obviously spoke to Fia, whose attention was fixed on the chilled pear a servant had placed before her.

"I think honesty is vastly overrated," Fia murmured, delicately slicing off a thin piece. "I think Miss Donne would agree. Certainly her brother would. I know Carr does."

What did she mean by that? And what had Thomas had to do with her?

"Lady Fia?" She kept her voice calm.

"She insists on being provocative," Carr spoke before Fia could reply, his manner disgusted. "It's a child's trick but then she is a child. You'd be wise to remember that, Tunbridge, next time she involves you in her games."

If Carr thought to vex Fia he was doomed to disappointment. She lowered her head, a little smile playing about her lips.

"A child? Games?" Tunbridge trembled on the verge of saying more. His chair legs scraped the floorboards as he shoved his chair away from the table. He stood up, snapping forward slightly at the waist. "Forgive me, Miss Donne. I fear I am inadequate company tonight."

"Tonight?" Favor barely heard Fia say. Beside her Carr snickered. Favor's head swam, trying to find her way through all the undercurrents she perceived. She dined with jackals. Tunbridge, gutted and hung, could only turn and leave.

But Janet would be used to such behavior. And while Janet had not approved much of what Carr had done and said, she had never publicly chastised him. She had ignored what she did not approve. So said Muira.

"Wherever do you find pears in the Highlands, Lord Carr?" she said, and bit into the succulent fruit. It tasted like clay.

* * *

The night would not end. The clock struck the witching hour but the revelry wound tighter, like a watch in the hands of a feckless, spoiled child. Fia disappeared, her inexplicable interest in Favor as quickly gone as it had appeared.

The one-sided smile had petrified like rigor mortis in Favor's cheek. Her spine ached from trying to appear taller than she was and the belladonna Muira had dropped into her eyes to dilate her pupils caused her head to throb and her vision to swim.

Carr, too, had distanced himself. Ordinarily, Favor would have retired but though Carr had left her side, he still watched her. Intently, covertly, hour after hour. So Favor ignored her throbbing head and aching back and listened to Muira who bobbed and grinned and hissed instructions at her.

At two o'clock Carr finally approached her once again and asked her to dance. She obliged. He was a superb dancer, guiding her expertly and wordlessly through the intricate steps. At the end, as he led her back to where Muira sat feigning sleep with her chin sunk upon an ample false bosom, he finally spoke. "I found your scarf."

Favor scoured her memory for some point of reference, some scarf that Muira had told her about that Janet had owned. She could recall none. Perhaps he sought to trick or test her?

"I have lost no scarf, Lord Carr. I fear one of your other lady guests is missing it."

His face stilled. It had been no trick. He had expected some other reply. Damn Muira for this over-sight.

Too late to claim the scarf now. At least until she found out from Muira what it meant.

"Ah. My mistake. Thank you for the dance, Miss Donne," he said, and bowed before disappearing into the crowd.

"What was that all about?" Favor looked down. Muira's expression was muddled, like someone coming awake, but her low-pitched tone was hard-edged.

Favor was in no mood to accept Muira's carping criticism. She, too, could hiss through a smile. "The next time you leave one of Janet's scarves laying about for Carr to find, I suggest you inform me first."

Muira's genteel mask evaporated, leaving a hard middle-aged face staring at Favor in angry consterna-tion. "I didn't leave any scarf anywhere."

Moonlight bathed Favor's sleeping form, embossing her features with blue-white alchemy. Her head bur-rowed against her pillow, the inky hair spilling across the coverlet and down the side of the bed. Her lips parted slightly and a little frown puckered the skin be-tween her brows.

The tall, dark figure standing at the foot of the bed angled his head, studying her intently. She looked tired, even in sleep, Raine thought.

He'd watched her from above the ballroom most of the night. Her shoulders had drooped with fatigue long before the evening had ended. Even from where he'd been standing the white face powder had not concealed the dark smudges beneath her eyes. And she'd held her head as though it ached.

She shouldn't have come here, he thought. She shouldn't—

She moaned and stirred unhappily. The small sound of distress sent him forward, out of the shadows, his hand poised to bestow a comforting caress. Abruptly he stopped.

No, he realized. It was he who shouldn't have come.

Chapter 16

The afternoon sun slanted through the stained-glass oriel, piercing the cool dimness of the Lady's Chapel and casting a mosaic of warm color on the gray stone floor. Overhead, shallow niches flanked the small, grimy rosette window. Within these a pair of dust-mantled saints kept vigil. Though the castle's chapel had long been denuded of bench and altar, it had always had a certain solemn dignity. No longer.

Raine had finally found where his father had banished his mother's possessions. "Damn you, Carr."

He looked about, unprepared for the wash of sadness recognition brought with it. So many memories. Here was a blue dress she'd worn one Michaelmas. He recalled how lovely she'd looked hastening down the stairs, her crisp petticoats rustling. Now it was limp and yellow and housed a family of mice.

Near the bottom of a heap of haphazardly stacked furnishings he spied the bench that had sat before her dressing table, its red petit point tulips dull and moth-eaten. Her favorite fan lay atop it, the painted silk tatters clinging to it, ivory frets like the fragile bones of an ancient corpse.

All jumbled and discarded and abandoned. No careful folding of Janet McClairen's things. No sweet lavender sprigs to retard the inevitable march of decay—The chapel door opened on a loud protest and Favor swept in.

"So, 'twas you! I thought I heard something down here," she announced triumphantly. "This part of the castle echoes strangely, don't you think? I swear I heard you say 'damn' all the way at the other end of the corridor."

Her voice was bright with interest, as alive as these things were dead. She brought with her all the ruthless practicality of her youth. And she swept the sadness from his soul as heedlessly as the riptide scours the shore.

"What are you doing here?" he asked.

She'd angled her head back, looking around. "This is where the McClairens wed and were christened and from where they were buried," she murmured. "That rosette window was brought from Paris."

"How would you know that?" he asked dryly, curious as to how she would wiggle out of this revealing statement. Clearly she could not afford for anyone to discover she was a McClairen. Carr would have her ousted within an hour.

But Raine had underestimated her. Her wistful expression evaporated. "Oh, it's all in the diaries and journals I've found," she said. "Oh, my! Look. I believe this is Venetian lace. 'Tis criminal someone would leave it to rot like this."

The pleasure she found in the task to which he'd sentenced her was as unaccountable as it was captivating. This was her fourth day helping him search for McClairen's Trust and each day she appeared, she sparkled more. Of course, were he to charge her with such a thing she would deny it. But he doubted she'd deny it to herself. She was a gifted liar, but as with all gifted liars, she would have an uncanny ability to be truthful with herself.

"You're early." He'd told her noon and it was not ten o'clock yet here she was, eager and ravishing and vulnerable. So very, very vulnerable. She had no idea the thoughts taking root in his imagination.

"Sooner begun; sooner done," she quipped, but the sparkle in her eyes belied the indifference in her voice.

Damn his misplaced chivalry. He should seduce her and be done with it. But he wouldn't. For while he was all too certain of his reaction to her, he was uncertain of hers to him.

He assumed she found him somewhat attractive. He'd a wealth of memories that taught him the signs of female interest and Favor, bless her, met the criteria. But he knew nothing of what a convent-raised girl did with such an interest.

And, too, Raine wasn't certain he wished to jeopardize this . . . this whatever this was. In his experience such camaraderie between the genders was unique. He'd never been in a young woman's company without the specter of imminent seduction transforming each word they exchanged into double entendres and each look into mental disrobing.

The young women in his past had been interested in one thing, for one reason, which even then Raine had realized had more to do with his reputation than with any personal recommendation. They'd sought him precisely because of his inability to curb his wild impulses—

"Well?" Favor asked impatiently, her tone suggesting she was repeating herself.

"Pray, pardon me. What was it you asked?"

"Why are you staring at me?" She looked down at her dress in some consternation. "I couldn't very well wear that filthy smock again and it's cold in here."

"I'm not staring. I'm trying to decide how best to put your rather negligible skills to work."

She accepted his excuse, completely unmoved by his criticism. She looked about the room and spied the book he'd placed on a shelf in the huge, teetering armoire near the door.

Like a cat drawn by a piece of yarn, her expression sharpened with interest, she hastened over to it. Gingerly, she opened the first page, catching her lower lip beneath the edge of her slightly crooked front teeth. They added a piquant note to her countenance. A once fierce countenance, he thought, deploring the artificial arc that stood in place of the once proud, slashing brows.

She read avidly and he watched her, feeling ridiculously pleased. He purposely sought such items for her to find, hoping to give her access to the history her clansmen hadn't lived to relate.

If he recalled correctly her father, Colin, had been a second son who'd left the Highlands early in life to seek fame and fortune. Instead, he founded a family—a wife and three children whom he'd sent home to Scotland while he continued seeking that ever-elusive fortune.

He came home in disappointment some years later to find his sons imprisoned for their part in their uncle Ian's Jacobite plottings. Ian had already been executed, and for a short time Colin had been laird.

Favor, Raine recalled, had never even lived at Wanton's Blush, her mother, dispossessed by Carr, awaiting her husband's return in an old deserted tower on the headland. The tower where Raine had been dragged so many years before.

The memory diminished his earlier pleasure. As though she sensed his darkening mood, Favor looked up from the page she'd been perusing. She closed the book, the resultant puff of dust causing her nose to wrinkle. "It's a sort of account book with personal notations. But it's not by Duart McClairen."

"Pray who might Duart McClairen be?"

"The little boy whose diary I found the other day."

"I see. And why did you think it might be young Duart's?"

"Oh, I don't know." She shrugged. How the holy Sisters must have bemoaned that particular mannerism. "I guess it was wishful thinking. I was rather hoping to discover what happened to Duart after he grew up."

"As I recall you were good for no work that day, your nose being stuck between the pages of the little heathen's memoirs."

"How do you know Duart was a little heathen?"

Because whatever interests you, I find interests me.

"There's not much to do come nightfall. Sometimes I read. Pray, try to compose your expression into bland acceptance, Favor; such ill-mannered surprise speaks poorly of the good Sisters. I can read . . . if I take care to sound out the words. But pray, don't let me interfere with your own reading."

If she noted his sarcasm, she did not reveal it. "No, thank you. I'll read it later. In my room." She tilted her head sideways. "Who exactly are you, Rafe?"

Since that night in the carriage in Dieppe she'd never asked him anything personal. It was as though she feared what she would discover. He turned up his palms. "You already named me. I am a blackmailer and a thief. There's nothing more to tell."

"You are awfully well spoken for a common thief."

"I should hope there's nothing common about me," he said haughtily, drawing a smile from her.

"Then you must be the, er, unacknowledged progeny of some personage?"

"Why, Miss Donne, are you asking whether or not I am a bastard?"

"Excuse me," she mumbled, blushing fiercely, the unexpectedness of it charming him in spite of himself.

"I'm not a bastard. But I'm no longer acknowledged by my father." It was near enough the truth.

"Because of your thieving propensities?"

He stood very still, thinking. He could tell her the truth. It had started out so nobly, so simply. He would anonymously aid the girl to whose life he had brought tragedy. But it was quickly becoming a deeper game he played and he wasn't at all sure what he'd anted or what was at stake. He *should* tell her who he was and let the chips fall where they may.

But then she would leave.

"Just so," he said.

She nodded, her smile an odd mixture of relief and suspicion. A naive liar; an innocent jade. She presented a riveting enigma.

"What about your mother?"

"She's dead." It came out more sharply than he'd intended. He looked up to see Favor's stricken countenance and immediately realized her conjecture.

"No, Favor, she didn't die from heartbreak over her son's criminal propensities. She died well before my *entrée* into the criminal underworld."

"I'm sorry." Her voice was tender with commiseration. "My mother died when I was young, too."

He could not think how to answer her. He remembered well Favor's mother's death.

"What was your mother like?" Favor asked.

"Beautiful. Capricious. A bit vain. Too romantic. Perhaps she was callow. She struggled mightily to believe in fairy tales." He remembered being angry when she asked him and Ash how they'd come by their bruises. She never hesitated to ask but then they'd never hesitated to lie. She never pressed; they never offered more.

"You did not like her very much."

"Like her?" He considered. "I don't know. She was totally absorbed with my father. But when she was with us . . . no one was more entertaining. She was cultured and honest and irreverent." He looked down at the fan in his hand. One could still make out part of the Greek temple painted on one of the sections. "For example, though she loved classical things, she didn't pretend to venerate them. She christened the Greek folly in our garden the Part of None, after the Parthenon, mocking her pretensions."

"You loved her."

"Yes." He set the fan down. "Come, we've work to do and you won't wriggle out of it by such transparent devices."

She grinned. "Since you are so determined to press me into service, O Master Most Severe, where wouldst thou I begin?"

"Did you bring my clothes?" he asked, knowing his tone would dampen her whimsical mood but having no idea how else to alleviate its effect on him.

Either I suppress some of that brilliant vivacity or you pay the consequences, little falcon, he silently abjured her. She'd saved his life and he would not repay her by seducing her no matter how often he flirted with the idea.

"No." She turned away but not before he saw the hurt in her expression. Better a small hurt than a deep wound. "I have no idea where I am to find clothes for you. You're too"—she flung her hand out—"large. Besides, even if I should find some monolithic dandy, I can't very well sneak into his room while he sleeps and pilfer his small clothes."

Monolithic dandy?

"You're a resourceful girl," he returned. "I'm sure you'll think of something. By tomorrow. I'm getting tired of wearing these clothes and I refuse to trick myself out in bygone glory."

"Why not?" she asked. "It seems a commendable notion to me. There are so many clothes here."

"It would amuse you far too much," he answered loftily. "Add to that the fact that you are—or so you tell me—my victim. Victims are not allowed to be amused by their victimizers. 'Tisn't done. I'm certain if there were a rule book for victims and their victimizers, it would be one of the first principles cited."

Her extraordinary eyes widened during this speech and at the end she burst out laughing. *Good God*, he was losing what little mind he possessed. First, he purposefully depressed the girl's spirits and then, not a minute later, unable to bear the downward tilt of her mouth, he wasn't content until he'd returned it to merriment.

"You can help me over here," he said. "The furniture is stacked too high. I cannot reach the top."

"How can I help?" she asked.

"Come here and I'll show you."

She approached him warily, which was amusing seeing how he'd come damn near electing himself to sainthood on the merits of his self-restraint where she was concerned. "Well?"

"I'll lift you up and you take down the smaller items."

"You'll lift me?" she repeated, eyeing him doubtfully.

"Yes. Enough wary glares, Favor. Come here."

She shuffled up to him, tilting her head back and looking squarely in his face, trying to gauge his intention. He glimpsed the edge of that crooked front tooth, a sliver of white in the warm, dark secret of her mouth. At the base of her throat, her pulse fluttered. Her skin there would be warm and satiny.

They were alone.

No matter what he'd told himself, he was no saint, had never aspired to sainthood. She shivered and he felt every muscle in his body tighten instantly in response, a cat watching a fledgling suddenly beat its wings.

If she shivered again he would pounce, as intransigently as that cat lured by that fledgling's helplessness. Dear God. He was a prison-hardened knave. What the hell was she doing here with him? He lowered his head, his gaze hooded and alive to opportunity. *Any* opportunity. Let her pulse quicken, let her eyes darken, let her part her lips . . .

It didn't. They didn't. She didn't. She turned, presenting him with her back and said, "I'm ready."

His hands trembled as they circled her waist. The homely dress she'd worn to work in had been a mistake. Not nearly enough separated him from her. No corset stiffened the bodice; no heavy busk acted as armor separating them. Just simple blue worsted wool suffused with her heat.

He felt each breath she took, each rise of her rib cage, the shallow plane of her belly under his fingertips. Only the texture of her skin remained a mystery.

He closed his eyes. A tavern is what he needed . . . and a tavern wench. There used to be a place called The Red Rose a dozen miles east of the north highway. Strong drink and willing wenches, both available for the right price.

"Well?" She sounded breathless.

He lifted her, determinedly pinning his thoughts on unmet ladies with welcoming smiles. He jounced her up onto his shoulder.

"Oh!" She wobbled atop her perch. Her arms flayed out as she sought to keep her balance. He clamped an arm about her legs, and thrust up his free hand. "Take hold of my hand!"

There was a flurry of little adjustments. She grabbed his hand. Her feet beat against his chest and he clasped hold of one delicate ankle and pinned it against his stomach. "Calm down!" he bellowed.

She scrambled instead of calmed.

"Damn it! Do you *want* to fall?" Silk pooled over his wrist as her garter came undone and her stocking fell down her calf and covered his hand.

"Stop wiggling!" He drove his hand up through layers of petticoats until he found her knee and climbed higher, gripping her thigh securely.

She went as still as a heart-struck doe.

Her thighs were smooth and firm, lithe and long-muscled. A young woman who walked more than rode. A satin-skinned siren.

"Has the unhappy Orville shown any further interest?" He had no idea where the words came from. Unplanned. Not even thought before voiced.

"Orville is gone." Her voice sounded faint.

"Good." He heard the gloat of possessiveness, abhorred it, tried again for a neutral tone but it was hard to do when her leg was a smooth, tapering column that begged to be stroked. "I mean, good for him. Married wasn't he? Waste of time pursuing you, then."

"He left because his face powder could not cover the bruises you gave him."

"Oh."

She shifted and a warm, womanly fragrance rippled forth, escaping from beneath the lace ruffles and the silk stocking sagging about her ankle. Jasmine and heated flesh and earthier, more provocative scents. His grip tightened. Her hand clenched his.

"Favor."

"What?"

He didn't know "what." He only knew their present positions were untenable. He dipped his shoulder, tumbling her from her perch and into his arms, one arm linked under her knees, the other beneath her shoulders. Her hair, dense and matte as a London midnight, escaped its cap and coiled down over her chaste bodice. He caught a handful of it, his knuckles pressed against the soft cushion of her breast.

"Wash it off."

"What?"

"Your hair. It's bright and gleams like molten gold. Wash the black out."

She stared up at him, a shade frightened, a bit anxious and, yes, a little tantalized. "I can't. She . . . I can't."

For a long minute he gazed down at her fresh lovely face, scrubbed clean of powder, her eyes blue not abnormally black. It was too quiet. She would hear the thunder of his heartbeat. He knew because he heard it himself.

Only it wasn't his heartbeat. He lifted his head, listening. It was something else. Something growing closer.

"What is that?" Favor asked.

"The echo you noted," he answered quietly. "Someone's coming down the hall."

He dropped her lightly to her feet and pushed her toward a low cupboard that stood behind where the altar had once been.

"Go through there. It's not a sacristy. It's a corridor that leads to the north wing. You mustn't be found here. Particularly by any of Carr's guests. Believe me, Orville was one of the better sort in this place.

"Hurry, damn it!" he said harshly when she hesitated. "I can't afford to rescue you again. I was lucky Orville's vanity kept him quiet about me."

"But how—"

"I can't fit through there, Favor," he said tersely.

"There's other places where I can conceal myself. But they're not big enough for two. Now *go*."

Only after the low, squat door shut behind her did he breathe again. The footsteps were louder now. Nearly to the chapel.

Raine did not bother looking around. He'd lied. There was no other place to hide. He stepped behind the mountain of furniture and waited. A few minutes later he heard the door swing open and then a short series of footsteps, moving slowly.

Whoever it was must not follow Favor through that door. Raine leapt out, fists raised, ready to strike—

A shriveled little woman stood just beyond the light coming through the rosette window.

"Raine!" Gunna crumpled to the floor.

Chapter 17

"*G*unna!" Raine sprang to the old lady's side and carefully lifted her in his arms. Weakly, she batted at him. She weighed next to nothing. Her thick, homely clothing gave only the impression of weight.

She still wore a thick mantle draped across her face, leaving only one side of her disfigured countenance exposed. She peered up at him through a sunken eye. She no longer looked as hideous as he remembered, only sadly distorted, like a watercolor portrait left out in the rain.

"Is it really ye, Raine Merrick, and not a ghost?" she whispered. Tears leaked from the corner of her eye and found a deep crevasse to course down.

He pressed a kiss against her cheek. "No ghost, old

woman. Just the same brat, back to make your life a misery again."

The gap-toothed mouth turned up at the corner in a weak grin. She closed her eyes and let her head relax against his chest. Contentment flowed from her like resin from spring pines. He gazed down at the wee old woman, both moved and disconcerted. The Gunna he remembered had little time for displays of *"waistie luve."*

As if she'd read his mind, her eyelid snapped open and her tender smile evaporated. She squirmed, struggling to right herself in his arms, swatting and muttering, "Leave me down! I heard ye were in prison. What sort of prison might that be, I'm askin', tha has built ye up like a prize bull?"

Apparently, she hadn't changed much after all.

Raine lowered her to her feet. Immediately, she dashed away any evidence of tears with the back of her elegantly shaped hand. Those gracefully wrought hands had ever been Gunna's only claim to beauty. She set them on her hips now, glaring up at him. "Well? How long have ye been out of that French prison, then?"

"Six months. Near seven."

"And here? How long here without . . . ? How long here?" It struck him that she was hurt, truly, genuinely hurt that he hadn't informed her of his presence. It never occurred to him that she might have fretted over him.

"A few weeks."

She pressed her lips together.

"I'm sorry."

With his heartfelt apology the anger lifted from her expression. "No need to be sorry, Raine. I'm just so . . ." She broke off, embarrassed by such sentiment. She began again. "I'm glad yer here and well and lookin' fit. Yer brother wrote and said he'd gone to pay yer ransom but ye weren't there. I . . . we feared ye'd been killed by the French."

"Ash went to France to ransom me?" Raine echoed. Once more the old woman confounded him. In quick succession, Raine discovered not one but two people who'd cared for him through all those dark years of his imprisonment. The intimacy of such a tie unnerved him.

"Yes." Gunna nodded. "Carr ransomed him near a year ago. Ash set out at once to earn the means to ransom ye. Succeeded, too, much to Carr's chagrin, and won himself a bride in doing so."

"A bride?" Raine asked in amazement. His older brother hardly seemed husband material.

"Aye. Yer father's ward what Ash snatched from whatever plots Carr had devised fer the chit. Ye should have seen yer brother, Raine. Fair besotted with the girl and she with him. And her a Russell lassie, no less." Gunna shook her head, cackling with evident pleasure. "The Russells were some that answered the McClairen call for the Bonny Prince."

"A Jacobite?" Raine asked, amused. "Father must have loved that."

Gunna pulled a grimace. "I'd be surprised if he even remembers the girl's name. That which doesna touch yer da doesn't much exist, to his way of thinkin'. Once Ash married—Well, yer father's not so dull-witted as to think there's ever a chance of him seein' his eldest son agin." She snorted. "At least not in this life."

Raine hesitated. "And Fia?" She'd been such a beautiful child with her black hair and rosy lips. She'd also been his father's little shadow. He waited now to hear to whom Carr had 'sold' her. Which duke, earl, or foreign prince. For clearly that had been Carr's plan.

"Here she be still. For a few months yet. Then it's to London with her. And him, too. Or so he says."

"I thought that King George had forbidden Carr to return to London."

"Aye. Yer da's last wife was the queen's own godchild, and doesn't yer father wish he'd known that before he lost her like the other two. But ye canna hang a peer for murder without proof and who would speak against Carr? So the king banished Carr here," Gunna said. "But now Carr's swearing Fia will make her bow this spring." She shot a glance up at him. "Have ye spoken with her?"

"No. I never imagined she wouldn't have been married by now." Had he seen her? Raine wondered, surprised by his eagerness. He scoured his memory, trying to match a mature face to the youthful one he recalled.

Had one of the women in the ballroom he'd watched from the high overhead been his sister? Would she remember him? Was she even more Carr's creation now than she'd been four years before? Sadness replaced his earlier expectancy. Of course she would be. He shook his head. "I wouldn't know what to say. No one knows I'm here, Gunna. And I'd as soon it remained that way."

"I wouldn't rely too much on that notion, Raine. Carr has been seeing 'things' lately, meaning ghosts and now I'm thinkin' it's ye he's been seein'."

Raine stared at her a minute before breaking out in laughter. "He thinks I'm a ghost? How perfect. He leaves me to rot in prison and then, catching sight of me, expects I'm dead and come back to haunt him?"

His mouth flattened in abrupt and savage bitterness. "He gives himself too much status. Were I dead and doomed to wander this earth for eternity, the last bit of ground I would go near would be the one he occupied—as either man or corpse."

"I don't think he believes it's yer ghost haunting him, Raine." Gunna said quietly. "He thinks it's another."

"What other?"

"His dead wife."

Bitter amusement filled him. "Oh? Which one?"

At this, Gunna *tched* loudly, her expression aggrieved. "Speak gently of the dead, Raine Merrick. Particularly those poor, cursed brides."

"Forgive me. I have only to be reminded of my paternity and its influence exerts itself. Now, which bride does Carr think cannot stand to be separated from him?"

"Yer mother. That's why I'm here." She shuffled toward an open box, its contents strewn untidily from the top. Her hand moved gently over the contents. "I knew this is where Carr had her things removed and when one of the stable lads claimed to have seen a light in the chapel last night I thought . . ."

"You thought I was Janet? So you came to petition Janet's spirit on Carr's behalf? I hadn't realized you were so devoted to him. I'd always assumed it was Fia who owned your loyalty."

The old woman answered his mockery by swinging around and cuffing his ear. He backed off with a yelp.

"And so she does," she said. "If someone is trying to convince Carr his dead wife is haunting him, it may be not to Miss Fia's best interest."

"You're still her champion," Raine said.

"I've had to be." The old woman hesitated. "Did ye . . . did ye feel it, then, havin' no champion of yer own?"

Raine stared, amazed, and Gunna immediately misread his silence as condemnation.

"Ye were strapping lads when I come to work here," she said defensively. "Both reckless and hotheaded but fer all that yer own creatures entirely. Ye can thank God yer father cared naught fer ye. It let ye become who ye were and not who he would have made ye."

And yet there was a time that Raine would have been glad of that, would have done anything to gain Carr's approval.

"But Fia . . ." Gunna's hands twisted the coarse material of her skirts. "So beautiful and so sad. She was just a wee wraith yer father spoon-fed lies and treachery. Someone had to stand between him and what he would have made of her."

"And that had to be you?"

"Who else?"

"Why?"

The old woman touched her ruined face. "They do say the ugly are powerless to resist the beautiful," she said simply. "But never doubt I cared fer ye and Ash, too. Who was it do ye think that found out the McClairens were plannin' to lynch ye and made sure Carr learned of it?"

Raine returned her unhappy gaze steadily. "Carr hardly came to rescue me, Gunna."

Gunna spat on the stone underfoot. "Of course he wouldna! But he would go after ye quick enough if he thought he could use those pitiful fool McClairens' attack on ye as an excuse to rid himself of the last of their lot. And so he did! Be happy he had that excuse, and forgive the McClairens for not sharing yer joy!" she finished, fierce and vastly upset.

But Carr *hadn't* achieved genocide, Raine thought. Favor and her brother lived. "Carr has much to answer for regarding the McClairens. No wonder he sees ghosts."

"Aye," Gunna returned. "But lately some of Carr's guests has been seeing' things, too. And Carr is actin' odd. Excited. And I coulda sworn I heard a woman's voice as I come down the hall."

"I assure you I was not sharing the chapel with a ghost, female or otherwise." He needed to get Gunna out of here in case Favor should take it into her mind to return. While he did not doubt Gunna's affection, she had made clear where her loyalty lay. If she realized Favor was a McClairen she might decide that she posed a threat to Fia. After all, all McClairens must hate all Merricks.

"As for Carr's guests, they must have seen me." He smiled charmingly. "I shall strive to be less obvious."

She'd always scented a diversion as keenly as a hound does a hare. She sidled nearer, watching him closely. "Aye. Might be so." She tapped his chest with one long finger. "What are ye doin' here, Raine Merrick? Clearly ye've not come for a family reunion."

"Haven't I?" He took her accusing finger and wrapped it in his fist, and dropped a kiss on its tip. "Perhaps I came just for one more hug from you, Gunna."

"Ye never got hugs from me to begin with so why would ye be thinkin' to get them now?" she said, but her gruffness could not completely mask her pleasure. "Out with it or I'll stay until ye tell me."

He released her finger and she wagged it beneath his chin. "Don't ever think to fool me, Raine Merrick. Yer in a lather to have me gone and gone I'll be soon enough if ye'll tell me why yer searching through yer mother's things."

The decision to tell her took no great deliberation. She would think him as daft as Favor did. Besides Gunna might know where Carr had dumped the rest of Janet's things.

"I'm looking for the McClairen's Trust."

"The what?" More lines added themselves to her already furrowed brow. "What's that be?"

Of course, Gunna must never have heard about the gems. As Favor had remarked, it was only a local legend. And Gunna was not a McClairen. She'd arrived from the north some years after his mother's death, seeking any kind of employment. Carr, seeing how Fia took to her, had hired her immediately. A woman with Gunna's mien worked cheap.

"My mother had a set of jewels, Gunna, which she held in trust for her clansmen."

Gunna shrugged eloquently. "Then Carr's got them now."

"No. He never knew about them. I only know about them because I saw her take them out once."

Gunna looked doubtful.

Raine went on. "There was a necklace and some other pieces. A brooch fashioned in the shape of a lion, embedded with rough stones. It wasn't fine craftsmanship, even my child's eyes could see that. But the gold was as thick as my thumb and the gems were as large as cat's eyes."

"Go on!" Gunna guffawed.

He smiled. "She kept them in a sort of oriental box. Do you remember ever having seen such a thing lying about here or in another room?"

Gunna squinted at the ceiling, rubbing her flattened nose with her thumb. She pondered several moments before shrugging apologetically. "Nay, Raine. I'm sorry. I don't recall ever seein' such a thing. But that don't mean it don't exist. There's so much that lays about in these rooms."

Her words sentenced him to long days of searching through endless piles of cast-offs, litter, and odds-and-ends. Probably many such days.

All in the company of his little "victim."

For whatever reason, he did not find the realization disheartening.

The girl had an aversion to him.

Carr led Favor Donne up toward the picture gallery. Earlier she'd claimed she would not be happy until she'd viewed it and then only under his tutelage.

Her fingers danced above his sleeve on the point of breaking contact. Very odd conduct if she were, indeed, occupied by the spirit of his wife, a wife who'd loved him devotedly, passionately and yes, demonstratively. At least in the earlier years of their marriage.

He was still wondering what to do with her should she prove to be Janet. He couldn't very well marry the chit. What if he did and a *real* accident befell her? He could offer her a position as his mistress, but Janet had, when all was said and done, been a prude about such things. She would not let him touch her until after they'd read their vows. And, too, as he'd already noted, the girl could barely tolerate touching him.

He was not wrong. He'd seduced many women. Yet all evening she'd put herself in his way. How to account for that, except with Pala's explanation, that the girl was directed by Janet's spirit.

He'd had his doubts after the scarf incident but her pursuit of him had been so persistent, having such an element of compulsion, nay, desperation, in it that he'd begun to believe Pala. Besides, the girl did not even know her body housed another tenant.

So he'd acquiesced and here they were, standing before one of Titian's conceits. He'd invested much of his wealth in artwork, jewels, and manuscripts.

"I like the color blue. Particularly peacock blue," Favor said, glancing sideways at him. Dark eyes, he noted, overly dilated and nearly black. Like her hair. Fetching but odd.

"A lovely shade," he allowed.

During the course of their walk here, she'd made several such random comments. She liked shellfish. She found violin music stirring. She announced that she'd read Jonathan Swift and Henry Fielding and clearly expected him to be scandalized. He told her he'd never read either and that he found reading tiresome. Clearly disconcerted, she fell into a lengthy silence from which she roused herself only to make more sporadic, disconnected comments.

The girl could not have so little—or such inane— conversation. Earlier, he'd overhead her talking easily and rather wittily to Tunbridge. Perhaps what he was seeing was Janet's unseen influence and these burbles of erupting nonsense were the result of being possessed.

They stood staring up at Titian's masterpiece some minutes before he grew bored. "Shall we continue?"

He led her by a deplorably murky Flemish painting to something he truly enjoyed, a landscape of near mathematical precision by Poussin, entitled *Dionysus at the City Gates*. The Greek theme appealed to him no less than the analytical purity of the composition. He'd always admired Greek architecture and, to some extent, the Greeks. Not as much as the Romans, of course.

"Lovely," Favor murmured.

"Not only lovely but precise," he instructed. "See these buildings in the background. They are all structures represented in their correct location in Athens."

"Really? I do not read Greek. Nor Latin. I have some French. Less German."

Carr barely heard her. He would have made a fine Greek aristocrat. Or perhaps a Greek philosopher. Or a Greek politician. He would have orated just . . . there.

"See, m'dear? There is the Acropolis and there, just so, the Parthenon."

She replied under her breath. He turned, his gaze sharpening. Her expression was both distant and tender. Her mouth held the promise of a smile yet to be born and her eyes were soft.

"What did you say?" he asked, dipping his head to be certain he heard her correctly. *"What did you say?"*

"Part of None," she murmured, as though recalling something foolish and sweet.

His breath caught; a painful hammering began beating in his chest. He hadn't really believed it. Not really. Not until now.

Janet had returned.

"I bid you good even', Miss Donne."

"Lord Carr." She smiled, entered her room and shut the door behind her. Her eyes squeezed shut as she listened for the sound of his leaving. A full five minutes passed before she finally heard his footsteps retreating down the hall.

With a sob, she slumped against the door; her shoulders hit the panel with a thud. She shoved her knuckles against her mouth, trying to compose herself, failing miserably.

She'd done it. She'd secured Lord Carr's interest. More than secured it. He'd fixated on her. Somewhere in that long, dismal picture gallery he'd become convinced that Janet McClairen's spirit lived within her.

He'd touched her. Stroked her cheek with the back of his hand. God! Her legs began trembling, her joints felt watery. She sank to the floor, upbraiding herself for such childish histrionics.

Of course he touched her! If all went as they'd planned, he'd do much more than touch her. That had been her goal and purpose from the start. For Carr to marry her. It still was.

Tears fell from her eyes. More of them followed and more still, a torrent of tears impossible to check. They coursed down her cheeks and lips, dripping from her chin and jaw, soaking the delicate lace edging her bodice. Treacherous tears, betraying tears, tears impervious to plans and goals and purposes and intentions.

If only, she thought helplessly, Rafe hadn't touched her first.

Chapter 18

"Not many of us here yet, are there?" Lady Fia smiled at Favor, a sweet smile that did all the right things to her lovely face and yet managed to make a mockery of its own gentleness.

Favor, standing beside Fia as they awaited the rest of the company, paid the girl little heed. Rafe would wonder where she'd gone. Why she hadn't brought the clothes he'd made her promise to bring him. Perhaps he would curse her and rant against her.

Perhaps he would miss her.

She blinked, amazed by her absurdity. She must force away such thoughts. She'd best find the means to smile before Carr arrived to lead the company to their *déjeuner* alfresco.

The late-October day had been born bright and unseasonably warm. Overnight, the wind had shifted and now meandered up from the south, amiable and unhurried as a maid on a Sunday stroll.

Lady Fia, ever chimerical, had arranged a picnic. Early this morning she'd issued invitations. Even now the more jaded *habitués* of Wanton's Blush slept, their invitations unread. But most of Fia's devoted retinue—having instructed their servants that any *communiqué* from Lady Fia was to be brought immediately to their attention had sent their acceptance.

Favor was one of the few guests who hadn't been sleeping when the invitation arrived, for the simple expedient that she hadn't slept. She had accepted reluctantly, knowing that by doing so she sentenced herself to the day in Carr's company when she could have been on a treasure hunt with Rafe.

But avoiding Carr only meant delaying what she must do. So now she awaited Carr's arrival, Carr's interest, and ultimately Carr's suit. And her thoughts were as dull and leaden as this fine day was sweet and clear.

"Miss Donne," Lady Fia exclaimed. " 'Struth you look unwell. Perhaps you'd best remain at Wanton's Blush?"

"No."

Lady Fia smiled obliquely. "If you choose to quit our party, I guarantee you won't suffer any lost opportunity for your absence."

"Lady Fia?" Favor queried, finally awakened to the subtle derision in the girl's voice.

"My father, Miss Donne, does not ride."

Favor was immediately alert, shedding her emotional somnambulism as one would a sodden winter cloak. That Lady Fia had noted Favor's attention in her father mattered less than the fact that he would not be among their number today.

"Lord Carr won't be going with us?"

"No," Lady Fia said, studying her. "He seldom rises before noon."

She leaned closer, smiling with falsely conspiratorial glee. "There, a bit of useful information for you. Of course, I could give you even better advice, but then, I doubt you'd take it, would you?"

Before Favor could reply, masculine voices hailed them. Fia twirled to return the greeting. Dozens of determined merrymakers surrounded them, sweeping the young women out of the castle's front doors, Favor still bemused by the news of her unexpected reprieve.

An entire day free. Free of Muira's badgering, of Carr's obsessive ardency, and even free of Rafe's troubling magnetism. Her sense of release was nearly palpable. She smiled at Tunbridge, returned another swain's sally, and chatted with the older woman next to her.

They arrived at the stables to find dozens of horses dancing on the end of their leads, tricked into fresh spirits by the springlike weather. The stable master stood among them, gauging the ability of the various riders and matching them with appropriate mounts.

Favor glimpsed Jamie Craigg's gigantic figure lumbering toward her, leading a docile-looking mare. Her spirits sank at this reminder of Muira's far-reaching influence and far-ranging eye. She'd nearly forgotten Jamie's masquerade as Thomas's driver. He looked out of place here on land, the sea seeming to be a more natural element for him. Not for the first time, Favor wondered whether the others whose lives Muira had orchestrated and overturned ever resented her manipulations.

Jamie halted before her, his expression closed. Perhaps, if she asked he wouldn't tell Muira she'd played truant for a day. "Jamie, please—"

"Don't worry none, Miss Donne." Jamie broke in warningly, his gaze fixed over her shoulder. "I put a kinder bit in 'er mouth."

She turned her head. Lord Tunbridge was close behind.

"Of course. Thank you, Jamie. You may tell my aunt . . ."

"Ach, Miss! Yer aunt is bound to be sleepin' until yer return. I'll send a maid to wake her if ye insist but, beggin' me pardon fer me presumption, I'd let the grand lady remain innocent of yer doin's." He gave her a quick, furtive wink. Bless him! He approved. She returned his wink with a gay smile, her spirits fully restored.

She lifted her skirts and waited for Jamie to assist her but before he had taken a step, thin, hard fingers encircled her waist.

"Miss Donne." Tunbridge's breath fanned her ear a second before he smoothly tossed her into the saddle.

She cast a startled glance down into the man's pale, upturned face. "Thank you, Lord Tunbridge."

Tunbridge's thin mouth formed an admiring smile. "May I be so bold as to remark on your rare good looks this day, Miss Donne?"

Perhaps he wasn't so terrible, Favor decided and, remembering his painful infatuation with Lady Fia and that lady's mockery of it, Favor smiled at him. "Thank you, sir."

Without glancing in Jamie's direction, Tunbridge dug a coin from his purse and flipped it in the giant's direction. Mumbling thanks and bobbing his massive head in a fair imitation of humble gratitude, Jamie backed away.

Tunbridge's gaze remained locked on Favor. "You're every bit as lovely as she," she thought she heard Tunbridge mutter beneath his breath, "Damned, if you aren't."

The sound of a boy's voice raised in panic finally severed his regard. "Damn. You'll excuse me, Miss Donne," Tunbridge said. "One of the stable boys is having rather a time with my stallion. Bad-tempered brute. Nasty habit of biting those who cinch his girth. I suppose I best see that he doesn't kill the brat. Put a bit of a pall on the luncheon."

Favor's momentary favor with Tunbridge evaporated. "You're truly a humanitarian, milord."

He smirked and moved away and shortly Favor's pleasure in the day returned. A little while later the others finished mounting and Lady Fia raised her gloved hand.

"Follow me, now!" she called out. "Riders, follow me!"

* * *

"Miss Donne rides out with Fia and the rest of her raucous crowd," Carr said, looking down from the tower window as forty riders came milling around the corner of the castle. With an imperious gesture, Fia raised her lace kerchief above her head and whipped it in a circle. As one the group broke, the riders sending the frantic cattle from standstill to full gallop, as though they were beginning a steeplechase and not a jaunt to a picnic site.

"Lud." Carr expelled a gusty sigh. "No one ever rides at a leisurely pace anymore." Carr let the draperies fall back down, giving his attention to Pala. "Will Miss Donne ever recall more of her life as my wife?"

Pala cringed where she stood. She'd better cringe.

It had taken two days to ferret the old crone out. One of his men had finally found her trudging along the cliff path picking her vile weeds and such. How dare she vanish when he'd things he wanted to know?

He tamped down his irritation. "I will assume that you didn't hear me. Now, once more, will Miss Donne ever remember specific incidents as Janet McClairen?"

Pala rubbed the red welt on her cheek. "I don't know."

Carr picked up his riding crop and bounced it in his hand. "Guess." He smiled mildly. "But guess correctly."

The hag flinched. "Please, my lord. I guess . . . no. These things she feels, she . . . *feels*. She doesn't know why."

"Hm." It made a certain sense.

"You not like my guess. I sorry. *I sorry!*" Pala whimpered, ducking her head.

"I'm not." It would make things even more difficult if Janet—Miss Donne—damnation, but this was a coil!—recalled the events of her last day on earth. But then, whose last day on earth had it actually been? Certainly not Miss Donne's and apparently not Janet's. The conundrum fascinated him.

Janet. They could be together, here at Wanton's Blush where it had all begun. He could set things right. If only he could persuade Miss Donne . . .

"In some respects Janet's lack of—what shall we say? presence?—creates a bit of a problem."

Pala flashed him a look of fearful inquiry. Her gray hair hung in filthy ropes on either side of sallow sunken cheeks. "What is that, Lord Carr? What can Pala do? How can she help her most generous Lord Carr?"

She crept closer, the strands of shells and odd bright stones clicking around her throat, her heavy skirts leaving a leaf-strewn trail on the otherwise clean floor. "What is Lord Carr's desire?"

"Well . . ." Carr murmured, examining his nails, "as hard as it is to believe, I have come to the conclusion that Miss Donne dislikes me. I see that you are shocked. I read it in your face. I empathize with your astonishment."

"Y-y-yes, milord!"

" 'Tis, nonetheless, true. Miss Donne has an aversion to my person."

As testament to her incredulity, Pala's head had

sprung straight up on the meager stalk of her neck. She met his gaze with her own wide, amazed one. "But how . . . I mean, you tell me she seeks you out. She puts herself in your way! Maybe you only seeing a young girl's shyness and *thinking* it dislike?"

He gave her a dry smile. "I believe I have ample enough experience to be able to distinguish virginal coyness from antipathy."

"But . . . ! I no understand. Why she seek you if she not like you?"

Carr seated himself on the room's only chair, carefully making sure not to rumple the skirts of his new coat. "You, Pala, are but a primitive Gypsy. How could you understand? Still, while explaining a philosophical nicety to such as you may well prove impossible, I have never refused an intellectual challenge. So, attend, Pala, and I shall endeavor to explain."

The old woman nodded eagerly.

"Janet's spirit has survived buried within Miss Donne's body rather like a wharf rat that secretes itself aboard a ship, unsuspected and unwilling to make itself known. Yet from this vantage Janet somehow causes Miss Donne to react to me, again rather like that rat might infect the crew with fleas of the ship upon which he hides. Miss Donne is *infected* with Janet's feelings for me, feelings so deep and intense Miss Donne finds them frightening.

"Thus, Miss Donne desires me—thanks to my former wife—yet has an aversion to me." He held up his hand, forestalling Pala's certain objection. "Hard to believe, isn't it?"

Pala, apparently not conversant with etiquette, merely stared at him dumbly rather than murmuring the expected assent. He sighed forlornly. People were such a disappointment to him.

"If I know my Janet, she is issuing Miss Donne her . . . emotional directives in a most forceful manner." He leaned forward confidingly. "Such passion as Janet had for me might very well overwhelm the delicate sensibilities of a gently raised young girl. How can Miss Donne help but be frightened, directed by what she must consider carnal impulses? Thus, she reacts by stubbornly resisting Janet's directives and forming an aversion to the man who engenders these feelings. *N'est-ce pas?*"

Beneath its coat of grime, Pala's face was utterly blank.

Pearls before swine, Carr thought. Ah well, she was, after all, little more than an animal. But, as many animals, she had her uses. He'd wasted enough time.

"You don't understand, do you? Thankfully, you don't need to understand. All you need do, Pala, is one thing."

"What be that, Lord Carr?" Pala choked out, her voice thick with awe.

Probably still trying to digest that bit about Miss Donne disliking him. 'Struth it was rather incredible.

"You must make me a love potion."

Muira shoved the footstool into the bright midday light coming through the stable door and plopped down on it. She held out her hand in an imperious manner and Jamie placed a mirror in it. She angled her face to better see herself.

"Curse the man!" The pain Carr's blow had caused her was incidental. The mark his crop had left on her face was much harder to bear. It meant a delay in plans and just when things were coursing along so very, very well.

"Damn the man! Damn his black soul to hell!"

"I thought that was yer aim and goal, Muira," Jamie said. "Damning his soul to hell."

Abruptly Muira giggled, an unnerving sound, particularly so hard on the heels of her rage. "Aye, Jamie Craigg. 'Tis. And soon now, soon."

The giant tucked his thumbs into the waistband of his breeches, looming over the small old woman. "Is it, now?" he said. "And here we've all been thinkin' that the plan had more to do with returning to the clan what was stolen from us than yer own personal cravin' for revenge."

Muira shot him a venomous glare. "If I can achieve both, why are you suddenly so reluctant?"

"Because ye haven't told the girl what it is ye plan to do."

Muira's gaze grew flat. She reached beneath her multiple layers of dirty skirts and tore a piece of flounce loose, using it to wipe her face. "She knows."

"Ye told her?"

"I didn't need to tell her. She must know but if she sleeps easier at night by telling herself Carr will live a long life after she weds and leaves him, fine. If it makes it possible for her to do what needs doing, then I'm for it."

Jamie watched her dip the rag into the water bucket and scrub violently at her face. "Yer half mad with what happened that night, Muira Dougal. Ye know that, don't ye?"

She grinned up at him, correctly reading his weary tone as one of capitulation. "And even half mad I'm cannier than most sane, eh?"

He snorted but finally nodded in answer. Immediately the humor left her expression.

"Remember, Jamie Craigg, 'twas me who tended you and the others that survived the demon earl's ride. 'Twas me that found the means to bring back those McClairens that were exported for their 'crimes.' It's me who brought those McClairens to the village on the north coast, that village where you hide your contraband.

"I did it. *Me*. We'll get back the land. A McClairen will live in Wanton's Blush again. And Lord Carr will die. *I swear it*." Her voice shook with vehemence.

Jamie's brow furrowed as he looked down at the old woman shaking with rage, but he said nothing. For all the years she'd led the clan and held the clan together by force of her will alone, he'd said nothing. Now, just because he looked at Favor McClairen and remembered a time when Highland lassies were courageous and blithe, free-spirited and generous, he had no right to speak. Even if Muira and her plots destroyed her.

"Damnation!" Muira exclaimed, her gaze once

more on the mirror, "This mark will never fade by nightfall and no amount of paint will conceal it. The girl will have to plead the headache tonight. Thankfully, tomorrow is the masque and believe me, I shall be wearing one!"

Chapter 19

"Innkeep! Another mug of ale," the stranger shouted.

"Me, too," Franny cooed.

The handsome, bruising brute didn't appear to hear her; he kept staring at the foamy waste in the bottom of his mug. She was about to repeat her demand when he raised his head. He stared at her startled-like, as though he'd forgotten she was on his lap. At twelve stone, few men forgot if Franny was on their lap.

It was a testament to the fellow's own big, manly build. Franny wriggled in pleasure. The man held up two fingers. "Her, too, Innkeep."

"Right you are, sir. Be but a minute. Gots to tap another keg, here, and I don't have no help to take care of the place whilst I do it, tha' help be currently helpin' herself to the contents of yer pocket, sir, if yer not careful," the innkeeper returned, shooting Franny a venomous glare.

"I never stole a penny from a gentleman, and well you know, it!" Fran squalled, but her protest was lost on the innkeeper, who was manfully upending another keg. Not that Fran cared a fig for what the innkeeper liked or didn't like. The rough-looking stranger had a look of generosity about him and Fran wasn't one to make a mistake about such a thing. He'd come in an hour before, set on getting drunk if she knew anything about it . . . which she did. Ill-humored, vexed, and needing a release. She'd decided to offer herself as a likely one.

Because, besides being generous-looking, weren't he handsome? Rugged sort of handsome. A bit of wear on him for all that he looked young, but then, she'd a bit of wear on herself, too.

"You. Sir!" A voice called from across the sun-dabbed room. "Are you from these parts or just traveling through?"

The stranger's head swung around at the sound of the slurred male voice and Fran's mouth twitched with irritation. Damn Davie Duff, anyway. He rose unsteadily, snagged his beer mug with his free hand and lumbered over. "Well?" he demanded.

The stranger regarded him evenly. "Why do you ask, friend?"

"Because," Davie said, peering down, "you remind me of someone I knew once. Bosom companion of my misspent youth." He seemed to like the sound of the phrase, for he repeated it several times. "Mis-spent youth. Misspent. Youth."

"Do I?" The stranger readjusted Fran on his lap. "Forgive me for not rising."

"Never!" Fran crowed, thrilled with her witticism. Davie leered appreciatively.

"And who might this lost companion be?" the stranger asked, not nearly interested enough in the bounty she sought to display.

"Fellow named Raine Merrick. But you're not him, are you?" Davie asked.

"Are you so sure?" the stranger asked, and something in his voice made Fran turn her head and look hard at him.

Only took a second to decide he was twitting Davie. He weren't Raine Merrick. She'd known Raine Merrick. Not well, but well enough to enjoy a tumble or two with the lad. He'd been a big lad, square and brawny.

This man was taller than Raine and though wide-shouldered, lean made. His hair was darker and his face more angular than Raine's. But most of all, she remembered the driving anger in Raine. He hummed with it like a piece of metal before a lightning storm. Biting words, clenched fist, bitter laugh—that's what she remembered about Raine Merrick.

Not that this fellow looked like he'd be a stranger to clenched fists. But this fellow looked like he owned the devil, whereas Raine Merrick had looked like the devil owned him.

Which, seeing how Lord Carr was his father, was probably close to the truth.

"—lucky you aren't Raine Merrick. Heard he died in some French crib," Davie was saying.

"Clearly, you grieve for him," the stranger answered with a touch of mockery.

"Me? Nah! He weren't really a chum, mind you. I only said that thinkin' you were him. He was just a lad always had a notion to spite his da, poor bastard. Only time his father even noticed him was when he nearly got himself hanged for raping a nun."

The stranger's head shot up at that.

"Ach! Davie, why'd ye want to go dredging up that poor, sordid tale?" the innkeeper called out.

" 'Cause that's the only sort of tales there are about Raine Merrick!" Davie cackled.

"Sounds the very devil," the stranger said.

"Well, that's what the McClairen clan thought sure enough—they're the ones that almost snapped his neck," Davie said. " 'Twas a McClairen lass the lad was supposed to have raped."

The stranger had returned his attention to his beer.

"But wouldn't they have been red in the face if'n they *had* stretched the lad?" Davie chuckled.

"Why do you say that?" the big man asked dully.

"Because it come out later that Merrick didn't rape no one."

"*What?*"

Davie nodded. "Merry McClairen, the girl they caught with him, confessed a few years afterward that she and Raine had been lovers. Said she couldn't live with the lie no longer."

"What did they do to her?"

"Do to her?" Davie looked confused. "Nuthin'. First off, 'cause there was no one much left to do anything anyway and, second off, because what are you going to do to a Mother Superior?"

The stranger's sherry-colored eyes had gone wide. "You jest."

"Nope." Franny confirmed Davie's tale. "Mother Perpetua Augusta of the Sacred Order of—ach! Some sacred order or other. Runs the abbey about a half day's ride south of here. We keeps discreet up here. No one mentions the abbey, nor Mother Augusta's tame priest."

The stranger smiled, then began to laugh. "Well, if nothing else your Raine Merrick had the devil's own luck."

"Since he was heir to a demon, makes sense, don't it?" Fran said, finding herself caught up in the story.

"Ah, yes. Carr. The Demon Earl," the tall man said. "I've heard of him."

"You and everyone else," Davie said smugly. "But *I* knew him. *And* Raine."

Fran nodded wistfully. "Aye. 'Tis sad. Raine weren't evil, you know. Just . . . poisoned like."

"I'll tell you about him for the price of a brandy, Mister . . ." Davie suggested.

Fran, abandoning tender reflections on past lovers, decided it was time to concentrate on the present ones. "Clear off, David Duff!" she exclaimed, "yer not wanted here. The gentleman and I are quite cozy enough without yer company. Besides, who'd want to hear stories about some poor sot of a dead boy?"

"Why, indeed?" the gentleman murmured, smiling down into his empty mug. "Best leave, Davie."

Thwarted, Davie snatched his mug from the table, nursing it to his chest. "Ah, now that I see you, you look nuthin' like him," he said, and with that parting salvo, slunk back to his original companions.

Finally, the innkeeper arrived at their table and thumped two overflowing mugs on the sticky surface. The stranger placed one in her hand. She nudged her thigh between his legs, wriggling deeper onto his lap.

"Ah," she breathed, her eyes lighting with discovery. "There ye are. I was wonderin' when ye'd make yerself known, if ye catch me meaning."

He moved his mouth a few inches from her ear. "I'd sooner make a proper accounting of myself, Franny."

She glanced at the door that led to the only private room the inn boasted. "'Sblood, I'd like to get to know you better, too . . . but I gots to work."

He tickled her chin. "There's not so many here that you'll be missed for a while."

"A short while?" she asked, tempted.

"If I'm to give a proper account of myself, I demand enough time to do so. I'd hate to rush the process."

She would, too, but she'd always prided herself on her practicality and if this young buck wanted more than a quarter hour of her time, he was going to have to convince her of it. "As sad a thing as it is, 'tis a fact that pleasure don't pay the landlord."

There was nothing overt. Nothing so apparent as a grimace, yet something rueful seeped into his expression. Still, he whispered, "Pleasure might not, but I will."

She promptly shoved herself from his lap and took hold of one of his large hands and tugged him upright. "Well then, come on, love," she said. "Follow me."

A flotilla of fat-bellied white clouds drifted overhead in a slow procession. There would be hours more sun to enjoy before October remembered herself and took her role as winter's vanguard more seriously.

The picnickers from Wanton's Blush took the warmth for granted, being far more interested in earthy diversions. They lounged on wool blankets, masculine heads lolling on female laps, tongues wetting lips, signals flashing amid ribald repartee, assignations covertly arranged.

Raine Merrick stood with his hand on his horse's bridle 'neath the branches of a rowan tree. He was well inured to such behavior, having been raised among its most avid practitioners. He waited a few minutes longer, scanning the party for her.

If she thought to sneak off for a spot of slap-and-tickle with some would-be suitor, she'd best think again. He had no intention of releasing her from their search. His knuckles stretched the black leather of his glove as his hand tightened into a fist. Somehow she'd arrived at the misguided notion that she and he were compatriots of a sort, and that she could follow her own whims, decide when and where she would attend him. She'd soon learn the error of that idea.

He looped his mount's rein over a tree branch, anger building in him and with it his sense of offense at her . . . her faithlessness. And if it occurred to him that he'd originally intended to keep her near him only that he might discover some way in which to repay his debt to her, he did not let that inconsistency trouble him.

As far as he was concerned, she had much to answer for, did Favor McClairen. She infiltrated his thoughts and dreams, disrupted his stratagems, undermined his intentions, and destroyed his desire to bed another woman—damn her to hell! There was no possible way he was going to allow her to indulge herself when he could not.

He'd find her, by God, even if it meant questioning each one of these bejeweled mannequins. He cared little that someone might note he had not been one of their original number. He cared less for the consequences of such a discovery.

He strode toward a small clutch of lounging revelers. A few gentleman watched his approach incuriously. Several of the women noted him with a good deal more interest.

"Where is the wench?" he said in a loud, exasperated voice as he drew near. A dandy, his chin propped in his hand inches from a brunette woman's bosom, raised his brows questioningly.

"We've a veritable buffet of wenches, sir," the

dandy said. "Which delectable morsel would you be seeking?"

"Miss Donne."

The dandy *tched* softly. "Too bad, old son. I fear Miss Donne is being . . . sampled even as we speak."

"Really?" Thank God, years of prison had stood him in good stead. He was still smiling. After a manner.

"Coo! Don't 'e look nasty?" A beauty in blue silk breathed, revealing origins that had never included silk. "Don't worry, sir. With your looks you won't 'ave too long a wait afore you find yourself another."

Raine ignored her. "By whom?"

"Tunbridge," another man answered wistfully. "Lucky bastard."

"And where is the happy couple?" Raine asked, less than pleasantly.

The beauty with the dockyard accent pointed. "That way they went, quarter hour at most."

The dandy glanced up at Raine and smiled nastily. "If you run you might just make opening curtain, if you know what I mean. There still might be some good seats left—"

Raine seized a fistful of waistcoat, shirt, and skin. The dandy yelped and thrashed his arms, dangling horizontally three feet above the ground.

The rest grew hushed. The dandy kept yelping. Raine bent over him. "I dislike your manners, sir. Perhaps your friends here"—he cast a harsh smile around the group, daring any interference—"consider your filth wit. I do not. I suggest you remember that."

Raine dropped the dandy. He scuttled away on his bootheels, clutching at his chest. "Who the bloody hell do you think you are?" he ground out, fear and fury matched in his quavering voice.

Raine, already moving in the direction the girl had indicated, did not stop. "No one," he muttered. "No one at all."

Chapter 20

 $\mathcal{L}$ ord Tunbridge intended seduction. An unfortunate intention in Favor's estimation, as nature had not endowed him with those attributes she found necessary for a man to be considered desirable. At least to her.

Warm toffee-brown eyes that crinkled at the corners, *they* were alluring. And glossy dark hair that became ringlets where it touched a strong, broad neck. And a lean, square jaw. And a wry wit. And an impetuous devil-may-care streak. The sort of temperament a man who chased after rumored treasure must own. Now *those* were tempting.

Tunbridge made a guttural sound, drawing Favor's attention. He'd posed beside a lichen-covered outcrop, his hand braced at head level on the rock, one leg bent foot forward, toe angled just so. He leered down at her where he'd seated her, like an actor onstage playing to the front row audience.

"You're a vastly pretty gel, Miss Donne." One of his gingery brown brows rose while the other dipped.

Whatever was she doing here with him? She'd been enjoying her freedom so much that she'd simply floated blithely along with the current and that current happened to have contained Lord Tunbridge.

When his eyebrows' acrobatics failed to entice her, he tried a different tack. "I've always been partial to black-haired chits." He wet his lips. "Bespeaks a fiery temperament, a passionate nature, and an adventure-some—"

Enough of this rubbish, Favor thought.

"My hair isn't black. It's actually quite light," she said blandly. "I dye it."

He dropped his hand and straightened, his expression slackening in surprise. "Oh?"

"I'm sorry to disappoint but I'd hate to have you think I'd . . . led you on. Now, Lady Fia," she added naughtily, "*she* has naturally black hair. I'm sure you noticed. Such a pretty *child*."

"I don't wish to discuss that hell-bred bit of baggage." Tunbridge's nostrils pinched and his eyes narrowed.

The change in demeanor was so startling and so abrupt that Favor was taken aback. She'd assumed Tunbridge nothing more than Lady Fia's pathetic, lovelorn castoff. She saw now a dangerous man, his expression revealing he was well aware of her mockery.

She scrambled to her feet, the huge bell of her skirts

hampering her efforts. His thin fingers closed about her upper arm.

"Allow me." He helped her to rise, his thin frame belying the strength in his grip.

She murmured her thanks, and this time *she* was the recipient of the mocking gaze. He did not release her.

"Miss Fia has a powerful parent," Tunbridge said. "It allows her a latitude of behavior that others shouldn't emulate, because they haven't the same guarantee that their taunts will go unanswered."

She'd been a fool and now she needed to retrieve the situation. "You're correct," she apologized. "It was unconscionable of me."

"Unconscionable." He tested the word, disliked it. His grip tightened. "Stupid."

"That, too." She agreed wholeheartedly. Her thoughts raced to find some way out of the danger. "I set a barb without thinking. It's just that this past week I, too, received a set down from one I . . . I am interested in. It rather makes one sharpish."

She'd caught him off guard. His fingers loosened. "You?"

She looked past him, as though pride kept her from meeting his gaze. "Yes. Me."

"But, who?" he asked, clearly surprised. "You haven't shown any favoritism among your followers. In fact, there's even a betting book dedicated to naming the man who first—"

He stopped. Apparently even Tunbridge still owned some decorum, for he obviously regretted revealing what Favor imagined were wagers on who would first bed her. Not that such things mattered. Not if she could use them to her advantage.

"First what?" she prodded sweetly, pleased to have him off balance. "Shall we say, 'breach my defenses?'" She twisted. He let her go.

"Yes," he admitted.

"I wouldn't expect you or your lot to have identified my . . ." Favor let the sentence hang. "He isn't one of your number."

Tunbridge stared at her a second before bursting out laughing. "Don't say he's a groom or a stable boy? Not a footman! Good God, you're not another Lady Orville, are you?"

"No!" she snapped.

Tunbridge's amusement faded. A speculative gleam entered his eyes. "I could make quite a tidy sum if I was to correctly name the fellow who's captured your fancy, Miss Donne."

Of course. Pleasure palace it may well be, but first and foremost, Wanton's Blush was an exalted gaming hell. And Lord Tunbridge one of its deepest players.

"You . . . you rakehell!" Favor breathed in high dudgeon, not in the least displeased with the direction the conversation had taken. She had adroitly side-stepped a potentially ugly confrontation and in doing so set up a perfect opportunity to further pique Carr's interest.

All she had to do now was name Carr her would-be swain. Tunbridge, eager to find favor with Lady Fia's sire, would run to him immediately with the news.

What man could resist knowing he was a lady's rumored object of fascination?

"We could, say, split the winnings," Tunbridge suggested slyly.

She gasped. Not because she was shocked but because she couldn't think of anything else to do. She couldn't give up Carr's name quite that easily. Not if she was to be believed. Favor, who was as adept at tale-telling as any minstrel, knew the value of good timing.

Tunbridge sidled closer and she presented him with her back. He touched her lightly on the shoulder, a furtive, conspiratorial touch, nothing of passion in it. She made herself stand still. She felt him bend his head close to hers. His breath tickled her ear.

"Just a first name?"

Now was the time. She'd only to whisper a forlorn "Ronald" to draw Carr to her as surely as iron filings to a magnet. She'd misplayed Carr last night. She'd said the right things, she'd endured his touch, and she'd listened to his every word. But without enthusiasm. He'd known it and it had made him suspicious.

She could easily rectify that error.

Say his name. Tunbridge pressed her shoulder encouragingly.

"Who is he?" he whispered.

She conjured his face, preparing to whisper the answer but instead of Carr's haughty, handsome visage it was Rafe's face that formed behind her closed eyelids.

No, she thought desperately. *Not Rafe. Carr. Say it.* Her lips parted. She took a breath. "He's—"

Tunbridge's hand was snatched from her shoulder.

At the same time she heard him make a sound of angry protest. She spun around. Her heartbeat quickened; happiness raced through her.

Rafe stood before Tunbridge, smiling. It took Favor a second to realize Rafe's smile was far from pleasant.

"Sorry, dear fellow," Rafe drawled. "Didn't want to see the lady's shoulder dampened by your . . . enthusiasm."

The delight she'd experienced on seeing him, a delight she was in no way prepared to examine, faded. He was deliberately provoking Tunbridge. Reality doused her in cold truths. She'd had the matter well in hand. His interference could only cause trouble and the great lout didn't seem to realize that most of that trouble would be his own.

"You insolent cur!" Tunbridge spat.

"At least I don't drool," Rafe answered lightly, but his posture was far from nonchalant. He stood in an attitude of readiness, body angled sideways, weight forward, and arms loose at his sides.

"Who the hell are you?" Tunbridge demanded.

"Just another worshiper at Miss Donne's shrine."

Tunbridge looked as confused as he did angry. Abruptly Favor saw Rafe through Tunbridge's eyes. For Carr's guests, appearance was of paramount importance. Rafe, attired in worn, somewhat shabby but well-cut clothes, clearly hadn't the means for dandification.

"The hell you say! What do you mean by interrupting this lady and myself?" Tunbridge said. "Can you not see we were engaged in a private conversation?"

"Really?" Rafe asked innocently. "I'm *de trop*, am I?"

"Decidedly."

She had to do something and quickly. Rafe mustn't provoke Tunbridge any further. The man was rumored to have skewered five men to their deaths.

"Oh!" she said.

Neither man appeared to hear her breathy gasp of distress.

She redoubled her effort. "Oh! My! *You!*"

At this squawk both men turned. Rafe frowned, apparently displeased she'd interfered with his masculine posturing. She ignored him, keeping her attention on Tunbridge and saw the moment comprehension seeped into his expression.

"*Him?*" Tunbridge breathed.

She nodded, eyes wide, not having to reach very deep to produce a shuddering inhalation. "Him."

"Lucky bastard!" Tunbridge said admiringly, new appreciation in his expression.

"What the devil are you talking about?" Rafe demanded.

"Please." Favor lifted her head, striving to emulate pride before the fall. "As you are a gentleman, Lord Tunbridge, I ask you to honor my confidences."

Tunbridge, all eager anticipation, slumped as if she'd pulled a trump card from nowhere in a game of hazard. "Well . . ."

"Sir!"

"Yes. Fine. Confidence shall be kept. Blast. Damn. Hell."

She didn't believe him for a minute. But she did believe that at this moment he honestly believed he would keep her secret. He'd at least that much of honor left. That's all she needed. A little time in which Rafe might get away. The rash, impetuous . . . *man*.

"Your language, sir, is not fit for this lady's ears," Rafe said.

Favor, who'd heard far worse from Rafe, stared at him, trying to discern if he'd suddenly decided to make a jest. Clearly not. He was glaring at Tunbridge, who stood poised to fly to his confederates and learn the identity of the big, ill-dressed man he'd somehow over-looked these past weeks. He looked about as trustwor-thy as a cat near an open bird cage.

"My pardon," Tunbridge muttered hurriedly. "Dis-respectful of me. I am unspeakable. A pig. Forgive me, Miss Donne and Mister . . . Mister? Sorry, sir. I didn't catch your name—"

"You didn't and you won't!" Favor stated emphati-cally. "Not from either of us, Lord Tunbridge! Please, sir. Leave us!"

Luckily Raine finally decided it might prove wise to take his cue from her. He positioned himself between Favor and Tunbridge, his attitude growing even more threatening. "I believe you heard the lady's request, Tunbridge. Leave."

Tunbridge looked from one to the other. "Damn!" he burst out. "I don't know why you won't reveal the fellow's name. Since he's a guest of Carr's it won't be all that bloody hard to discover and you'll save me a bit of time."

Favor placed her fingertips over her chest and closed her eyes. "I will not make my tender heart the object of filthy speculation," she whispered dramatically.

"What?" Rafe's head snapped around.

"Fine," Tunbridge bit out, and without another word stalked off in the direction from whence they'd come.

They waited in silence until Tunbridge disappeared, before turning to face one another.

"What the hell was that all about?" Rafe asked in bewilderment.

Favor burst out laughing.

She braced her hands on her knees, laughing in that full rich way of hers and there was nothing he could do but smile and then chuckle and then laugh himself. And that was the last thing he'd been expecting to do.

When he'd seen that ass's hand on her he'd reacted instinctively, viscerally, jerking it away from her. He'd expected her to be furious that he'd thwarted her *tête-à-tête*. But when she'd turned he'd seen the welcome in her expression, the surprised second of—God help him—what looked like joy in the smile that sprang full blown to her lips . . . for *him* . . .

And later while he tried to figure out what sort of lies she'd been telling Tunbridge so that he could appropriately play his part, she'd caught his eye and the immediate sense of understanding, the rightness of it, had been like homecoming.

The realization rushed into his thoughts and soul, filling the empty and hollow parts of his life. When he was with Favor, his past did not exist. He felt no anger or bitterness or hatred. He thought of Carr and his mother without choking on the need for redress or recompense. His eye turned out, toward the morrow: not in, toward the past.

And now she made him laugh.

What more could she do to him?

Except make him love her.

"Ah! Me," she finally sniffed, wiping the tears away with the back of her hand. She sighed and smiled at him. "Well, you'd best be off before Tunbridge comes hurrying back bringing witnesses to my deflowering."

"What?"

Favor valiantly withstood another wave of laughter.

"Oh, yes. That's what he was doing whispering in my ear, trying to coax from me the name of the fellow who'd caught my fancy."

She nodded happily, unaware of the havoc she was causing in his heart. "They've a betting book on it, you see. Poor Tunbridge, after discovering he was not destined to be my paramour, decided he might as well make the best of the situation and find out the name of the fellow who was. Being a lady, I, of course, declined to name names and refused to say more than that my beau was not among Tunbridge's circle of friends. Then you arrived. I could not have asked for better timing."

"You jest."

"No!" She grinned broadly, tapping him lightly on the chest with her finger, winsome, naughty, and utterly engaging. "I couldn't make up so rich a tale."

"I'm afraid I have more faith in your skills than you," he said dryly.

"Well, perhaps I could come up with *as* good a tale, but none better," she allowed modestly. "Why *did* you come?"

He wasn't about to tell her he'd come because he'd made the frustrating discovery that he wanted no other woman but her. He glanced about for inspiration.

"Clothes. You were to get me clothes. This afternoon. At one. It's"—he yanked his timepiece from his pocket—"three o'clock."

She drew back and he cursed the distance that separated them even though it was but a mere foot or so.

"You mean you came charging over here because I failed to deliver your clothes at the exact hour you'd decreed? Of all the reckless, self-important, vainglorious masculine— Oh!"

He wasn't attending her words as well as he ought, though something in her tone cautioned him. He was simply too busy enjoying the sight of her, hair tossed by a suddenly capricious breeze, color fresh in her cheeks and lips, eyes as clear as wood violets. "It wasn't that reckless."

"Ah!" Her hands flew up in exasperation.

A thought interrupted the pleasure he took in the picture she made. "Why would that Tunbridge fellow think you had chosen a paramour?"

"Because I told him so."

"You were lying."

Her brow cleared. She smiled sunnily.

Damn. He may as well hand her his heart on a platter and what the bloody good that useless organ would do either of them was, and would forever remain, a mystery. He would do no such thing, for it could only result in more harm to her.

And worse harm for me, an inner voice cautioned. *An irreparably, irredeemably worse harm.*

"Was I?" she asked archly.

He did rise to her bait although it took much effort to stand motionless while she sashayed up to him, tossing her head.

"But of course you were," he said with carefully measured indifference. "If you had found your gull, you'd hardly be out here cavorting with Tunbridge. You'd be close by the poor dupe, setting up a wind what with fluttering all those lashes."

Her impertinent smile wavered, dissolved. "Well, if you think that for one instant I believe you came storming out here simply to demand I produce your purloined wardrobe, you're sadly mistaken."

"Why else would I come here?" he asked coldly. "I thought to teach you that I am not to be discounted at your convenience. Certainly not because my demands interfere with your pleasures."

Her lips pressed tightly together, the full curve of her enticing lower lip disappearing.

"Having achieved my purpose," he went on, "I will now leave you to your . . . diversions. Tomorrow you will bring the clothes."

There. He'd sounded cold and threatening to his own ear. He needed only to leave. Except Favor's lower lip had reappeared and it trembled slightly and the hard brilliance of her eyes was no longer hard, but veiled by a wash of unshed tears, angry tears but tears nonetheless. He couldn't remember when he'd last seen a woman cry. It undid him entirely.

"Why do we always end up fighting?" The words escaping her lips were rife with unhappiness.

He gave up. Reaching out, he captured her easily and spun her about, bending her over his arm.

"Little falcon, don't you honestly know?" he asked. "Why, so *this* won't happen."

And he kissed her.

Chapter 21

Rafe's lips moved over hers. His arms were strong and his body an anchor she could cling to and not for an instance did she consider trying to free herself from his embrace. With a sigh, she gave herself up to his kiss, wrapping her arms around his neck and pulling him down.

She closed her eyes, soaking up all of the delicious sensations not only surrounding but filling her. Like a dry sponge thrown in an ocean, her awareness expanded with the influx of perceptions. She cupped his hard jaw, holding his face to hers, alive to each inch of beard-rough skin abrading her palms.

Her pawn. Her blackmailer. Her thief.

His muscular arms, the sinew in the thigh pressed against her hip, the hard chest flattening her own breasts, all of these set her skin tingling with the need to arch closer, rubbing against him like a cat. His scent filled her nostrils, crushed grass and dry pine, astringent soap, mysterious male musk.

And kisses. Kisses such as she'd never known nor dreamed existed: the feathering gentleness of velvety nibbles; the shivery carnality of moist, softly drawing kisses; and, finally, a deep, soul-searing kiss as he angled his mouth sideways over hers and tilted her chin, urging her mouth open. She needed no further encouragement. His tongue stroked the sleek lining of her cheeks, playing with her own tongue: wet, warm, and infinitely wicked.

Abruptly sensation exceeded experience. She'd no words to record the feelings rocketing through her, no terms to even identify them.

Her head fell back and wedged in the lee of his arm. Her eyelids fluttered open, allowing her a glimpse of his rugged face, tense and intent. Then he was kissing her again. But surely kisses alone could not account for the surge of pleasure coursing through her, as sweet and heady as hot mead. Kisses couldn't set a pulse beating high between her thighs, or rouse an aching in the very tips of her breasts.

She wanted to *melt* into him, to feel his body surround hers, to absorb him into herself. She tried. Lord knows, she tried.

She moved her hands around his torso and up his back, clasping the hard, mounded shoulder muscles and pulling herself as close as humanly possible. Her hips burrowed into the niche created by his splayed stance. A sound rumbled from deep in Rafe's chest. He pulled away from her. She voiced an unintelligible but vehement protest, her eyes opening to flash a disbelieving glare at him.

Why would he want to stop? Why, in the name of all the saints, would anyone *ever* want to stop something so wonderful?

He lifted his head and stared down at her. His breath rushed out in pants to fan her hot cheeks and swollen lips.

"Oh, no," he said, sounding amused and winded and angry and tender all at once. "Kisses, yes," he said and rained a dozen lightning-fast busses over her temple, cheeks, and eyelids. Her mouth turned to intercept them but could not. She made a sound of frustration.

"Dear Lord," he whispered, capturing the back of her head in one broad hand and pressing her forehead to his.

"Kisses," he whispered. "Nothing more." He laughed. "I seem to have acquired a taste for punishment. I knew how inadequate kisses would—No! Stay, you!" he commanded as she tipped her chin seeking his lips. "I am no saint and you, lady, are a far greater temptation than this poor mortal flesh has ever endeavored to resist."

She didn't understand the meaning of his words, or why, though his gaze roved like a stalking thing over her countenance, he held himself back. She knew only that a moment earlier she'd been vibrantly whole, and as each moment passed her pleasure dissolved like footprints lapped by an incoming tide.

She'd had too little happiness of late. She'd forgotten its flavor. She worked her hands up to his face, bracketing the tense jaw between her hands and polishing his lips with hers.

"Kiss me," she whispered. He stared down at her, the shadows of his lashes making mysteries of his warm brown eyes. She could read nothing there. The very world seemed to hold its breath. She brushed her fingertip across the silky sable fringe of his lashes. "Kiss me."

His head moved slowly down—

" 'Sblood! Tunbridge was right!" A woman's voice broke Favor's hushed anticipation.

Instantly, Rafe straightened, carrying her to his side and behind him, shielding her from curiosity seekers.

"Pray excuse us." His voice was vitriolic and cold, like burning ice. "I hadn't realized we were being offered as voyeuristic entertainment," he said, "or I should have endeavored a more licentious tableau."

Silently, Favor cursed the intruders, far more furious at their interruption than embarrassed by it. She raised her chin to a haughty angle and stepped from behind Rafe's broad back.

"Lady Fia." She acknowledged the slender girl and brace of snickering men on either side of her. "Were you seeking me?"

But Fia didn't appear to hear Favor. Her gaze was trained on Rafe, as blank and fixed as a sleepwalker's.

"Fia?" Rafe echoed, scowling.

One of the swains—a handsome blond man whose name Favor could not recall but whose fetid breath she did—stepped forward. His lip curled in derision. "The Lady Fia Merrick. Lord Carr's daughter. You do know Lord Carr, don't you, fellow? For either he's your host"—he turned to Fia, doubtless so he could witness the appreciation his next sally was sure to bring—"or your employer."

The other swain, a green lad who'd the previous night confessed to Favor his fervent desire "to be baptized in the ways of sin," took his blond friend's cue.

He shot a quick, guilty glance in Favor's direction before averting his eyes and addressing her. "Miss Donne, never say your taste for rural pleasures is what's kept you from sampling a more cosmopolitan fare. I didn't believe Tunbridge when he claimed it so, but"—he hid his mouth behind his hand—"I can scarce doubt my own eyes."

"You must have gone to some trouble to locate me, Lady Fia." Favor tried once more to divert attention from Rafe. He'd been mad to walk into the center of one of Carr's parties. If she didn't think quickly, he'd be found out. "And in quite a hurry to do so. Lord Tunbridge left not ten minutes ago. Was there something imperative that you needed to see me about? Or were you eager to see *us*?" The innuendo was sharp and unflattering yet Fia barely glanced in her direction.

The men, either too dull-witted to catch the inference or simply uncaring, were watching Rafe, who had gone mute—strange behavior from a man who hadn't lacked for words a few minutes before. Favor studied him. But though at first glance one might have supposed that he, too, had fallen under Fia's siren spell,

there was nothing of desire in his gaze. It was searching and somehow sad.

"*Is* this brute one of your employees, Lady Fia?" the
youth asked. Favor held her breath, willing Rafe not to
take umbrage.

Fia answered without removing her gaze from Rafe.
"No."

"You know him, then?" the blond man said.

"I don't know," Fia said reflectively. "There's
something familiar about him." She stepped forward.

"Here now," she said imperiously, "do you know
me, sir?"

Rafe hesitated. The sorrow intensified in his eyes.
He shook his head. "No. I do not know you."

A shadow passed over Fia's countenance, making
her beauty suddenly tragic. Then it was gone and one
high-curving brow rose haughtily.

"I thought not. Nor do I know you." She turned
away but checked her step and turned her head. "Ah. I
have it. I know where I've seen this fellow. Do you
know my father?"

An unpleasant smile curved Rafe's wide lips. "Oh,
yes. Him I know."

Fia nodded, clearly satisfied. "There you are. He is
one of my father's special guests and that is why we
have not seen him. That, and his having apparently
been"—her gaze passed to Favor—"preoccupied with
other companions. Tell me, Miss Donne, does my father know you are dallying with his . . . guest? He
won't like it."

Favor's heart beat thickly. Silently she prayed Fia

would not reveal her interest in Carr to Rafe. Not yet. She needed time. Time to . . .

"He doesn't like sharing," Fia went on. "Never got the knack of it." Her three-point smile lit her smooth, youthful countenance and she motioned for her swains. They came like puppies to a milk bowl and she linked her arms to each, one on either side.

"Come, gentlemen. Despite Miss Donne's conviction that we were sneaking through the woods hoping to surprise her and this fellow in an indiscretion, I still desire to find the stag's antlers Mrs. Petrie claimed to have seen. Oh, yes. I heard your query, Miss Donne, and no, I did not come to *see* you."

She did not look back as she allowed her sniggering male companions to draw her away. In minutes they were lost to sight in the rocky, tree studded landscape.

Favor, flooded with relief that Rafe had escaped more dangerous notice, sank to the grassy floor.

"Why did she warn you about Carr?" Rafe asked, standing above her. "What did she mean?"

Her recent relief died. She should tell him the truth: that she was here to become affianced to Lord Carr. She kept her head averted, steeling herself to say the words. And why shouldn't she tell him? He already knew half of it: He'd accepted that she was seeking to make a brilliant match, to refill her clan's coffers with a rich husband's money. Why not Carr?

Carr's face rose in her mind's eye. Other girls had wed men with far more years than Carr. It wasn't age alone that stayed her tongue. It was the knowledge that she knowingly sought to take as her mate a man so evil.

But Rafe wouldn't know that. Rafe hadn't stood beneath Carr's lathered steed and stared up at him while he decided one's fate with less thought than he'd give to drowning a kitten. Rafe hadn't witnessed Carr's satisfaction as he'd ridden off with his devil's brood, leaving her alone in a blood-stained night rail among the dead and dying.

Rafe wouldn't know she maneuvered to become a monster's bride.

"Favor?"

How sweet her name sounded coming from him. But he couldn't match her Christian name with her surname. He didn't know it. Just as she didn't know his. And it didn't matter.

But it did. They'd followed their inclinations on instinct and emotion. Their relationship was a castle built on quicksand, doomed to disappear, swallowed by harsh realities and grim truth, surnames and pasts, obligations and penalties.

But she could not see it fall apart yet. Not yet. She could cling to whatever she had of happiness, stretch it out a few more hours or days or . . .

"I think she was talking about you, Rafe."

He'd squatted down on his heels beside her, his brow worried. "What?"

"When she said Carr didn't like sharing. I think she mistook you for one of the gamblers and I believe she meant Carr would not like sharing you with me. I might divert your attention from the tables."

"I see." He'd accepted her lie, too concerned about

her to give it much heed. "Are you all right? Did those men offend you? I can—"

"No!" She reached up, grabbing hold of his forearm. The muscle tightened beneath her grip. Sensual awareness ambushed her anew. She drew back her hand. "No. You can't do anything. You have to keep hidden or you'll be found out."

"No one will find me out."

"They almost did! You're safe now only because of Fia Merrick's certainty that no one could breach her father's castle."

That wholly engaging lopsided smile once more graced his bold features, making boyish what was normally so unremittingly male and mature. "Thank you for caring."

She made an exasperated face. "It's not as though I want to care."

His smile spread into a grin. "I'm sure of that."

He knelt down beside her on one knee and raised a hand to touch her cheek. She scooted backward on her seat. She could resist him if he didn't touch her. But why would she want to res—

Ah, no! she thought, *that way lies disaster!*

No similar cautionary thought seemed to occur to Rafe. He'd eased forward, prowling toward her. The smile still teased the corners of his mouth, a lazy smile now and quite, quite predatory. As were the dark eyes and intent gaze belying that charming, casual smile. He looked like the proverbial wolf come to court the lamb.

She gulped, scooted back again, slipped and landed

flat on her back. Before she could scramble up he was over her, arms braced on either side of her shoulders, blotting out the sky with his breadth.

He reached down and grinned as she flinched, but his hand moved harmlessly past the quivering agitation of her mouth and chest and tangled in her hair.

Her pulse galloped. The memory of his kisses was so fresh she could still feel his lips.

"Why would you conceal its true color?" The smile slowly vanished from his face. "Ah, yes. The would-be suitors like a dark lass."

He released the strand of black dyed hair and in one easy movement rose to his feet. He extended his hand down to her. She wriggled up onto her elbows, gazing blankly at his hand. Disappointment quickly replaced her trepidation. So, there was to be no dalliance, then?

"Let me help you up," he said mildly, as though he'd never held her, caressed her, molded her body to his and his lips to hers.

"No, thank you," she said, aware she sounded disgruntled.

As if he knew the reason for her glum expression he grinned. "Here, little falcon. I may not be one of Carr's well-heeled *roués* but at least my character is not so poor that I would ply my slight amorous skills here for any chance passerby to view. Neither, do I think, would you want that."

"Of course not!" she huffed, dusting off nonexistent pieces of grass, avoiding his amused eyes. Damn the man's arrogance!

"I don't know what momentary aberration clouded

my judgment, but you may be well assured there shan't be a second such lapse," she said.

She clambered to her feet, ignoring his offer of assistance and turned a quelling eye on him. She acknowledged with gratification his bow in deference to her terse statement.

And missed the smile his deferential pose concealed.

Chapter 22

*F*avor meandered toward her suite, peeling back her riding gloves as she went. She'd been away from Rafe only an hour and already she missed him. Not that she'd ever allow him to know that. And truly it had been insanity to let him kiss her.

Let him?

An impish smile appeared on her face, born of the knowledge that he was attracted to her far beyond what he was willing to admit. And if she suffered from similar pride—or fear—well, she didn't really care.

She'd just arrived at her chambers when the door swung open. Muira seized her wrist and yanked her inside, slamming the door behind her. Startled, Favor jerked away from her, only then realizing that Muira wore none of the makeup that created Pala or Mrs.

Douglas. Instead a livid red welt crossed one weathered cheek.

"What happened?" Favor asked in concern.

"What *hasn't* happened?" Muira snapped in reply. "While you've been licking icing from your fingers beneath some tree, 'Pala' had an audience with Carr."

"Did he do that?"

"Do what?" Muira asked irritably, and then, seeing the direction of Favor's shocked gaze, she touched her cheek. She made a dismissive sound. "This is nothing. We have far graver matters to consider."

"I don't understand."

"Of course not, you stupid girl," Muira said. "I'll tell you what you've done. Because you were too delicate, too sensitive to endure Carr's attentions, he's decided that he needs a *love* potion to make you more receptive."

"What!"

"Yes. A love potion. Which I will provide him. And later, when he hands you a drink, my girl, you will take it and drink it and within an hour act like his Cheapside doxy."

"I will not," Favor breathed, repelled.

"Don't worry," Muira sneered. "You'll have at least one day to practice puckering your lips. Carr made sure of that by marking me with this." She touched her cheek. "No paint will cover it and you can't appear unchaperoned. I'll send word that you have the headache. Tomorrow you'll be ready to play Carr's cooing lovebird."

Every fiber of her body rebelled at the notion. "No," she said. "I will not do it."

"By God, you will!" Muira's hand darted out with the speed of a striking snake, slapping Favor hard across the face.

Instinctively self-protective, Favor grabbed hold of Muira's arms above the elbow, stopping a second blow. Stunned, Muira stared at Favor's hands. Her mouth fell open.

Instinct might have incited Favor's action, anger caused her hands to tighten.

"Listen, old woman," she said in a low, hard voice. "Long ago, you assured me that simply showing interest in Carr would be enough. I've been able to carry my role this far only because I did *not* have to pretend I was smitten.

"I would *never* be able to carry off such a farce and not all your slaps or threats can make it so. I can barely tolerate his breath on my cheek! If you force me to try, you, and only you, will be responsible for the failure of your plan. Do you understand me?" She shook Muira, rage and pain and regret overwhelming her.

"Now," she grated out. "I shall not drink any vile brew and pretend that that bastard fills me with lust. Do we understand each other?"

Muira, eyes wide and unblinking, nodded. "But what shall we do? He trusts Pala to make him a potion. She dare not show up without one. And it must work or he will never again trust her."

Favor released Muira's arm and stood back, as disgusted with her violence toward the elderly woman as with Muira herself. She wondered if Muira was even aware that more and more often lately she spoke of Pala as if the character were a real woman.

"Make your potion," she said. "Deliver it to Carr. He'll have to combine it with drink or food he intends to give me. I shall find excuses not to eat or drink anything he offers me. At the same time, I'll make clear that the only time he will be alone with Janet is after he marries me."

"You think this will work?" Muira said, her shock at Favor's ferocity fading. She eyed the girl with hidden acrimony. *She* was the one who'd held the clan together for the last bleak decade, not this little uppity bitch. It was *her* plan that would return the McClairens to power and prestige, not this . . . *child*'s. She, Muira Dougal, was the dark heart of the clan. And now this barely weaned little slut challenged her.

"Yes," Favor said, unaware of the dark path of Muira's thoughts.

Muira, her gaze never leaving Favor's hard, determined countenance, nodded her compliance. And made plans of her own.

". . . and if what yer da says is true, ye'll be in London by Christmas," Gunna prattled on, she who was not given to chatter. Fia continued watching Gunna's reflection in the mirror hanging above the dressing table. The twisted old woman brushed through Fia's hair, turning the curly mass into a rippling, shimmering veil of black. "I'm thinking ye'll like London. What do ye think?"

"How can I fail to like it? It's not Wanton's Blush," Fia replied.

"Aye," Gunna said. "That's for certain and right ye are to be putting this wretched place behind ye. It's no but a mausoleum yer father's guests use like a brothel."

"What lovely imagery," Fia said, softly ironic. "You've such a gift for words, Gunna."

Gunna cackled. "Well, I have no love of the great gloomy place but"—her eye fixed on Fia—"I thought ye'd a bit of care fer it."

"I'd an interest," Fia corrected. "I should have liked to have known the castle when it was called Maiden's Blush. As a matter of curiosity."

Gunna did not reply, concentrating on a snarl. Moments passed. The setting sun filled the bedchamber with amber light. Outside, the bare limbs of the oak trees tapped lightly on the windows, like a lover come begging.

"You know he's here, don't you?" Fia said.

Gunna's hand checked. "Who be that?"

"Raine," Fia replied, and turned in her chair to search Gunna's face. The ravaged countenance gave little away. It never had. "You knew he was here, didn't you?"

"Aye," Gunna admitted.

Fia nodded as she turned back around, facing the mirror. She'd thought so. And that Gunna, whom she'd always trusted, had kept this from her caused only a small prick of anguish. She was used to being disillusioned. "When did you find out?"

"Yesterday. He's been here some weeks and me never knowing, nor anyone else neither."

"How enterprising of him. Not even Father?"

"No. I dinna tell ye because he did not want ye to know and I wouldna have ye hurt by his seeming indifference, though I do believe it's not indifference as much as mistrust." She caught Fia's eye. "He doesna know ye, Fia," she said flatly. "And what he remembers is that ye were yer father's shadow."

"He's quite right on both counts," Fia replied calmly. "He has no reason to show interest in me or to trust me."

"Do not act callous for my poor benefit, Fia Merrick. 'Tis a waste of a good performance. I know ye better than that."

"Do you?" Fia whispered suddenly. Her voice was that of a lost little girl unable to hide her wistful hope that deep within she really was decent and honorable and . . . good, when she knew how unlikely that to be. She bowed her head, ashamed of such emotions.

Gunna's hand hovered briefly above Fia's bowed head, hesitated and was retracted. She cleared her throat. "How did ye find out about Raine?"

Relieved that Gunna would not pursue other topics, Fia answered. "He was on the picnic this afternoon. Attending Miss Donne."

"Miss Donne?"

"Thomas Donne's sister."

"Aye. I remember ye remarking ye were surprised by yer father's interest in her. Ye thought it odd as he hadn't paid much attention to her until the last week or so."

"Yes. Apparently not only my father but my brother is interested in Miss Donne. The Donnes hold some sort of fatal magnetism for us Merricks." She regretted the words as soon as she'd said them. Even Gunna did not know exactly how much Thomas Donne had hurt her. She would just as soon not hint that the injury she'd sustained still bled.

She could still hear Thomas's voice, carrying above the gales blowing up from the sea to the garden where he'd led Rhiannon Russell for privacy. It had carried, too, over the garden wall where she'd knelt, listening:

"This isn't simply a rather nasty family. It's evil."

"Carr killed his first wife."

"Merrick skewered a man's hand just for cheating."

"His brother raped a nun."

"They are all as bad as their sire."

And finally, the mortal thrust,

"Fia is nothing but Carr's whore, groomed to fetch the largest marriage settlement possible."

Her entire body jerked in physical repudiation of the memory. She closed her eyes, hating that it still had such power, hating more that she, who'd spent her life building walls, was so vulnerable in this one last area. Once she'd loved Thomas Donne. But now, as with all love betrayed, she hated him with surpassing fervor.

If only she could stir within herself some animosity for his sister, she might find she liked the taste of revenge. But she couldn't.

She glanced at Gunna. The old woman stood motionless, the half of her face revealed by her mantilla taut with concentration. "What is it, Gunna?"

"What was Raine doing at yer picnic?"

Fia lifted her shoulders. "I don't know. He pretended not to know me and I returned the favor. Why is he here, Gunna? What is going on?"

"He's looking fer some treasure he says his mother had keep of. He came to find it without yer father's knowledge and to take it away."

Fia smiled, slightly bemused, a trifle sad. How in keeping with what she remembered of her brawny middle brother. Impetuous. Bold. Doomed.

"Ye say ye found Raine and this girl together?" Gunna asked.

"Like a dovetailed joint," Fia replied flatly, "fitted at the lips. Quite protective of her, he was. Nearly snapped my head off when we came upon them. And she . . . well, she was obviously intent on distracting me and my companions from asking too closely about him."

"I *thought* someone had been there with him," Gunna murmured.

"What?"

"I found him in the old chapel. Or he found me, is more like. Sprung at me, arms raised to strike and his face hard with violence. It makes sense now. *She'd* been with him and he'd been protecting her.

"And later, as we spoke his eyes kept moving about the room, touching on bits of trash and turning tender.

He was thinking of her." She passed her slender hand over her face. "Oh, Raine!"

"Why do you say that?" Fia asked, perplexed. "So, Raine has found himself a light-skirts. What of it? You can't be surprised? Not what with Raine's reputation. Even I have heard tales about him, tales old by the time he was sixteen."

"Ach!" Gunna shook her head, setting the mantilla swinging. "Ye never knew him at all if ye think that. He was ever the reckless one, set on racing the devil to damnation, but only because no one ever bade him stay. No one ever cared enough to stop him.

"He knew plenty about tupping, I'll grant ye that, but naught about love, either the giving or the receiving of it. But I always ken that once he'd learned to love, he'd do it as he did everything. Wholeheartedly, recklessly, without a thought to consequence or the risks to his heart."

"You think he *loves* Miss Donne?" Fia asked, taken aback.

"I don't know," Gunna answered flatly. "I do know he deserves to be loved. He's waited for it long enough."

Fia laughed, made nervous by the pity and confusion Gunna's revelation awakened in her heart. "And Miss Donne? Have you any thoughts on her emotional state?"

"Don't use that tone on me, Fia. Save it for yer sophisticated friends," Gunna reprimanded her sharply and Fia's eyes fell. "I know nothing of this girl; perhaps she's no better than she should be, but Raine . . . yer father's taken so much from him already. He mustn't take her, too."

Lord Carr uncorked the crude bottle a footman said had been delivered by a raggedy-looking tinker a few hours earlier. He waved it under his nose, his nostrils quivering.

Not too vile a brew: a hint of almond, a soupçon of orange blossoms. But then, Carr reminded himself, it was a love potion. What would it smell like, brimstone?

He lit the candles on his desk before working a key into the lock on one set of drawers. It was dusk and he'd need to hurry to finish his preparations.

He opened a drawer and removed a short tray. Several small vials clinked together as he set it on his desktop. He removed an empty one and fitted it with a small funnel, humming as he filled it with the potion. By midnight, Miss Donne—and Janet—would follow him anywhere.

Not that he couldn't have brought the girl round entirely with his own charms. But when so expeditious a solution was at hand, why exert oneself needlessly?

Having filled the vial, he sealed and pocketed it before returning the tray to its original location. He locked the drawer. He had to remember to take the tray with him when he vacated Wanton's Blush. Its contents might prove useful in London.

He chanced to catch sight of his reflection in the mirror and frowned. This would never do. One simply couldn't commence a seduction in a plain white periwig. He would see that the increasingly—and thank-fully—close-mouthed Rankle prepared a lavender powder for his new bagwig for this evening.

But first. . . . He moved to the wall and yanked on a silk bell pull. A footman arrived in a few minutes.

"Go to the conservatory and have the gardener cut several of whatever bloom is most exotic. Deliver them immediately to Miss Favor Donne with my regards and tell her I look forward to her company this even-ing."

"Ah. Er. Yes," the tall, strapping, and exceedingly ornamental young man said. "Ah. Sir?"

Unfortunately the best-looking of this sort were in-variably the most dull-witted.

"What?" Carr snapped irritably. He'd much to do before this evening's *soirée* began.

"Miss Donne ain't going to be coming down to dine this evening, sir. Her old auntie sent her regrets, saying as how the young lady had the headache and how the old lady would sit by her."

"Damnation!" Carr thundered. "Get out of here!" The footman began to bolt. "No. Wait. Go get the bloody flowers and deliver them to her anyway. With my regrets that she's feeling vaporish."

The footman ducked his head and backed out of the room. Carr slammed the door after him and com-menced pacing. *Headache?* He'd been all set for the next part of his plan and now she had a *headache*? Of all the gall.

Clearly, Janet had done this to the chit simply to

taunt him. Or maybe the chit had done this to Janet, simply to thwart her. It was hard enough understanding the primitive workings of one female mind but to have to deal with two conjointly! A lesser man would fail in so tortuous a task.

Chapter 23

"The momentary aberration" Favor had promised would not return the day before had, apparently, returned. Not only did it cloud Favor's mind, it had eclipsed her reason as well. Raine wasn't even certain how it was they'd started kissing. And he didn't care.

Then thought receded and pleasure took precedence as Favor's soft lips found the base of his neck. He groaned as she nibbled her way up the side of his throat to the angle of his chin, his small measure of self-restraint fast being depleted.

When she'd appeared in the room he'd been searching, her mouth sulky and succulent and the purloined men's garb draped over her arm, he'd promised himself he would treat her as the convent-bred lady she was, not the girl her presence in this Scottish Sodom declared her. It quickly became a task far more arduous than he'd imagined.

Favor sighed, her fingers exploring beneath his shirt with shattering eagerness. Her eyes were closed and her head had fallen against his shoulders, inviting more kisses. Genteel, sweet kisses, nectar when he was fast growing thirsty for a more potent brew. But he would be good. He would hold back. He would keep control of the hunger rumbling through his body like distant thunder. Not only because he was no longer a willful, irresponsible boy, not only because her upbringing cautioned any wooer to use restraint to bring this little falcon to hand, but because, just as Favor had never been wooed, he had never courted.

It was a rich, complicated dance and one not without its own subtle, piquant rewards. All of his early sexual experiences with women had ended in bed. All of it, the petting and licking and kissing, had been accomplished too hastily and most often frantically, an obligatory prelude to mating.

This was . . . exquisite.

Delectable. Ambrosial. Honeyed kisses, pulpy sweet, open-mouthed exchanges, wet and yearning and deep. Caresses like satin. Smooth, deep polishing strokes. Skimming feathering touches. He'd never known such delicious torment.

She nestled trustingly in his embrace, unskilled yet wise in a way no woman in his past had ever been wise—with a deep understanding of unselfishness, of pleasure gained through pleasure given. She was a treasure.

"Treasure," he murmured against her forehead.

Her eyes opened. "Yes." She sighed. "You're right. We should get back to it."

"I . . . I didn't mean—" He stopped. What was he going to do, admit he'd been speaking about her? Unwise. Not with everything so bloody complicated and daily growing more so.

She didn't appear to note his stumbling near-confession. Her arms slid languidly away from his throat. She smiled regretfully. Regretfully, he released her.

"I have to leave. Tonight is Carr's masque." Her cheeks colored and he knew she was remembering his comments on masques and their attendees.

"You don't have to go," he said.

Her gaze was fixed on the opposite wall. She'd pinned a faux smile to her countenance. He hated it.

"You should leave Wanton's Blush," he said, unable to keep his frustration from sounding like anger. "Pack up your aunt and go back to your brother's home.

"If you must find a rich husband, go to London when your brother returns. I assure you, this isn't the only society that would welcome you. There are better hunting grounds, Favor. You don't have to be *here*."

She turned her head toward him. She looked weary, in some unfathomable manner depleted, as though all her reserves had suddenly found an end.

"There you're wrong. I need to . . . marry soon."

"Why? Can't your family fend for themselves for an additional few months?" he asked angrily. "Are they such poor specimens that they would sacrifice you to provide them an easier life for a few weeks more?"

Her blue eyes quickened with anger. Better lightning than emptiness. "You don't know anything about it!"

"Then tell me!"

"Ach!" She backed away, driven off by his words. But he wouldn't retreat. He couldn't.

"Tell me."

She crossed her arms under her breasts and glared at him. "Men! You think you have a monopoly on honor. That only males need the catharsis of discharging a debt. But you're wrong."

"Why would you need catharsis?" he asked, holding his breath, afraid she'd tell him, terrified she wouldn't. He wanted her trust. He didn't deserve it. He hadn't even told her who he was. "Why?"

"I did something. Years ago." She hesitated. He searched her face and saw a young woman, little more than a girl, torn by indecision, wanting desperately to share the most intimate details of her life with a man she knew next to nothing about. Desperate because there was no one else to tell.

How alone she must be to have come to such a pass. How achingly alone.

"My actions cost my . . . it cost people their lives," she said finally.

"Did you know they would pay such a price?"

"No!"

"Then if unintentional, you cannot be blamed."

"Ignorance is no excuse." She recited the words in such a way that he knew she'd heard them many, many times.

He started toward her but she held up her hand, denying him, stopping him. "Explain."

"I . . . I was a child," she mumbled, eyes averted. "My . . . people were seeing that a criminal was brought to justice."

"A criminal?"

"A rapist."

Odd he should flinch now, upon hearing that label on her lips, when years ago he'd not only refused to flinch but had endured blow after blow without giving satisfaction.

She misunderstood his recoil and nodded. "They brought him to where we lived to see justice meted out by my father. But he was gone and my mother, who was a lady of standing, bade me stop them."

"Why?"

"Because she feared that if they hanged this rapist, my brothers would be killed in retaliation."

"I see."

"I did what she asked. I stopped them"—her arms tightened about her—"just long enough for *his* family to arrive with armed men. They killed most all of those people. Slaughtered them. Cut them down like wheat before the scythe. I found out later that my brother was already dead."

Her eyes were dazed, her expression ravaged, stunned anew by the memory. He had to draw her back from that terrible inner vista he knew so well himself. "Bedamned, Favor! What else could you have done?"

Her brow puckered, looking for an answer to a riddle posed years before and never answered. "I should have let them kill the boy. If I hadn't stopped them they could have hanged him and been gone by the time the soldiers arrived. And even if they hadn't been gone, at least justice would have been served. A rapist would have died."

"You did what your mother asked," he said soberly. "It wasn't your fault."

He had the distinct impression that he'd failed her, that she'd been waiting hungrily for an answer she'd yet to hear.

"I know," she said, as though he were being purposefully obtuse. "But 'fault' isn't part of this. Nor blame. This is about what I can live with, what I need to do."

"And marrying a wealthy maggot is the only way you can live with yourself?" he asked, frustration spawning sarcasm.

"Aye." Her voice was distant.

"Why not don a hair shirt?" Raine asked bitterly. "I'm sure I can find a flail somewhere about to help aid you in your pleasure. This is Wanton's Blush after all."

"Don't," she said, not angry, not pricked, simply resigned. " 'Tis you who are being unreasonable, not I. I'm not the first woman who chooses a husband for what he can bring her family. Indeed, I have it better than most, for I do this of my own free will." She appealed to him helplessly. "Would you rather I disobeyed the dictates of my conscience just to please my selfish heart?"

Joy was a piercing blade, killing him with never-to-be's. He couldn't say a word. He could only stand, drinking in the implication of her words.

"Rafe." She smiled, shy and forlorn. He held out his hand. She pretended not to see it and turned and walked away. He closed his eyes.

"Raine," he whispered back in so low a voice she could not hear him. He knew now why poets spoke of a heart breaking for something spilled in his chest, something hot and hurtful. He opened his eyes. Her slender back was to him. The slope of her shoulders was burdened, her steps heavy.

She stopped, looking around the room, trying to find an excuse to stay, knowing she should go. "You." She cleared her voice, tried again. "You said you were looking for an oriental box." Her tone tried hopelessly for its former brightness.

He answered in kind, searching for a place hidden from the demands and machinations of the world outside, the place they'd found in these empty rooms, searching for a fabled treasure and finding another even greater, one they'd never sought and knew they could never keep.

"Yes," he said dully. "An oriental box."

"Dark? About two feet across?" Irrepressible interest flickered to life in her expression.

"Yes," he muttered. "A tea chest."

Her eyelids were stained mauve with fatigue. Her skin looked ethereal, clean of the white face powder she usually wore, fragile and all too mortal.

"Does it look like that?" She pointed.

He glanced in the direction she indicated. This

room was less crammed than the others: a pair of water-stained sideboards; a moldy rolled-up carpet; a leather-clad traveling trunk; and, against the wall, a huge bookcase, one door missing, the shelves dark and empty. Atop this monstrosity sat several boxes that, because of the bookcase's height, had hitherto gone unnoticed. Only now, looking up from across the room, could one see them.

One was intricately carved. Foreign in appearance. Black.

"Yes," Raine said, his heart beginning to race. Inside that box could be the answer to the dream he forced himself to forget upon waking each day. But now, with the box within reach, that dream emerged from the nether world he'd relegated it to and became dazzling potential.

With McClairen's Trust *he* would be wealthy. *He* would be a prize to any woman who would marry for money.

Immediately, he slaughtered the ridiculous notion. She was a McClairen. She held him accountable for her clan's massacre. Not ten minutes earlier she'd been regretting his having lived.

He grabbed hold of one of the mahogany sideboards and leaned into it, grunting as he shoved the mammoth piece across the floor toward the bookcase. He could not ask Favor for her hand but at least with McClairen's Trust in his possession he could make sure she didn't have to marry some bleeding idiot like Tunbridge. He could give her the bloody jewels.

He gave the sideboard a final heave, bringing it

within a few feet of the bookcase, and jumped atop it.
He peered at the dark box. It *was* his mother's tea
chest. He recalled the rippling inlaid back of the
dragon that danced across the lid. He pulled it into his
hands and jumped down.

An intricate bronze clasp swung listlessly from the
back hinge. One tiny set of drawers was completely
missing. But the top, the portion that had opened to
reveal the jewels, was still seamlessly closed.

"Do you really think it holds the treasure?" Favor
asked. Raine could not read either her tone or her odd,
unhappy expression.

"I don't know. Let's find out." He seized a heavy
candlestick holder and brought it smashing down on
the tea chest's lid. The fragile, delicately carved wood
splintered and flew apart.

Together Raine and Favor stared down at the shattered chest. For a full minute they stood. Slowly, Raine
reached down and lifted a large, covered tray from the
ruined box. He pulled it open, revealing a faded velvet
lining and nothing else. Favor knelt beside the splintered pieces, lifting and discarding splintered boards,
peering into the few interior trays that survived the
demolition. Raine nudged the last of the pieces with
his foot, turning them over. There was no place a ring
could hide let alone a complete parure of heavy gold
and gems.

"I'm . . . I'm sorry," he heard Favor whisper.

Desolation swept through him. He'd nothing left
now. Not pipe dreams. Not honorable intentions.

He stared in bemusement. He should leave. The

chances of his finding McClairin's Trust among the dozens of rooms crammed with hiding places was infinitesimal—assuming it still existed. But that wasn't the real reason he wanted to flee. How could he stay while she sought some other bastard for her spouse?

"I guess we'll just have to continue looking," he heard Favor say in a small, rough voice.

He looked up, read her face, and understood. As far as Favor was concerned, she'd found that place where they could be together, separated from debts and duty. And she found the excuse she needed to stay with him: searching for the Trust.

She wasn't smiling but guilty happiness illumined her face like sunlight.

He didn't stand a chance.

"Yes," he agreed softly.

Chapter 24

Tunbridge burst through Carr's library door. "Carr! Great news! At last!"

Carr, in the process of searching through a pile of promissory notes, deeds, wills, letters, and the occasional confession, looked up sharply. "Pray shut the door, Tunbridge," he said, and began stacking the papers.

He'd been looking for a particularly damning love letter but that could wait. It was more important that he must not seem overly concerned with the sheets on his desk. He mustn't let Tunbridge know that he was seeing the source upon which hung Carr's future power and prestige.

"Now," Carr said, snipping off a length of twine

and tying the papers into two separate bundles, "What is this wondrous news?"

"The king is dead! George is dead!" Tunbridge said. He braced his hands flat on the desk and leaned over it. "Do you hear me, Carr? George II died October 25. His grandson is now king."

"Grandson?" Carr repeated. After all these years finally . . .

"Yes." Tunbridge nodded vigorously. "And as all Hanovers hate their successors, George hated his grandson and the grandson returned the sentiment. This new king is young, Carr, malleable and eager."

"He will rescind his grandfather's edict concerning me?" Carr asked, careful not to reveal his anxiety.

"He wouldn't even *know* about it."

Carr surged forward, thrusting his face close to Tunbridge's smirking visage. "Be careful, sir. I will not be disappointed in this."

"I am certain of it!" Tunbridge avowed. "George spent so many of his last years abroad he barely knew the boy. The young king will have scant time for his grandfather's personal enmities, I assure you."

"Where did you hear this news?"

"From Lord Edgar, not an hour ago. I was leaving the castle as he arrived. He'd come directly from St. James's Palace itself."

"Where is he now?"

"In his chambers, asleep I should imagine. He's exhausted. Rode straight through."

Slowly, Carr straightened. "I see."

Tunbridge took a deep breath and pushed himself

upright from the desk. "I have served you well these many years, Carr."

"Ay? Oh. Yes," Carr acknowledged distractedly.

No more George. How very ironic. He'd intended to return to London this winter regardless of the old king's banishment of him. He'd finally accrued enough "influences"—his fingertips caressed the stack of papers to his right—to defy the edict that had exiled him to Scotland.

Now, with that sentence finally reprieved he could . . . by God! He could marry again!

"Your Grace?"

Tunbridge broke through his thoughts. He was inclined to feel magnanimous toward the bearer of such wonderful news. "Yes?"

"You'll want to alert your staff."

"Good idea, Tunbridge. I shall set them to packing forthwith. I don't suppose I can expect to leave before week's end?"

"Sir?" Tunbridge blinked.

"Well, you don't think I'd leave my treasures behind here? The place can burn for all I care but not before I divest it of its valuables." Carr pulled his stack of correspondence toward him. "I'll want all the silver and jewelry to come directly with me. The paintings and statuary should follow in wagons at the same time—art makes a fine investment and that's as good a piece of financial advice as ever you're likely to get."

"Ah, yes, sir. Thank you."

"Come, come, Tunbridge. Why do you look so confused?"

"I was speaking of alerting the staff to the matter of tonight's masque."

"What of the masque?" He would need to see about those tapestries, too. Hideous gloomy things but he'd been told they were worth a pretty penny.

"The king has died. The castle must go into mourning."

Mourning, when all he wanted to do was celebrate? Nonsense. Besides, with George's death things between him and Janet had suddenly, drastically, changed. The thought brought with it a smile.

He was rushing his fences. First he needed to summon Janet to him and in order to do that he needed to see Favor Donne. Alone. It had been a task he'd yet to achieve; it would prove impossible if she followed what would become an exodus heading back to London for the king's funeral.

"You say Edgar has retired to his chambers. Did he come with any others?"

"No."

"Did he speak to anyone else?"

"No," Tunbridge said thoughtfully. "The Highgates arrived with a large party as we spoke but poor Edgar was so exhausted he barely nodded before seeking his bed."

"Then the Highgates know nothing of the king's death."

"That's correct."

Carr's glance fell to the drawer that held his special elixirs. "Tunbridge, you will leave for London on the morrow. In the meantime keep to your room. That way no one can accuse you of keeping the sovereign's death secret, nor me of hearing and then disregarding it."

"You are risking a great deal," Tunbridge said. "There are those who would call knowingly holding a revelry during a period of national mourning sedition. What if Edgar tells someone?"

"Edgar," Carr said smoothly, "will not be waking anytime soon. His trip, which you already noted left him depleted, has turned into something more dire." He tapped his chin thoughtfully.

"But what of his servants?"

"I shall send them away. What with Edgar's undiagnosed malady, I cannot risk the health of my guests by exposing them to possible contaminants."

"They may already have told other servants."

Carr sighed. He was fast tiring of Tunbridge's fretfulness. Most unmanly. He'd been considering giving Tunbridge back the deed to his family manse. Now he saw that the fellow didn't deserve such a gift.

"Let them," Carr said. "There have been rumors of George's death half a dozen times in as many years. Who is going to blame me for not listening to servants' gossip?"

"You have, as always, accounted for every contingency," Tunbridge said admiringly.

"Yes," Carr said, "I have."

"And soon you will reign once more in London, powerful, respected, feared, courted—"

"Yes, yes, yes. Out with it, Tunbridge before your tongue rots the leather of my new boots."

The thin, pale man grew paler. Bloodless white outlined the flesh about his narrow lips.

"Well?"

"You've achieved your goal without having to threaten, blackmail, or coerce another man."

"Yes," Carr said, wondering a little at the dissatisfaction that suddenly crept over him. "So?"

"You don't need me anymore."

"I never did need you, Tunbridge. I found you convenient." Carr smiled. "I still do."

The heat was stultifying and the racket ear-splitting. The spectacle of three hundred people vying to be the brightest, the gaudiest, and the most outrageous hurt the eye and robbed breath from the lungs. Carr had declared this to be Wanton's Blush's Last Masque and since rumors had spread that Carr intended to quit Wanton's Blush for London, his guests were rabidly determined to make the ball memorable.

Encased in bizarre costumes, burdened by towering headdresses and extravagant wigs, they strutted about with a formality belied by the open leer that was their universal expression, made prim by clothes stiff with gems, brilliants, and paste. Like grotesque hedgehogs in bejeweled armor, they circled the rooms in a stately waddle, undressing each other with their eyes.

And, truth be told, they'd not much undressing to do. Skirts dragged the floor under the weight of pearl and crystal and heavy gold trim. Coats crunched as gemstones grated against each other with the slightest movement. But other parts of their anatomy were bare—both men's and women's—displaying only salved and scented flesh. A great deal of flesh.

There was no risk. For who could tell who hid beneath Prospero's black silk domino, or the feathered mask of the Swan Queen? And if the answer to that was "many," few would admit it. For anonymity was the *raison d'être* of a masque. Tonight no one would know with whom they flirted and danced and dallied.

Except Carr. He knew every one of his guests' identities. Later he would make certain they all knew it. At the moment, however, he cared little who groped whom. Only one woman concerned him. His little Scot.

He'd spotted her a few minutes earlier. He was still amazed by her audacity even though Miss Donne was one of the few women who had not contrived to bare at least one breast.

She'd found another way to excite the most jaded of interest.

She wore an *arisaid*, the traditional plaid scarf of the Highland Scotswoman, prohibited since 1747 in an act of Parliament. Or rather *they'd* dressed themselves in plaid. This could only be Janet's unbiddable spirit at work.

The long rectangular piece of rough silk plaid veiled her black hair and hung over the lose sacque gown she wore. Not a particularly modish dress, being in vogue some twenty years earlier, but attractive on her.

Favor was speaking to her doughy and doughty old aunt, a pudding in unstructured puce draperies with a serpent perched atop her cap and a semitransparent veil pinned over her mouth. 'Sblood, the woman was portraying Cleopatra.

Carr hailed a footman carrying a tray of punch-filled cups. It was time to address the problem posed by his dead—yet still amazingly obstinate—wife. He withdrew the vial containing Pala's elixir and emptied it into a cup and then, careful not to spill any, wove his way through the crowd.

"Mrs. Douglas," he greeted the old lady when he'd reached them. He inclined his head toward Favor. "Miss Donne."

She'd seen him coming. The mask she wore over her eyes did not conceal the way her full lower lip tightened with aversion. Before daylight, he swore, he would chew on that provocative lip and she would sigh with pleasure for it.

"Lord Carr!" The aunt giggled into her plump, glove-clad hand. "Such an extravagant *soirée*! I've never seen the like."

"Nor hope to again," Favor said sweetly, and then, in answer to her chaperone's gasp, "How could I? How could anything compare to . . . this?" She waved toward a satyr chasing Lucrezia Borgia. "I would never dare to imagine I could experience another like it."

Carr smiled. "You might experience its like and more, Miss Donne, if you continue to honor me with your presence."

"But that's most unlikely, isn't it?" the aunt interjected mournfully. "However much my dear niece might desire it otherwise."

"Why is that, Mrs. Douglas?"

"You'll be going to London soon, or so 'tis rumored, and we, perforce, will retire to Thomas's manor. We couldn't possibly venture to London without Thomas and heaven alone knows how long the dear boy will be gone. It may be months or years before he's back."

"I see." He stared into Favor's shadowed eyes. "Perhaps I can yet find some way to enjoy Miss Donne's company."

He heard the aunt's sharp inhalation, a response he'd hoped to draw from Favor. The girl must know he was implying marriage. And even if she had currently found his person distressing, shouldn't Janet be supplanting the girl's reaction with her own rapturous response to the hinted promise?

Instead Favor had frozen. Frowning, Carr sought an answer. Happily, one was not long in coming. She simply didn't dare believe that she'd understood him correctly. She was stunned by the honor he bestowed on her.

Given that, he would forgive her lack of enthusiasm.

"Miss Donne, I don't believe I've mentioned how delightful you look. I saw you across the room and remarked it immediately. But that"—he motioned toward the heathenish *arisaid*—"looks rather warm. So I've brought you a punch to cool you."

He held out the cup of punch.

"Thank you," Favor answered, and began reaching for the cup but suddenly changed her mind and withdrew her hand. Her smile became shy. She backed up a step, leaving him standing there with cup still extended.

"A minute, sir, before I accept your kind offer. Tell me"—she placed her hand on her hips, striking a winsome pose—"can you tell who I am?"

Damn the chit. He just wanted her to take the damn cup of punch and drain it down.

"No," he said as pleasantly as possible. "I can't. Here." He thrust the cup at her. She ignored it.

"Oh, *do* guess!" she pleaded, unexpectedly playful.

Her aunt, her gaze fixed on her niece, nodded slowly. "She's a child still," she said, "and will have her games as all children must. Pray indulge her, Lord Carr."

"I don't know," he exclaimed in exasperation. She was, indeed, frolicsome and girlish. He'd always found both qualities tiresome. "Queen Boadicea?"

"No . . ." She waggled her finger playfully.

"Enough," he snapped. "Who are you, then?"

"Janet McClairen. Your dead wife."

The cup fell from his hand and hit the floor; any sound it might have made swallowed by the surrounding din.

"What did you say?" He stepped toward her, crushing the cup beneath his foot. "*How came you by the idea to dress as my wife?*"

She shrank back, eyeing him fearfully.

"I found th-this in a box at the bottom of the—the chest in my b-bedchamber!"

"Impossible!" He'd had all of Janet's belongings removed and stored in the farthest reaches of the castle.

Nothing of hers remained in these inhabited wings. Unless Janet herself . . .

"*Why* did you dress as my first wife?"

"I found the *arisaid*. Someone had told me the story of the first ball held at Wanton's Blush"—her lip trembled—"and how your wife didn't come down and your guests went searching for her. I heard how they first found her scarf and then spied her but before they could get to her body, it was swept out to sea. I'd heard, too, how devoted you were and I thought—" She hesitated. "It just seemed right that for this last masque she should be here, too."

The aunt's gaze flickered nervously between them. "She didn't mean any harm. It's my fault if she's offended you. I should have asked her who she was impersonating."

"No," Carr replied. "I know she meant no harm. I was taken aback because I had been thinking of wives and marriage and how very alone I am." He reached out and secured one of Favor's hands. It lay limply in his own. "Then to suddenly hear my wife's name on Miss Donne's lips . . . ! It seemed more than happenstance, indeed, a sign.

"Ah!" The aunt clasped her hands at her ample bosom in an attitude of rapture.

Favor wet her lips. "I cannot begin to fathom your meaning, sir," she whispered.

"Really? I can," Fia pronounced. Carr looked around to find his daughter standing at his elbow. She was dressed all in silver and white satin, even to the slight mask over her eyes. Long, soft feathers plaited in her hair nodded in the soft currents of air. More feathers covered her shoulders and the long, tight sleeves of her dress. She'd dressed as the Swan Princess.

"I have years of experience in interpreting everything Carr says. Should I translate, Miss Donne?" Fia asked.

"Ah, Fia my dear," Carr acknowledged her coldly. "Forgive my daughter, ladies. One would think she was fresh from the nursery with such manners. I'm afraid I've overindulged her. She continually makes the unwarranted assumption that she is welcomed everywhere."

Instead of being cut to the quick as he'd intended, Fia laughed. He should have known his sarcasm would be lost on her.

"Don't fret, Carr. I shall take myself off before you"—she glanced at Favor—"end up on your knees." Before he could respond, she drifted away.

"Whatever could she mean?" the aunt chirped.

"I am sure I couldn't fathom," Favor said forcefully. Her skin had turned very pale.

"Soon you will not have to fathom anything. I will reveal all." He gazed tenderly down at her, cursing himself for dropping the love potion. Ah, well. The night was young. He'd simply refill the vial and return. Or he could try . . .

"Mrs. Douglas"—he smiled respectfully at the old woman—"though I am a man in the prime of my life and one of both experience and sophistication, I find myself in the odd position of having to beg your leave to be private with your niece."

"Oh?" The aunt blinked myopically. "Oh. Oh *no*, sir! Thomas would never forgive me were I to countenance such goings-on. My niece is a well-brought-up young girl, sir, not some light-skirts!"

So, the fluffy little lap pisser dared lift her lips and reveal her ancient teeth at him, eh? "Of course. How thoughtless of me."

"Thoughtless, indeed, sir. And one gets only one chance to be careless with so lovely a lady."

Carr turned irritably toward the male voice, prepared to spear the interloper with a quelling glare. He found himself staring into the broad tanned throat of a . . . well, damned if he knew what the Goliath-sized creature was supposed to be. A jinn, perhaps.

The newcomer wore a long coat in an oriental style, made of bronzy satin figured with geometric patterns. Over one broad shoulder hung a plum-colored cape. A huge turban wound above a face stained dark as a Moor's.

Jinn or Turk, Carr thought, eyeing the scimitar suspended from the man's waist. He looked up and met the rogue's interested gaze. He was unfamiliar. "You must have come with Highgate this afternoon, sir."

The tall man inclined his head.

"I don't have your name."

"You may call me Mahomet."

"May I?" Carr stretched his lips into a host's smile. "How gracious of you."

'Struth! Whose idiot idea had this bloody masque been anyway? Everywhere he met impertinence. He'd had enough of it. He'd find out this bastard's name tomorrow, if it still interested him. Right now he needed to refill that vial.

The Turk shouldered his way past Carr to Favor's side. She stared up at him with wide-eyed trepidation. "If I might have the pleasure of this lovely Scottish lassie's company I can promise nothing more unacceptable than a dance." Though he spoke to Mrs. Douglas his eyes never left Favor's pale face. "Miss?"

"Ach," demurred the auntie, clucking fearsomely. "I don't know you, sir and—"

"Ah!" The tall Turk swung his head around, displaying a very large, very white set of teeth. "But I came with Highgate, one of Lord Carr's special friends! Surely that's voucher enough?"

He'd caught the old bitch off guard and she knew it, Carr thought. His eyes narrowed appreciatively on this unexpected rival. Mrs. Douglas didn't dare refuse him now lest she insult her host.

"Miss Donne?" The Turk held out his hand.

Slowly, mutely, Favor nodded and laid her hand within his great, strong-looking paw. His fingers closed tightly on hers.

And she clenched his in turn.

"Ah! Allah blesses me!" The tall Turk laughed in triumph and took her arm, sweeping her into the crowd as he led her to the ballroom. Immediately, Mrs. Douglas mumbled an apology and hied off in pursuit, leaving Carr alone.

Yes. He would still be interested in the man's name come the morrow. He felt certain of it.

Chapter 25

"You must be mad!" Favor gasped as Rafe swung her in a dizzying circle. "Do you know who that was?"

"Who? The fellow in the lilac wig?" Rafe caught Favor's hand and laid it on his forearm. He kept his own hand over hers, his fingertips lightly stroking her wrists, sending shivers of pleasure coursing up her arm as they commenced the sedate promenade the dance prescribed.

"Favor?" His sherry-brown eyes warmed with knowledge.

"Hm?" Favor murmured, distracted by his caresses.

"Is that the fellow you meant?"

"Hm . . . ? Yes. Yes! That, my boy, was Lord Carr."

He drew back in mock horror. "Say not so! The

Demon Earl himself? But where is his tail? His horns?"

"Who could see horns under all that hideous purple hair?" Favor muttered, winning Rafe's laughter. She eyed him severely. "Aye. We'll see how amused you are when Carr has you hauled out and whipped until your back is nothing but shredded flesh."

He grinned. "Would you care?"

She felt herself blush and looked away. "No."

"You would."

She heard the tender smile in his voice and could not deny him. "Yes."

His hand pressed hers and she listed toward him, pulled by a need to be nearer, much nearer than this too public place allowed. A sense of urgency underscored that desire.

Carr was going to offer for her. Possibly tonight, but if not, soon. He'd all but declared himself already. Wherever he'd gone, soon he'd come back and expect her to fawn over him. As would Muira.

She couldn't be here when he returned. She glanced at Rafe. A lightness of expression had gentled his aggressive profile. Her declaration had pleased him because, she suddenly understood, he cared for her. She sensed it in the deepest part of her, knew the truth of it just as surely as she knew . . .

"I love you."

His head whipped around. He pulled up short in the middle of the dance floor, arrested in midstride. He gripped her arms, turning her to face him. He stared down at her, his brows snapped together in concentration as he searched her face.

Around them the other couples, thrown out of their patterned dance, milled and hesitated and finally split and flowed on either side of them, leaving them an island in a river of streaming satin.

"What?"

"I love you, Rafe. You knew that though, didn't you?" she said simply.

"No," he said faintly. "No. I didn't."

He looked up as though searching the heavens for inspiration. She tugged lightly on his arm; they'd already attracted far too much attention. Like a sleepwalker, Rafe moved back into the dance steps, his rhythm wanting, his steps mechanical and graceless.

On the far side of the room Favor glimpsed Muira's furious mien, her glare lethal enough to kill at any closer range. If Favor had her way, that's as near as Muira would come to her for the rest of the night.

She looked up at Rafe. He still appeared bemused. She supposed she ought to feel like a slattern for being so forward. She didn't. She'd no time to be less. She had one night. This night.

There would be no happy ending for her and Rafe. He was a thief and an escaped prisoner, without family, future, or even, she suspected in spite of his denial, a surname. Not that he need envy those.

She had a family . . . a clan to which she owed a debt that only one act could repay. She'd a surname . . . which kept her chained to her past as inescapably as Rafe's manacles had once chained him to the prison walls. And she had a future . . . as Lady Carr.

She owed her clan that. But she did not owe Carr anything. Including the privilege of breaking her maidenhead. That gift she would insist on giving in love, not sacrifice. To Rafe.

"Let's leave here," she whispered.

"What?" Dear, reckless, baffled Rafe.

"I want to be alone with you. But if my aunt makes it across the ballroom—a task she's presently engaged upon—I guarantee she'll keep me by her side the rest of the night." Rafe looked in the direction she indicated. Muira had waded into the thick ring of spectators lining the dance floor. Her step was determined, her mouth grim. "Not only will we be unable to share another dance but we won't trade another unchaperoned phrase."

It was threat enough. Without another word, Rafe took hold her arm, pulling her after him as he strode toward the opposite side of the room.

Muira elbowed her way through the last of the posing and primping fools that stood between her and the dance floor. She was sweating profusely under the layers of stuffing and wadding that formed "Mrs. Douglas's" matronly figure. Dark rings circled her armpits and she could feel the paste, made of sweat and powder, trickling down the side of her face.

Damn the girl to bloody hell! Now she'd need to go and repair her makeup before the welt on her cheek was laid bare. And where was the little bitch anyway? A moment ago she'd been panting up at that big, dark-skinned man as if she'd seen Robert the Bruce himself. And him looking down at her like a starving man at a feast . . .

She scanned the dance floor. It only took a few minutes to discern that they were no longer on it. Furiously, Muira began stalking the perimeter of the room but the crush was growing by the minute and soon she could see nothing.

She'd no choice but to give up. No one knew Wanton's Blush better than she, but the castle was huge and the places they might have gone too numerous to count. Besides, Carr would reappear soon. She couldn't take the chance of Favor's being with Carr unchaperoned. She didn't trust the chit not to make a bloody hash of it.

No. She would just have to wait, bide her time and bite her tongue. If Carr asked after Favor, she'd make excuses he would swallow. She'd spent too many years half-starved and half-frozen, plotting and planning and begging and stealing her way to this place, to this point in time. All for the sake of her clan. For the Mc-Clairens.

And tomorrow she would make sure Favor Mc-Clairen understood just what that meant.

"You don't even know me," Raine said. He clasped her shoulders lightly, pushing her back against the tapestry-covered wall. They were in one of the castle's solars, a chamber attached to what had once been the private quarters of Lizabet McClairen, the first lady of Maiden's Blush.

Favor touched his face. "I know you."

He shook his head in patent disbelief. She was young and he'd befriended her in a place populated by predators. Of course she thought she loved him.

"I am"—*dying with hope I know to be hopeless*—"honored by your words."

The gentle comedown he'd hoped to give her did not have the desired effect. She smiled tenderly.

"I should hope so. I don't give my heart readily." One fingertip swept along his lower lip. "Lud, you have a beautiful mouth."

"Stop that!" He sounded panicked, which he was. "You're mistaken. You must be. How can you give a thief and blackmailer, a man you mistrust—and with ample cause, I do admit—your love?"

"Had I any choice perhaps I would heed your sage advice," she murmured, "but my heart, graceless thing, did not ask my opinion. It loved without first seeking my counsel."

"You speak too sweetly and wake a craving for more such words." *Such sweet words that I would give anything to believe.*

He dared not move. Her hand brushed down his chin and traced his jaw, trailing a lightning strike of sensation. She covered the pulse beating at the base of his throat with her palm.

"Think you so? 'Tis you who make me a poetess then. And I thank Him who gave me so canny a tongue. But I must return the compliment yet complain, for, in truth, sir, your tongue has its own sweet tricks that I do crave to learn." Her other hand had moved up, unbuttoning the ancient Persian coat and pulling loose the strings tying his shirt.

"How can I get you to divulge your secrets? I would recite you more poetry but, sir," she whispered, "longing takes my breath away."

He groaned. His eyes shut. Her hand burrowed under his shirt, stroking his naked chest.

It was all too much.

With a growl, he wrapped his arms about her waist. He lifted her slight form, imprisoning her between the wall and his body. His mouth slanted over hers, his tongue thrust between her lips, seeking and finding the sweet, warm interior and—blessed bounty!—her own eager tongue.

She denied him nothing, either by word or act. He swept her loose frock from her shoulder, baring one of her breasts to his greedy eyes. He cupped the firm pale globe gently. She whimpered with pleasure, pushing the tightening nipple against his palm.

Hungry, desperate and half-dazed with the unexpected heat of her response, he lowered his mouth and swirled his tongue against the silky brown aureole. Her hands came to life on his shoulders, biting deep into his muscles as her gasp set the ripe flesh to jiggling against his tongue. He suckled greedily, sweeping a hand under her buttock and lifting her higher against the wool-softened wall. The rich, crisp cloth of her skirt crumpled in his fists. Gossamer lace drifted over his arms. A creamy smooth thigh slid beneath his hand.

"Yes," she whispered rapturously, her eyelids fluttering half shut. "Please. Yes."

"Yes," he echoed, his lips sliding to the outer arc of her breast. He would drown in her physical response.

"Oh! Please. Don't stop," she pleaded when he sought a less urgent pace and he, both supplicant and sovereign, gladly complied.

He rucked her skirt up about her waist, inhaling sharply when he felt the warmth of her mons press tight against him, separated from her nakedness only by his breeches' thin material. Instinctively, he thrust against her.

Her mouth parted, revealing the erotic unevenness of her front teeth. He rolled his hips and her thighs fell apart.

"Make love to me," she said.

Love. Dear God. Yes, he wanted to make love to her, to love her, to give her some of the physical pleasure he knew this act could bring and in doing so find for himself that deeper . . . *something* he suddenly had cause to believe existed.

He had to think but he couldn't, not with her dampness seeping through his breeches and her gaze sultry and inviting. He tore his mouth from hers. She made a sound of protest. Lightly, he clasped her chin, turning her face away and resting his forehead on the wall beside her head. She took his free hand and lifted it to her mouth.

"I want you." A siren call. She didn't know what she asked.

Once, a decade earlier, she'd saved his life. He

wouldn't ever again be the cause of her anguish or her guilt. He couldn't bed her and risk ruining her future. While he put no great store in virginity, most men did. And Favor, if what she'd told him had been true, had nothing else to offer a groom but the presumed paternity of her child. She herself had once told him it was the only thing of value she owned.

Bloody, bloody son of a bitch! If only he'd found the bleeding jewels. If only her name wasn't McClairen. If only she would tell him to stop . . .

But she didn't. She nipped the tender pads at the base of each finger before sucking on his thumb's knuckle. "You have the most beautiful hands. I want to know what artistry they might work on my flesh."

Good intentions faded. His clasp on her chin became a caress. "You don't want this. It isn't going to lead to some blessed union, Favor," he rasped out. "I have nothing. Nothing at all to offer you."

"You have your name," she suggested in a whisper as fearful as it was hesitant.

God, yes. His name. "I assure you, my name would be no recommendation to you."

She came back with a reply at once. "I don't care."

"I do! Damn it, don't you think I want to feel you under me, around me?" he ground out. "I want to drink your cries, I want to make you scream with pleasure. I want to take you. Now. Here."

"Yes!" One of her long thighs climbed up his leg and hooked over his hip. She rocked her pelvis against him. Desire careened through him, splintering his resolve.

"You can't. We can't." His breath had grown thick in his chest; his body burgeoned with need.

She tipped her upper body away from his and yanked his shirt open. Her expression was heated with desire, fixed with determination. She started at his throat and worked down his chest, her fingers flowing over his pectorals, her nails raking through the soft hair, past the thickened V of fur low at his waist, beneath the waistband of his breeches. He held his breath.

Her hand closed about his cock. He jerked at the contact, impaled by want, torn by conflicting desires. A rumbling growl issued from deep in his throat.

"You're a virgin," he panted, his eyes hot and accusing. It was an act of masochism holding himself still like this, fighting to retain his self-control.

Her hand tightened into a silky fist and slid down over his throbbing shaft. Sweat shimmered on his forehead and above his upper lip. His body trembled. She leaned back, still holding him, and whispered, "No, I'm not."

Her words shredded what was left of his resistance.

It ought to make no difference. He still had nothing to give her, no future, no name, no recompense for a childhood destroyed. But if he had nothing to give her, at least he couldn't hurt her by taking her virginity away.

"Please," she said, her hips rocking against him in a thought-destroying rhythm. She released him, pulling his head down to hers, her mouth open and seeking, the flavor of desperation on her tongue and in the tightness with which her arms wrapped around him.

He made no further attempts at chivalry. He reached between them and wrenched the cloth away from his straining manhood. Then he found her opening and pushed his finger into the sleek cleft, found her ready, wet and heated.

He moved his finger inside of her, testing, stimulating. Her interior muscles clamped tight about him, a little sob—pleasure? pain?—fanned his ear as she nestled her face against his throat. He withdrew his finger and found the nubbin hidden between the plump folds of her sex. He flicked it gingerly, eliciting from her a breathy series of gasps.

He prayed for strength and plucked again, in short, rhythmic pulls. She keened, trying to mount higher on him, her shoes falling to the floor with a dull thud, as her feet climbed the backs of his calves.

"Little falcon," he urged. "Let me pleasure you. Let me show you."

Her hips surged forward to comply in a rough, bucking rhythm. She moved in gorgeous abandonment, her head thrown back, her hair streaming past her hips, her arms taut with strain.

He licked the salty moisture from the base of her throat. His own arousal was near a fever pitch now, contained only by his need to see her climax, to be fully aware of each second of her crisis and to revel in the knowledge that he'd brought her there.

"Please!" she sobbed.

"Yes." His hand worked deftly between her legs, his gaze growing hot and fiercely possessive.

He'd not long to wait. Her thighs clamped about his hips, her toes flexed with exertion. She arched, her spine curving over his arm, her skirts piled about her waist, her breasts bare in the soft shadows.

"Oh, please. I can't . . . I can't . . ."

"Yes. Yes. And yes," he murmured, stroking the damp hair from her face as he drove her toward fulfillment.

Her gaze found his, focused. "Rafe!"

Rafe, not Raine. He refused to think. He would not think. He would just feel.

And then her fierce pants dissolved into a high cry of effort that broke into the sweetest sound he'd ever heard.

He positioned himself and pushed into her heated core. Her shallow pants of repletion became a single sob. She was tight. Some beast within purred with the evidence of her relative innocence. He pushed harder. Her arms tightened convulsively about his throat.

"Mine," he intoned, surging slowly forward.

She moved, not in unison with him, but as though to avoid the deeper coupling he sought. He hesitated.

"Yes," she whispered.

He set his hands beneath her thighs, spreading her legs wider and with one long thrust came up against a barrier. Her maidenhead. He clenched his teeth in a feral snarl, near violent with frustration, desire building to a near explosive pitch in his loins. He trembled. He swore.

"You're a bloody virgin! Aren't you?"

She was crying.

"Aren't you?"

"Yes!"

He jerked his swollen member out of her, heedless of his roughness until he heard her gasp of pain. He looked down. Her brilliant eyes were filled with despair. Tears streamed down her face. With a groan he wrapped his hand about the back of her head and dragged her into his arms.

She'd only wanted to gift him with her maidenhead. He could not rail against her for that. But rail he could against all else.

He threw back his head and cursed the heavens and his fate with every foul and blasphemous word he knew. He would have howled in fury but for fear of scaring her even more. So he simply stood, cursing in dark and vehement tones while stroking her head with exquisite tenderness.

Chapter 26

$\mathcal{M}$uira flung herself down from the carriage and reached back, grabbing hold of Favor's arm and jerking her out. Favor stumbled and fell to her knees in the mud, staining the bright scarlet skirts of her antique Highland gown.

"Where are we?" she asked, blinking into the bright morning sun, dazed with anguish and lack of sleep. She'd returned to her room last night to find Muira waiting in the hall. Wordlessly, Muira had seized her arm and dragged her down the corridor, ignoring Favor's stammered demands for an explanation as well as the speculative gazes that followed them out the back door to the stable yard where Jamie had awaited them atop Thomas's carriage.

Favor had resisted then, but Muira had backhanded

her across the face, stunning her with the brutal strength of her blow. She'd shoved Favor into the carriage and followed her in, yanking the door shut and slamming her hand against the ceiling, calling out for Jamie to whip up the horses.

They'd driven most of the night. Muira had settled in the corner and stabbed Favor with a malevolent glare. Favor had been bitterly unsurprised by how quickly she'd gone from Rafe's passionate embrace and heated words to this cold, silent carriage on a nameless road.

"Where are we?" Favor repeated now.

"You don't know?" Muira seized hold of Favor's hair and yanked her head up, half hauling her to her feet. "Look around!"

"Muira, careful. She's but a girl . . ." Jamie objected from atop the carriage.

Muira swung round, bruising Favor's upper arm. "*Girl*, is she?" she hissed. "Well, this *girl* has jeopardized everything we've worked and sacrificed for, all so she can rut with some pretty English hound!"

An expression of shocked betrayal flashed over Jamie's rough features at Muira's accusation. "Not quite the little novitiate you'd imagined, is she, Jamie me boy?"

Jamie turned his head, fixing his gaze on the horizon.

"It wasn't like that," Favor whispered.

"Wasn't like what?" Muira turned on her. "Wasn't he any good then, lassie? Didn't he spread your legs wide and make you scream with it?"

Favor bit hard on the inner flesh of her cheeks. She wouldn't weep. Not in front of this woman. No matter how much she wanted to—and God knew she wanted to break down and cry.

When she'd agreed to Muira's plan she hadn't known what she would be giving up. Now she did. Now she knew just what and just whom she was losing. And that knowledge threatened to swallow her whole.

"Well?" Muira demanded brightly. "Didna scream, eh?" She pointed behind Favor. "*They* did."

She said it so matter-of-factly, so conversationally, that for a moment Favor did not grasp her meaning.

With a sense of inevitability, she looked around. Backed by a swollen leaden sky, a tower's rough shell stood wearily in the misting rain. The roof was gone, the western wall tumbled, exposing the rooms on the second story. Within, black rotted beams leaned against bare interior walls. It was the room where Favor's mother had birthed her stillborn brother and then, dying in the process, given Favor her fateful charge. The rain's soft susurration could not conceal her mother's weak voice.

"*They're killing my sons!*" She'd grasped Favor's hand, but her clasp was weak and her skin hot and dry. "*You* must *stop them, Favor. There's no one else.*"

"*How?*"

"*I don't know!*" her mother's voice had risen frantically. "*But you must. If they kill Carr's son, the king will never have mercy on mine. They'll be gutted and hanged by month's end and not all your father's pleading will stop it. Go, Favor. Stop them!*"

And she had.

"Do you know where you are now?" Muira's voice had lost its savagery, becoming nearly gentle. She released Favor's arm and moved about the muddy ground with a dazed look of wonder, like a Muslim in Mecca.

"There is where Cam McClairen died," she said, pointing. "That great rock there, that split his head as he fell from a soldier's blow."

She turned, her skirts belling out as lightly as a girl on a dance floor. "And here is where my Bobbie was killed. He was my youngest, ever falling over his own feet."

She smiled at Favor in bizarre camaraderie, as though they were two women chatting about their family's foibles. "He took a lead ball in his brain." She pursed her lip and nodded. "Quick at least, not like his father, whose gut was split open and took three days to die."

Favor's stomach rose, sickened by the light voice reciting the horrendous memories she shared: screaming men, horses impaled, blood licked by torchlight, and the pure snow glistening on the mountainside far away.

Muira returned and wrapped her arm about Favor's waist. Pulling lightly, she began walking her toward the tower's arched gate. "Did you see who fell and who didn't? Who gave as good as he got? I would have stayed and fought, but as soon as we saw the redcoats the men shoved us down into the moat to hide."

She cocked her head. "I didn't see much. But you

. . . you were right in the thick of it the whole time, clinging to that Merrick boy like a limpet. I always wanted to know if my men acquitted themselves well. Did they?"

"I couldn't say," Favor whispered, images of horrors piling up in her mind's eye.

Muira nodded understandingly. "Aye. It was dark and over so quick and you didn't know any of those men now, did you?"

She stopped just short of the gate. Favor began to tremble. Muira didn't appear to notice; she was scowling. "Jamie? Was it Russell who was cut down here? 'Faith, I be growing old for I canna remember whether it was Russell or Gavin Fraser. 'Twas Russell, was it not?"

"Aye," Jamie called back. "Russell."

Muira brightened, sighing with pleasure. "I dinna forget then," she said, and tugged Favor back into motion. "Jamie was here, too, did you know? Being so big, they made him hold the cattle. But when the redcoats came down the horses panicked and bolted and just plain ran over Jamie Craigg. He came to his senses a few days later. In my house."

Her knees felt liquid and weak. The mud sucked at her shoes as she stumbled forth. The mist soaked her uncovered head, condensed on her frozen flesh, and leaked down her cheeks.

"I have it all in here," Muira confided, touching her free hand to her temple. "Each moment. Each cry. Like acid it burned its way into my brain so that everything I see, I see overlaid with the images from that night. Like a shadow play on my every thought . . ." Her voice trailed off.

The shivering in Favor's body had become shaking. She could hear her teeth clattering against each other. They stopped at the gate.

"Right here is where you stood." She gave Favor a little shove and then backed up. "I stood . . . yes. Right there. Imagine that, Favor. For a few minutes nine years ago I was within reach of you . . . and him. And after, when they'd taken him away and left you standing here, barefoot and cold, your night rail soaked with blood, I could have taken my wounded and gone, leaving you here."

The smile twisted, became ugly. "I would have, too, if I'd known you would betray us twice."

She *was* going to be sick. Her head spun and her knees knocked together. She didn't want to be here. She'd never wanted to come back here. All that was here was terror, terror and a boy's filthy, blood-slick torso, the shouts of men, the stench of gunpowder, and . . . and the gentle, pitying brush of a rapist's lips against the top of her head—the only bit of comfort in that night, given by her enemy and yet one she'd gladly accepted, one she'd never forgive herself for accepting.

She wrapped her arms around her waist and hugged tightly, afraid that if she let go she would burst into a million fragments and be lost in a black, all-consuming abyss.

"You see it again now, don't you, Favor?" Muira asked gently. "You'd forgotten, hadn't you? Aye, I thought it was so. I didn't think anyone who remembered could fail us."

Numbly she nodded.

"Seventeen men and boys of clan McClairen died that night. Those that didn't die, I patched together. Two died later. That's what saving that rapist did, Favor."

"Muira!" Jamie suddenly called out, his voice worried.

The gentleness bled from Muira's eyes. "Quiet you, Jamie! She saved the life of a rapist and nineteen died because of it."

Muira turned back to Favor, her expression fierce and commanding.

"The nine men that lived have worked as hard as I for restitution. They're smugglers and thieves, hard laborers and servants now, struggling to earn enough not only for the families of them that died, but also for you. So that *you* could become Lady Carr and return the land and the castle to us.

"That's where the money for your convent and your clothes and your jewels came from, Favor. That's who you've betrayed."

"No!" Favor cried weakly. How could she have forgotten? How could she have for a minute risked what they'd worked so hard to achieve?

"Are you ready to be Carr's bride?"

Numbly, Favor nodded.

Raine prowled through the shrouded empty rooms and dark echoing corridors, an animal set loose in a graveyard. Favor had not come to him yesterday, nor had she come today. Last night, he'd waited high above the ballroom for her to appear, suffused with a feeling such as he'd never known. His heart thumped thickly in his chest; his breath lodged in his throat.

He was, he realized, afraid. Afraid she'd regretted it. All of it. Her words, her passion . . . her love. But then she'd entered at Carr's side, clinging to his arm like an invalid. Her face was white, her gait unsteady.

A new fear swelled, eclipsing the other. Was she ill? The thought tormented him until finally, late last night, he'd gone to her room. She wasn't there and a word with a scurrying maid informed him that she slept in her chaperone's room.

All day he'd watched, trying to catch sight of her. At noon he'd seen her being hustled from the orangery by her aunt. Again her gait had been unsteady.

Now it was late afternoon. If he did not speak to her and discover if she was, indeed, unwell and if so, with what and to what extent, he would go mad. He *was* going mad. And he'd never been one to wait.

Without another thought, he strode to the room where he slept and snatched his coat from the table where he'd thrown it. He shrugged into it, heading down the empty hallway to the tower door. From there he followed the spiraling staircase to the main floor and opened the door leading to the north wing.

Few people were about in the great salon. A cluster of aged *roués* played hazard at a green baize-covered table while a single footman kept watch on the decanter sitting on the floor beside them. A woman attended by a phalanx of gentlemen stood at the great leaded window looking out over the terrace below. She turned and caught sight of him.

It was his sister, Fia. He wished that he'd known her better as a child. But Carr had always kept the little princess far away from her brothers and when they had seen her, she'd seldom spoken, only watched them with the same considering expression she now wore. Or had that expression been wistfulness?

A little frown turned her lips; she glanced outside and then came toward him. The men at her side began to follow, but she bade them stay. Raine watched her approach.

"Ah, Mister . . . ?" She waited. He regarded her evenly. "Mr. Mystery." She smiled. "But not Miss Donne's Mr. Mystery anymore, eh?"

"I do not take your meaning," he replied. "Do you know where Miss Donne is?"

"Oh, yes. I do, indeed," she said, snapping open the pearl-handled fan that hung from her wrist. "But first, aren't you curious about why I say you are no longer Miss Donne's . . . well, anything, I should imagine."

"Not particularly. I dislike word games."

"Oh, yes. I recall." At his startled look her dimples deepened. "From our previous encounter. The thing is, sir, I *do* like games. They hone one's intellect."

"Miss Fia, I am sure your gamesmanship is unsurpassed. Now, please—"

"You aren't Miss Donne's anything anymore because," Fia cut in, leaning close and raising her fan to conceal what she was about to say, "she's somebody else's something now. Somebody who would dislike very much finding out that she'd had a somebody before him." Her smile was buttery soft and innocent.

He stared at her, frozen. "Who?"

"That's the amazing part. If I hadn't heard him all but propose myself, I wouldn't have believed it!"

"Who?" he demanded.

"Why, my father." Abruptly her voice went flat. "Lord Carr."

No. She couldn't. He couldn't. No.

The word rolled through his mind, his thoughts, his heart. His entire being hummed denial. *No. No. No.*

"Fascinating creature, Miss Donne," Fia continued. "Why right this minute she's keeping company with a quart of gin, either celebrating her imminent engagement . . . or consoling herself."

"Where is she?"

"She's down below, on the terrace—" He'd left so there was no reason to give further direction. The brittle smile faded from Fia's face. "—brother."

"You can pack a trunk of my clothes for London tonight, Gunna. I shall be leaving on the morrow."

Gunna paused in helping Fia off with her day gown. "I didn't ken that yer father's plans had come so quick to profit," she said in amazement. "Still and all, how can he leave so sudden? There's so much to do."

"Carr knows nothing about my leaving," Fia said uninterestedly. "I shall be staying with Lady and Lord

Wente. They have been kind enough to extend to me an open-ended invitation to be their guest."

She untied the ribbons around her waist. Her hoops collapsed to the floor. Gracefully, she stepped out of them. "Of course," she said, "Lord Wente's well-documented indebtedness to Tunbridge has, I fear, more to do with their gracious invitation than my own, ineluctable charm. Be that as it may, I intend to take them up on the offer. At least until I can secure my own establishment. Then I'll send for you, Gunna."

The chill left her expression and a degree of human warmth softened the hard brilliance of her eyes. "I promise, it won't be long."

"I don't understand," Gunna said, untying Fia's corset with trembling fingers. "Yer own establishment? Yer a girl, Fia, not a woman."

"Oh, Gunna," Fia said, "I've never been a 'girl' and well you know it."

"But it isn't done! Ye can't have yer own establishment. Carr will insist ye live with him. He'd never allow anything different. I . . ." She hesitated, her half-exposed face lined with worry. "I don't even know if he'll allow me to come to London."

The glimpse of vulnerability disappeared from Fia's face, leaving it coolly serene. "I will handle Carr, Gunna. I will handle everything: the house, the funds, and your arrival."

Gunna had no choice but to believe her. Fia had never made an idle promise in her life. "But why? Why now? Why not wait?"

Once more a shadow of the young girl that might

have been crept into Fia's expression, looking out through the smooth, artificial, and ravishing visage with infinite sadness. "Because I am tired unto death of tragedies and I don't wish to stay and witness the one unfolding now."

Chapter 27

*F*avor tucked the heavy wool blanket around her legs and gazed with sullen satisfaction at the storm swelling above the castle turrets. She did not think she could quite endure a bright, clear day.

Morosely she motioned a servant to her side and indicated the empty glass on the wrought-iron table before her. He filled it from the bottle standing beside it again, bowed, and left. Favor lifted the glass in both hands and took a long draught before returning it unsteadily to its place.

The courtyard, which had been set up for a late-afternoon repast when the day had promised better, held only a few people. Indeed, it seemed to Favor that the castle was quickly emptying of its population. Everywhere, people were in the process of leaving this place. Godspeed to them.

Those left sat in little groups at tables, warming their palms on china cups filled with tea or coffee while Favor attempted to warm a deeper chill with a more potent distillation. She sat alone, her table somewhat removed from the others, the expression on her face dissuading any approach.

That's the way she wanted it. Getting drunk, Favor had decided, was a solitary occupation. She swept the glass up once more, tipped its contents into her mouth and grimaced as she swallowed.

"Does it help?"

Favor closed her eyes, despair sweeping over her. Of course he would come. Why should he stay away? Why would she think for a moment that common sense would have any influence at all over him and that he might realize the risk of discovery he ran?

"Go away," she muttered, refusing to look at him.

"I asked you if it helped." His voice was low and quite savage, as enraged as he'd sounded when he'd discovered her virginity two days before. But then he'd held her as though she were the most precious thing he'd ever known. He'd made love to her. She must cling to that sole benefit in this vile stew. Longings struggled to rise from deep in the cold, dark place she'd buried them.

She kept her eyes tightly shut, trying not to cry. Her nails dug fiercely into her palms. She would focus on that pain—but how, when this other one so utterly eclipsed it? She must just send him away. She'd not shed tears for Muira, she wouldn't shed them now.

He was waiting. She braced herself. She was a good liar. The best the convent of Sacré Coeur had ever known. She opened her eyes. He loomed above her table, his clenched fists planted on either side of her on the tabletop. His feet were spread wide as though bracing himself for a fight.

"Help with what?" she asked, furtively cataloguing each beloved feature—the amber color of his eyes, the texture of his beard-rough jaw, the breadth and height of him—hungrily hoarding each impression so that she would have his image for all time.

She did not worry about remembering his touch. The tensile strength in his fingers, the warmth of his mouth, his kiss, his whispered words, these were part of her now. She would no sooner forget them than she would forget how to breathe.

For a long moment they stared at each.

"Is it true?" he finally asked.

She'd begun shivering. She hadn't shivered since Muira had brought her back from the tower even though she was cold, so cold she doubted she'd ever be warm again.

"Is what true?" she asked feebly, dull-witted with gin. Ah, yes. Gin. The promised void. She snagged the glass and brought it to her lips. He seized her wrist and slammed it down on the table. The liquid leapt from the glass, spilling over the linen table covering.

She tried to pull free. Around them the low murmur

of conversation died. Interested faces turned in their direction.

"Stop!" she whispered hoarsely. "The footman will be on you in a minute if you continue like this!"

His smile was feral and dark. "Let him."

"No, I beg you," she said. "You'll only be found out. Leave. *Please.*"

"Not before you tell me whether it's true," he ground out between clenched teeth. "Are you going to marry Carr?"

"What does it matter who I wed?" she asked in a low, taut voice. "You knew I was trolling for a trophy. What grander trophy than Carr? Who wealthier?"

"You little fool," he said, his eyes blazing. "You don't know what you're doing. You can't."

"Why are you suddenly so loathe to see me marry?" she asked bitterly, unable to contain her words. "Remember? You have nothing to offer in substitute. Not even a name. Or should I just acquiesce to your demands, give you *carte blanche* and become your mistress?"

He leaned forward. She could see his braced arms tremble with barely contained emotion. "If I don't already have a place in hell, that would surely win it," he said in a low, intense voice, "but by God, if that is what you want . . . if that would keep you from him . . . my hand is yours, Madame."

Hand, not heart.

"My path is set," she said vacantly. "I've other masters to serve besides myself."

His bronze skin dulled. He straightened, towering over her. "Carr will destroy you."

She shook her head. "I can manage Carr. You see, I have been *bred* to manage Carr."

"You fool," he said again with quiet venom. "You don't know what you're dealing with. If you won't have me, have some other knave. I swear to God, I could gladly give you to another if by doing so I kept you from him."

"I won't have another."

"Vanity or suicide; which one?" His eyes condemned her, his knuckles were white where he gripped the edge of the table.

"Neither. My family."

"Oh, Favor," he said, suddenly appealing to her. "Refuse them. You'll be doing them a benefit by setting them free from their expectations of you. Let them find their own fate and not rely on you to find it for them."

She stared at the sodden linen, soaked with the spilled oblivion she'd been courting to no avail all afternoon. The wind had picked up, driving most of the others in the courtyard inside though a few remained seated at a distance. One of them would tell Carr. Rafe would be exposed.

She rose unsteadily to her feet, separated from him by a table and a decade of obligation. "I have a debt I need to repay."

"A curse on your damned debt!" he grated out.

Too late. Already damned. She made a last appeal to him, trying to make him understand. "How could I live with myself if I asked less of myself than you would ask of yourself?"

He slammed his fist down on the table once more. His face was flushed, his teeth bared. "I don't give a bloody damn about your moral conscience. This is *Carr*. A man who's known to have killed three wives already. Is it your desire to be the fourth?"

"I will die—"

"Bloody right."

"—long after we marry. I will outlive him. I'm far younger than he—"

He surged across the table, grabbing her hand and dragging her halfway across it. She did not resist, even when he thrust his face within inches of hers. "You are a little girl," he said tightly. "A foolish little girl raised on stupid romantic notions about sacrificing yourself for a lofty and noble purpose. But you won't just sacrifice your youth, your beauty, your bravery and—Damn you! You'll sacrifice your *life*, Favor!

"You'll *die* at Carr's convenience and the only thing lofty about it will be the heights from which he'll pitch you like he did m—his first bride."

His words scared her, undermined her resolve, and she couldn't let that happen. She closed her eyes, forcing herself to return to that tower, to see her clansmen's broken bodies and hear their dying screams.

She'd been raised with this one purpose. And she would fulfill it but, the Blessed Virgin help her, she could no longer stand to see the bitter condemnation in Rafe's expression or hear the contempt in his voice. He'd been a lover. He deserved the truth.

"My name is Favor McClairen," she said dully. "The Earl of Carr robbed my family of this island, this castle. He stole not only our wealth but our heritage."

He was watching her, not only unimpressed but unsurprised. "Why must you be the one to regain it?"

"Because," she said, "ten years ago I was responsible for the massacre of those who could have fought for it."

"No." He shook his head.

"Carr's son had raped a novitiate and they brought him to—but you'd know, wouldn't you?" she asked. "If Ash Merrick told you about something as paltry as the Trust, he surely recited to you that fascinating bit of his family history. I see I'm right." Her smile felt like a grimace. "Well, Rafe, *I* was the girl who saved Raine Merrick's life. I delayed his hanging long enough for Carr to ride down on my clan with a hundred redcoats."

His face was hard, intractable. "You can't repay the dead with your life."

"I'm repaying the living," she said tiredly. "I'll marry Carr and I'll leave him. I'll return to France. He wouldn't dare follow me there. I'll wait for him to die and then—"

"And then what?" Rafe sneered.

"Then McClairen's Isle will belong to the McClairens once more. In Scotland a widow inherits her husband's property."

He shook his head, his eyes bleak, and shook his head again. "You cannot be so naive," he whispered.

"Whoever put you to this cannot be so naive. 'Wait for Carr to die?' "

"It's what I'll do," she said. "It's what will happen."

He kept shaking his head, his lips curled back to reveal the edge of his teeth, a pulse pounding in his temple. "No," he said. "No. I'll stop it."

"No. You can't. You're too late." Her gaze fell before his, her voice dropped to a harsh whisper. "Carr proposed this morning. I accepted."

He went absolutely still. She closed her eyes, unable to stand the condemnation in his expression. His contempt washed over her like a physical thing. Not that she could blame him. It was why she was here with this bottle of gin when she did not drink spirits. It was why she'd drunk Carr's gift—a carafe of Madeira doubtless laced with Muira's "love potion"—throughout luncheon. It was why she would stay here, drinking, after he left. She opened her eyes. He was still there.

"I will ask you this and, damn you, you'd better answer," he said in a hard voice, "Did you declare yourselves? Were witnesses there?"

She understood then. He thought Carr had tricked her into the old Scottish custom of declaration and that they'd already wed.

"Did you?" he shouted, rattling the heavy iron furniture like a piece of tin.

"What difference does it make?" she said.

"I'll ask once more 'ere I throttle you, Madame—and be warned, I have never so desired to do a person harm as I do you at this moment."

"I assure you, I hurt every bit as much as you could

want," she replied softly. He jerked forward and caught himself short as though held by invisible chains.

"Did you declare?"

"No," she said tiredly. "No. I would have and so, too, would Carr but Muira—Mrs. Douglas—insisted on finding a priest. She said the McClairens would not accept the marriage as real unless it had been sanctioned by the Church."

She lifted tragic eyes to him. "Is that not funny? Do you not see the joke? They want this marriage blessed when it is from its conception cursed."

A sound of anguish and fury rose in Rafe's throat, frightening the hollow humor from her.

"You can't stop it, Rafe," she whispered. "A priest rides for Wanton's Blush even as we speak."

His fury erupted in a roar of pain. He seized the table and pitched it over, hurling it across the terrace. Without another glance at her, he strode from the windswept courtyard.

Gunna was waiting for Raine when he reached the room he'd been using for sleep. "They say the king is dead!" she greeted him.

Raine didn't reply. He moved past her and began a hurried hunt through a pile of discarded clothing.

"Everyone is leaving Wanton's Blush. Everyone!" Gunna went on. "Fia is already gone. The house is in an uproar: servants scurrying everywhere, packing trunks; the grooms and stable boys working round the clock to hitch the proper horses to the proper carriage."

He found his greatcoat and swung it over his shoulder, stopped in the middle of the room, and looked about for the small leather purse containing all the wealth he owned, a dozen gold guineas.

"And Carr prowls the castle like an aged badger, snarling and gloating, and while all his guests leave he keeps servants in the tower looking for the arrival of a carriage!"

"Aye," Raine swept the debris from a table. His purse wasn't there. "He's sent for a priest."

"Why?" Gunna asked, her confusion mirrored in her ravaged face.

"To marry him and Miss Donne."

He heard the sharp whistle of her indrawn breath. "Aye. A new stepmama for Fia and myself. Aren't we lucky?" He spied the purse on the windowsill. He snagged it, tossing it in the air with a predacious smile.

"Oh, Raine. I am sorry," Gunna said softly.

"Don't be. You'd be wasting your pity. She'll not wed Carr. I swear it."

"But, Raine, how can you stop them?"

He shoved the purse into his belt and wheeled around, grasping her by the shoulders. "I'll be gone for a while, a couple of days at the most. If you ever had any affection for me, I need you to do something for me now, Gunna. And never fail."

She studied his face, saw something there that caused her breath to catch in her scarred old lungs. "Of course, Raine. But where are you going?"

His expression turned hard. "There's an old debt I have to collect."

Chapter 28

$\mathcal{W}$ake up!"

Favor rolled onto her side, swatting at the hands pulling her. She blinked owlishly into the dark. It was still night. Her mouth was cottony and rancid, her eyes crusted with the residual salt from countless tears. And she was still half-drunk.

Not that it helped.

She remembered each eternal moment since yesterday when Rafe had left. She must not think of Rafe. He was gone. "Go 'way," she mumbled.

"Nay!" Muira grabbed her arm and hauled her upright. The sound of a flint strike preceded the flash of a flame as Muira lit a candle. "The priest is here. You're to be wed in an hour's time."

Favor came wide awake, snatching herself out of the

old woman's grip and scooting to the far side of the bed, yards of rumpled and stained pink satin heaped about her. She stared at them uncomprehendingly until she recognized the skirts of last night's gown. She hadn't taken it off before falling into her bed last night and no maid had disrobed her.

"No," she mumbled, tucking her knees to her chest. "Carr is too sick. He's been abed since yesterday. So sick he hasn't even come to see his guests off."

"He must have gotten better," Muira said, seizing Favor's ankle and dragging her across the bed. "He sent word a few minutes ago. He's found a priest but the man won't stay long, fearing the antipapists at Wanton's Blush. You must get up!"

"I am cursed then," Favor said, and as Muira began to drag her farther she reached down and pried her fingers from her ankle. "I'll come. I said I would marry him and I will, now let me be."

"Stupid girl! You can't appear like that! Look at you. I've ordered a bath brought up." She pointed at a tub standing in the center of the room. "You'll use it and clean yourself!"

Favor's lip curled back. "If you think to deck me out like some virgin sacrifice, you'll get no satisfaction, I promise you. I'd sooner go to him dressed in black."

The old woman's mouth flattened with impatience. "Ach! Fine, then. Carr isn't marrying you anyway, he's marrying Janet."

She stood back, waiting while Favor pulled herself to the edge of the bed and stood. Her head swam and she closed her eyes against the ache in her temple.

When she opened them she caught sight of herself in a dark mirror on the far wall.

She was ghastly white, her eyes sunk deep and ringed with shadows. Her hair fell in thick black ropes about her face and shoulders, lending her a feral appearance. She glared at her image with satisfaction. A worthy bride for a murderer. With a sharp movement, she gestured Muira ahead of her.

Muttering, Muira led her down empty black halls and long-echoing corridors. Already Wanton's Blush wore an air of abandonment, her denizens having fled in a steady stream over the last few days.

"They're in here, waiting," Muira whispered. "I'll look over the marriage certificate. You bob your head when the priest bids you do so and then, finally, it will be done." She opened the door and waited for Favor to enter and followed her in.

The room was small and dark and of indeterminate usage. The few lit candles did little to chase the shadows from the corners. At least it is not a chapel, Favor thought. A priest, sitting on a hardback chair near the doorway, rose as they entered, his gaze darting anxiously. A small man stood beside the priest, his expression closed. Probably a witness.

Favor looked about. No one else was in the room. Certainly not Carr. Relief flooded through her. Perhaps he was, indeed, too sick to leave his room. Perhaps he'd overestimated his strength. Perhaps he wouldn't come. Hope uncoiled in Favor's heart.

"Where's His Lordship?" Muira asked, her honeyed 'Mrs. Douglas' tones so unlike her real voice that for a second Favor did not realize who'd spoken.

"His Lordship is too ill to leave his bed." The small man beside the priest stepped forward.

"Ah!" An involuntary cry, small and quickly smothered, rose from Muira.

"But," he said, "His Lordship is most anxious, indeed, *most* anxious to wed Miss Donne, and as the priest"—his gaze flickered derisively at the silent man—"is afraid to leave his sanctuary for long, Lord Carr insists we do not delay."

"I don't understand," Muira snapped, in her confusion over this unforeseen turn of events forgetting her harmless mien.

"If it pleases you, he would like to go through with the ceremony by proxy," the small man continued. "I will stand for him. My name is Rankle. I am His Lordship's valet."

"His *valet*? This is most irregular," Muira exclaimed. "Some would say ridiculous. Why I doubt such a marriage is legal or"—she looked at the priest—"even valid."

"I can assure you as to its validity, Madame," the priest said quietly, "and as far as the world is concerned, you know that a simple declaration before witnesses is all that Scottish law requires to marry."

"I want to see the certificate," Muira said, holding out her hand.

Wordlessly, Rankle gave it to her. She tilted the paper into the candlelight while Favor held her breath, praying she would find some irregularity, a few more days in which—if God would but show mercy—Rafe's face would begin to fade from memory.

Muira raised her face, a gloating smirk on her lips. Favor's hope died.

"It's legal and it's clear as day. Aye!" Muira said. She grasped Favor's elbow and propelled her forward. "Say your piece, priest, and make sure to heed her answer well."

She could not say what held her upright, Muira's grasp or her own will. With Muira's triumph her last bit of hope died. The room faded to a dim stage, the others became caricatures mumbling unintelligible lines in a play in which she had no interest. She stared at the candles' haloes, heard the priest's voice drone above the dull throbbing in her temples. Her limbs seemed liquid, her thoughts disjointed. She answered in a faint voice when prodded, nodding in continual agreement while deep inside she chanted his name like an incantation against the devil: *Rafe. Rafe. Rafe.*

And then it was done. Rankle wished her well and plopped a purse into the priest's outstretched hand. Muira, eyes ablaze with triumph, folded the certificate and stuffed it into her bodice.

"I must go at once and show this to those left of the clan."

"Don't leave," Favor whispered, and knew she had finally reached the end of her strength, for she was asking for Muira's aid. She should have known she wouldn't receive any.

Muira grasped her chin between her thumb and forefinger and shook it with horrible playfulness.

"Don't be ridiculous. The village where the last Mc-Clairens live is less than a five-hour drive. There's no reason for you to become all over vaporish, m'girl." She leaned close, whispering in Favor's ear, "Carr is too ill to perform his husbandly duties." She smiled thinly. "If you're very lucky, he'll die and never will."

Favor stared at the old woman as she swept from the room. The priest followed her, his face taut with worry.

"Lady Carr." Rankle bowed and he, too, left.

She was alone.

She stood until her gaze slowly focused on a dark, oily lock snaking across her bodice. She lifted the tress as one would a dead thing. It filled her with revulsion.

She'd dyed her hair black to ensnare Carr. She'd achieved that goal. Now she wanted only to rid herself of the noxious stain. Rafe had hated it.

She must clean it off now. She *had* to get it off.

She returned to her room and undressed, dropping the foul garments about her feet and peeling stays, chemise, and petticoats from her body. Then, naked, she scooped water from the hipbath Muira had ordered into a smaller basin. She dunked her head.

She began slowly, using the bar of harsh soap Muira had used to clean off her own makeup. With numb fingers, she worked the soap deep into her hair. But as the water grew dark, so grew her eagerness to be rid of the dye. Harder and faster she scrubbed, digging her fingers into the sodden mass, working up a thick lather of gray foam.

Desire became obsession. She dumped the dirty water on the floor and stood in the spreading pool, refilling the basin with clear water. Again and again she washed and rinsed her hair, until finally the lather remained white and the water held no tint of color. Only then did she fall exhausted and trembling to her knees, wrapping her arms around her middle and rocking back and forth. Because though she'd removed the blight from her hair, she still felt unclean.

Warmth flowed over her. Slowly, Favor opened her eyes. A hazy glow filled her room. Dawn had finally come.

"Favor, beloved, wake up."

She turned her head, certain she was dreaming. She was not.

Rafe stood over her, the gentle sunlight revealing each harsh and beloved feature. No anger remained in his expression, all the rage was gone; he knew he'd lost. They'd lost.

"Your hair," he murmured, tenderness filling his voice. He reached down and fingered a tress. " 'Tis as bright as I recall. Brighter."

"You're too late," she whispered.

"Aye," he answered sadly. "Years too late 'twould seem."

Reality sliced through the languor binding her. She struggled to rise, heedless of her nakedness beneath the bedsheets. "You must go! If you're found—"

"Gently, sweet falcon." He grasped her shoulders, sitting down on the bed beside her and pushing her against the pillows. "There's no cause for alarm. Your dragon *doyenne* is gone, the servants are otherwise occupied, and Carr is sick in his den."

Relief flowed through her and hard on its heels, gratitude. She'd never expected to see him again, yet here he was, filled with such poignance, such loss. She turned her head and kissed the back of his hand where it still lightly cupped her shoulder.

Without hesitation he wrapped his long fingers around the back of her head and brought her mouth to his. Surprise briefly touched her; he'd taken this kiss, not courted it, and he was a man not given to taking. But then his lips moved over hers and she couldn't think beyond the moment. 'Twas her beloved who embraced her, kissed her, caressed her. 'Twas Rafe.

With a sob, she wrapped her arms about his throat, deepening the kiss. His hands moved up and tilted her face, gently urging her mouth to open. She complied and his tongue plundered deep within, finding hers and mating with it. Her head spun, her body burned bright as the sun outside and was just as ignorant of morality.

"You're mine, Favor," he whispered against her mouth.

Her body was ignorant, but she was not. "I'm married, Rafe."

"I know." His tone was serrated with anguish. He pulled back and stared into her eyes, ferocity flickering to life in the amber depths of his own. "It doesn't matter. You are mine, Favor. You always will be no matter what name you take or where you flee. I love you."

Yes, she thought hopelessly. *Yes*. His words speared her with their essential truth. She could not deny them any more than she could deny her own heart. But she could not acknowledge them either.

Rafe's she might be, and he her own love, but still she *did* have another name and she *would* soon flee to France. . . .

But not now. Not yet. She'd been granted a few hours' reprieve, a few hours to make enough memories to last a lifetime. Her embrace tightened.

It was enough of an answer. He eased her onto her back, following her down. His body had been her anchor before, a rock she'd clung to as he'd held her upright, buffeted by a tempest of sensations as he'd pleasured her. Now she learned the weight and breadth of him covering her and gloried in it.

His fingers skated lightly over her collarbone and found the pulse at the base of her throat. He measured the rapid beat with his lips, trailing lower, just above the line of the blanket. She arched upward, wanting more, wanting what he'd given her just a few nights before, wanting what she thought she would never know again. He brushed the linen away, exposing her breasts to his hungry gaze.

He inhaled sharply. "Let me take my shirt off, Favor. Let me feel your skin naked against mine. Please."

She nodded. She could do nothing else; her voice was lost. He stripped his shirt off over his head, the movement feline and graceful, the muscles cloaking his laddered ribs sliding smoothly beneath velvety skin. His chest and belly were as hard and muscular as her caresses had described them, his arms long and power-ful-looking, capped by thick dense muscle.

Dark hair covered his chest and thickened into a dark line that traveled beneath the waist of his breeches. Her gaze traveled lower. She caught her breath. His breeches were tight, too small and old, and the faded cloth hugged the big bulge of his sex closely, clearly revealing his arousal.

Her eyes fluttered shut remembering the feel of him pressed inside her. It had ached. Now that ache had returned but this time it seemed only the instrument that had then caused the ache could now ease it.

"Favor?"

She opened her eyes, swallowed hard. He was watching her intently, his expression taut.

"Is it . . . can I . . ." He trailed off and speared a hand through his hair, further rumpling the glossy sable locks. "Favor, I would not frighten you. I swear—"

She reached for him. He dropped to one knee, slid-ing his arms beneath her and lifting her clear off the linens, crushing her to his naked flesh. He inhaled sharply. "Dear God, you feel good."

She twisted in his embrace, dragging her nipples across his chest. The sensation was carnal, the sweet abrasion causing the peaks of her breasts to throb. She rubbed them again in the soft hair on his chest, as-suaging the ache.

He clenched his teeth, his eyes narrowing with plea-sure. She threaded her fingers through his hair and pulled his head close, drinking in the scent of him, the crisp, silky texture of the loose curls between her fingers.

"You are beautiful, too beautiful, and I want you too much," he whispered, and she realized that he worried he would hurt her.

She didn't. He'd shown her the most exquisite care, given her profound pleasure, and taught her passion. She'd taken all he'd had to give and offered nothing in return. Except her love, and that she gave in abundance. Now she wanted to please him, to show him her love in the most intimate way possible.

She gripped his upper arms, reveling in the feel of his muscles bunching beneath the clear, smooth skin. She pushed. He was heavy. She would never have been able to dislodge him by her strength alone and yet he shifted at once, his gaze quiet and askance, allowing her whatever she would have of him. Or not have.

She pushed again, harder, and he acquiesced to the unspoken command by rolling on his back, catching her to keep her from falling on top of him. But that's where she wanted to be. She snuggled down, lying fully on him, her breasts flattened against his chest, her hair a shimmering curtain flowing on either side of his rib cage.

She lowered her head and kissed his flat belly. It jerked into taut delineation. His hands, barely clasping her shoulders, tightened painfully. She opened her mouth and flicked the heated skin with the tip of her tongue.

"Favor!" The choked word came out a warning.

Her longing preempted his caution. She curled her

fingers beneath the waist of his breeches, tugging the cloth down over his narrow hips. His sex sprang free. Touch alone had not prepared her for the sight of him, big, swollen, and rigid. She raised her eyes in apprehension and found Rafe watching her, his smile rueful. Instantly, her fears disappeared.

"I swear I won't hurt you," he said hoarsely, trying to pull her up.

She would have none of it. She twisted out of his grip and scooted farther down. Lightly, she clasped him between her palms. His hips bucked slightly in response.

She lowered her head, placing a fleeting kiss on the thick tip. He made a throaty sound, half anguish, half pleasure. It was all the impetus she needed. She opened her lips over his sex and took him into her mouth. He pulsed, silky and smooth against her tongue—

His hands swooped down to bracket her face. "No, Favor. You don't—" Whatever else he'd been about to say was lost in a shuddering groan.

Carnal satisfaction flooded her. This strong, broad man, this huge male, trembled with the pleasure she gave him. She reveled in the power. Her ability to inspire his desire was intoxicating.

She glazed the head of his sex with her tongue. His fists twisted in her hair, his knuckles shivering against her temples in his efforts to control the building lust she drew forth with each long, sultry pull of her mouth. She did not want his restraint; she wanted his passion. She tasted the salty essence, drawing him deeper—

With a low, guttural roar, he grabbed her upper arms and hauled her up and over him, holding her upper body suspended above him. His biceps trembled, veins roping thickly under the tanned skin.

"My turn." He lifted his head to her breast and opened his mouth wide over her nipple, sucking the velvety peak deep into his mouth.

She gasped, her hips undulated instinctively against his thick staff. Liquid warmth seeped from between her legs.

He released her nipple and clamped his big hands on either hip, repositioning her higher on his body. She bowed backward, her hands seeking purchase and finding it on his own hips, her swinging curtain of hair lightly teasing his thighs.

He pressed his mouth to the soft flesh of her inner thigh and nibbled higher, closer to the jointure— Her eyes flew open. He'd covered her mound with his mouth, and was sucking softly.

Dear God! His tongue swept deep within the folds, grazing the nubbin buried within, robbing her of cohesive thought. Lightning raced along her nerves, spun behind the black shield of her eyelids, taunting her with the promise of more.

She moaned, no longer able to tell what he did or how. Her whole body was caught in a vortex of driving need, the pitch to the crescendo building within her with painful intensity . . .

The crisis broke. Her cry rose to a soundless keen as the climax engulfed her, narrowing all sensation down to one essential point. She tensed, impaled on the very apex of pleasure, rocking slightly until the feel of his tongue, flickering lightly over her sex, became too acute. She shivered, drew back. Gently he shifted and lowered her to the mattress, covering her with his body.

He came into her on a long, smooth thrust, breaking through the thin barrier of her maidenhead without hesitation. The pain was sharp and brief, supplanted by a quickening need. He stopped deep within her.

Her eyes fluttered open. He was watching her, his breathing harsh, his bronze skin dusky. He reached down and lifted first one then the other of her hands, and set them on his shoulders.

"Hold on to me, Favor. Please. Cling to me. Want me. For the love of God, hold on to me this one time." And then he moved.

The pace he set was hard and brutal, his thrusts deep. He stretched and filled her, yet still she wanted, needed. Her recalcitrant hands strayed from his shoulders and swept down the muscular straining back to his taut buttocks. She dug her fingers into the hard round muscle, wrapped her thighs about his hips and tilted her pelvis in ancient welcome, greedily absorbing the agressiveness of his possession.

Just this one time. Just once to last the rest of her life.

Climax after climax seized her and carried her like a scrap on a tidal wave, peaking and crashing, wild and tumultuous and exquisite. Suddenly Rafe tensed. He rose like Vulcan, hard and burnished beneath the sheen of sweat, masterful and potent. He braced himself on his arms, and with a deep cry, pushed deep within her. He held himself still, his body shuddering with his release.

When it was over he sank down on her, heavy with repletion. He slid his arms beneath her, cradling her tenderly.

She started to rise.

"Stay, Favor," he said softly. "Rest with me. It isn't only sex I would have but its sweet aftermath, too. Stay."

"I can't. He'll send a servant. We'll be found."

She tried once again to free herself but her attempt was a pitiful parody. His sadness bound her to him. She allowed him to draw her back down to his side and wrap his long arms around her. She laid her head on his chest and listened to the low, deep beat of his heart. And there, against all chance, she fell asleep.

"Raine! Rouse yerself! Carr is up!" Gunna stood in the bedchamber doorway, the light from the hall making a black silhouette of her misshapen figure.

Raine surged upright, carrying Favor with him. Instinctively, he shielded her.

"Rafe?" He heard her voice, soft and groggy, yet a sliver of fear sliced through it.

"It's all right, Favor." He mouthed the words knowing them for a lie. It was not all right. How could it be? She would hate him and he would have to live with that hatred the rest of his life.

"But who is that? What does she say?"

"Raine," Gunna repeated. "There's no time for this.

He's up and he's looking for her. 'Tis only a matter of time before he comes here."

"Why does she call you Raine?" Favor whispered. "Why. . . . Dear God."

He closed his eyes. He'd hoped . . . for what? Another hour before he was destroyed?

"Because that is my name. Raine. Raine Merrick."

Chapter 29

$\mathcal{R}$aine felt her scuttle away from him, dragging the bed linen with her. He turned. She was staring at him with wide, uncomprehending eyes, her golden hair streaming about her bare shoulders.

"No." She shook her head. "It cannot be."

"Yes. I'm . . . I'm so damn sorry."

"Sorry? Dear God, that's how you knew about the Trust and the castle and all about Carr and what he . . . why?" The last word was a heart-wrenching whisper. "Why?"

"I didn't want Carr to know I was here. Then I found you and later I discovered who you were. I owed you my life, Favor. I thought that if you knew my name you wouldn't allow me to help you—"

"Help me?" she echoed, lifting the pitiful sheet as

though that could somehow hide her from him. "And making me an adulteress is how you *helped* me? By cuckolding your father?"

She scooted off the far side of the bed, backing away from him. Her eyes revealed her horror.

"Raine!" Gunna shut the door and hobbled forward.

"You said you'd kept him sick with some drug!" Raine said desperately, keeping his gaze on Favor who trembled before him. "That he'd be abed. You're probably misinformed. He's probably still sick."

"Nay!" Gunna said. "I saw him myself. He must not have drunk the drugged water this morning. If Carr finds ye in here with her he'll kill ye!"

A sob broke from Favor, dispelling all other considerations. "What sort of hellish family is this? Did you see bedding me after my marriage to him as a chance to pay him back for the years you spent in prison?"

"No, Favor, I swear it's not so." He stretched out his hand; only on seeing her expression did he realize he was still naked. With a snarl he rose, snatching up his breeches and pulling them on. Gunna grabbed his forearm. "Raine!"

Angrily he shook her off and went to Favor. She backed away from him, panic suffusing her lovely features. "No. No. Oh God, how could you?"

He'd no choice but to tell her now, with Gunna hovering. "You're not an adulteress, Favor."

"What?" Favor whispered.

"You married *me* last night, Favor. Not Carr."

"No," she breathed. "Impossible."

" 'Tis true. Gunna kept Carr drugged while I rode to an abbey south of here. The Abbess there owed me a good deed. She sent her priest here."

"But the valet . . ." She was trembling, her skin blanched white as cream. He longed to enfold her in his arms, took a step forward, and saw her gaze dart wildly about, seeking escape. He had to keep talking, trying to explain.

"Rankle stood proxy for me, knowing that while he played the part of Carr's stand-in he was in truth acting for me."

"Why?"

"You've seen how Carr treats his servants. Rankle was only too happy to repay him in kind."

"But the certificate! Muira said it was all in order!"

"Muira believed what she wanted to see. The certificate named R. Merrick as your husband. It gave no peer's title."

"R. Merrick. Raine Merrick." She swayed slightly.

"I couldn't let you marry him, Favor. He would have killed you. This plan, this godforsaken plan of yours, could never have worked."

"*You* stopped it from working. You stopped me from repaying my obligation," she said, a new horror in her voice. "You ruined it all. Why . . . Oh God." Her head shot up and she gazed at him out of terrible, wounded eyes. "You even made love to me this morning to ensure the marriage couldn't be annulled. Didn't you?"

He could not deny the charge. In truth he had entered her room with just such a motive. But that motive hadn't survived the passion that had ignited as soon as he'd seen her. Then his only consideration had been to make love to her, to find in a life rife with pain and regret and sorrow one short interlude for love. But she was right, that hadn't been his plan when he'd gone to her. She read the guilt on his face and flinched.

"Not in the end," he whispered hoarsely. "Not—"

"Go!" she panted desperately. "Get out of here! Leave me! Go!"

"Favor, please, I beg you—"

"Go! Haven't you done enough? Stolen my heart, my honor, and my pride and—go!" She crumpled to the floor, sobbing. Her slender back, so vulnerable and pale, shook with a tempest of tears.

"Heed her," Gunna insisted, yanking on his arm. "Ye'll do no good here, Raine, and ye'll surely do her no good dead!"

"Won't I?" Raine asked numbly, staring at the slight figure at his feet, afraid to touch her, unable to leave.

"Think!" Gunna ground out. "Carr will kill ye and take yer place, Raine. No one knows yet about the marriage. Rankle can be silenced and Carr's Christian name still begins with an 'R'."

She was right. He couldn't die. He had to leave.

"Favor . . ."

She huddled closer, refusing to look at him. With an oath, he swung away and strode from the room.

She heard him leaving with the old hunched woman in the veil. For a long moment she lay where she'd fallen, huddled among the tangled bedsheets still scented with their lovemaking.

Raine Merrick: Rapist. Her enemy's son. Her betrayer. Her husband. And soon Carr would come . . . and he would want to know . . . and Muira was gone . . . and she was alone, far more alone than she'd ever been before because even last night she'd had Raf—Raine. She jerked upright, the thought a physical pain.

She had to get out of there. Leave. But where? All her life she'd been shunted from place to place. The small town of her birth, these fatal shores, the French convent. She had no home. She'd only had her goal and that had been rendered unattainable. She only knew she couldn't stay here.

She rose and dressed with trembling haste. Quickly she donned a cloak, then she opened the door to the hallway and peeked outside. No one moved. She crept down the corridor, past the main staircase to the servants' stairwell, and descended on clattering heels. Downstairs she hastened through the kitchens and larders, the curtseys and bobs of startled servants following her progress.

She burst through the back door and raced across the small open courtyard for the stables. There she stole inside. A surprised groom harnessing a team of matched grays stumbled to a halt and tugged his forelock submissively.

"Where is Jamie Craigg?" she asked him.

"He be—"

"Right here, Miss Donne." The giant emerged from a stall, wiping his huge paws on a leather apron.

"Where's Muira?"

Jamie darted a warning glance at the groomsman. What matter? It was all over now.

"*Mrs. Douglas* drove herself out early this morning," he said. "She said she was going to visit relatives up north and would be back by dinner. Beggin' yer pardon, Miss, but ye don't look so well. Are ye all right?" His craggy face was riddled with concern.

"Yes," she whispered. "Except I have a desire . . . that is I *need* to go away." She prayed he would not ask her where, for she did not have any idea. She only knew she had to leave and Jamie was her only hope.

"Now, Miss?"

"Oh yes, please, Jamie."

Again he darted an anxious look at the groom, who stood watching with undisguised interest.

"Please."

"Of course, Miss. Right away, Miss. I'll just hitch the carriage and we'll be off." He turned away, his gaze passing scathingly over the eavesdropping groom. "Ye can tell me where once we're on our way."

In the end there was no place to go except her brother's manor twenty miles inland.

"What has happened? I returned to the castle to find Carr beside himself and the two of you missing." Favor heard Muira's voice rise stridently from the small entry hall below. She heard Jamie's low rumble in reply.

She rose from her chair. She would not hide up here

from Muira. Muira no longer mattered. Nothing mattered.

"What did Carr say?" Jamie asked.

"I didn't speak to Carr, you great oaf! I couldn't very well show up without his doting bride, now could I? Nor tell him she'd fled like a rabbit from a hound. I come straight here to fetch her back and that's exactly what I'll do."

"The girl is sick, Muira," Jamie muttered. "As white as new snow and eyes as bleak and deep as a new dug grave."

"I don't care. Where is the silly bitch? I'll teach her to—"

"I'm here, Muira."

The old woman swung around and looked up at where Favor stood on the landing. "Get your cloak on!" she spat. "Your husband's waiting for you."

"No. He's not."

"Stupid girl, he's not had you yet. He can still have the marriage annulled. Now get down here!"

Favor laughed, a hopeless choked sound. In response, Muira stormed up the steps, grabbed her arm in a viselike grip and wrenched her forward.

"No." Favor shook her head frantically. "No! Listen to me, Muira! Listen!" Her shout had the desired effect. Muira dropped her arm.

"I didn't marry Carr. I married his son, Raine!"

Muira turned to Jamie. His forehead rippled with a fierce frown of confusion. "And you said *I* was daft," she muttered grimly. "Well, mad or no, she'll lay beneath Carr this day."

"I will not. I've already lain with his son. My husband."

The supreme confidence in Muira's expression faltered. "She's mad."

Favor looked past her to Jamie. " 'Twas Raine Merrick who we finagled from that French prison. He came to Wanton's Blush without Carr's knowledge, seeking McClairen's Trust. He found me instead. But he didn't tell me who he was, I swear it."

"Oh, lassie," Jamie breathed.

"Ignore her," Muira said flatly, but something skittered behind her opaque eyes. "She's just looking for some way out. And she'll not find it."

"You foolish old woman! 'Twas Raine who danced with me at the masque. 'Twas Raine whom I stayed with that night. 'Twas Raine's name on that certificate."

She could see Muira's throat working convulsively. "No."

"Look at it!" Favor said, and the old woman withdrew the folded sheet from her bodice with trembling fingers. "It says 'R' Merrick, 'R' for Raine not Ronald. If it were Carr I'd married, the paper would read 'Merrick, Earl of Carr.' Look! What date does it give for my groom's birth?"

Her answer was a howl of rage that rose from the depths of Muira's belly. Fearfully, Favor backed away. Muira crumpled the certificate into her fist and tore at the rumpled wad, tearing it to pieces with hands whose bones showed white. When she was done she hurled the pieces to the hall below and swung around.

"NO! I won't let this happen. All the years, the planning, the sacrifices and scratching to make . . . No! McClairen's Isle will be the McClairens' once more!"

Jamie, his face still and wary, moved cautiously up the steep flight of stairs. "It's over, Muira," he said.

"No, it's not," she panted, her gaze wild and staring. "It's not over. There has to be a way . . ." She swung on Favor. "You vile thing. You wretched curse on our clan!"

Her words beat at Favor, each word a blow. "For what did you sell out your honor and your debt?" Muira demanded.

"I didn't know. God help me, 'tis true I love . . . loved him but I swear I didn't know who he was. I didn't know 'twas Raine Merrick I married. I swear I thought I'd wed Carr! I only learned of his duplicity this morning after he . . ."

"Tupped you," Muira finished in tones so ugly Favor closed her eyes. "Who else knows of your filthy betrayal?"

Favor flinched before the raw hatred in Muira's voice. "No one. Only the priest and the valet and Raine."

"*Raine*," she sneered. "Could you not have waited to lay with him? A few months and I would have made you a widow."

She laughed at Favor's bewildered expression, a dark and hideous sound. "Oh, so innocent! Did you not ken that was part of the plan, dearie? Did you honestly believe I'd trust God to take Carr's life before yours?

God is not to be trusted. I planned to kill Carr within the week.

Murder? She should have known. She should have realized. But she hadn't. Yet another thing she was guilty of, but at least in marrying Raine she had been spared a part in murder. "I would never have agreed to let you kill Carr," she whispered. "No matter how evil he is."

"Of course not," Muira sneered. "You haven't the guts. You've too much blood of your whey-faced mother in you and not enough McClairen. You sold us out to squirm beneath a rapist, to grow a belly full of Merrick demon. May the fires of hell consume you!"

"Leave off, Muira!" Jamie said, his voice cold with warning. "Merrick never raped that nun and well you know it. Merry confessed her guilt and absolved him."

"What?" Favor asked. "All these years you had me think I'd traded my people's lives for a rapist."

"What matter?" Muira sneered. "He's demon spawn and I'll see him to his rightful home in hell. There's time yet to make this work. The valet and priest can be dealt with later. And once I find—"

"No!" Immediately Favor grasped the black permutations of Muira's mad thoughts. "No, you—"

Muira swung, all her rage invested in the blow that caught Favor across the temple and sent her tumbling down the stairs. The world was gone before she reached the bottom.

Chapter 30

"Where's Muira?" Favor asked faintly. Her head throbbed and a burning pain drove through her back to her shoulder blades. Blackness skirted about her consciousness, beckoning her toward oblivion.

"She's gone too far," she heard Jamie mutter. "No piece of land is worth the price of yer soul."

The darkness swallowed her. When it released her again she grew slowly aware that someone held her, pressing a cool, moist cloth against her forehead. "Raine," she whispered.

"I'm sorry, Favor McClairen," Jamie said. "I'm sorry fer all we done to ye. The boy was no rapist. Ye saved us from the sin of murdering an innocent lad. And that's all ye did. Carr would have found another way to rid us from his land. Ye were just convenient."

"Please," she said trying to turn. She had to stop Muira. Raine. Dear God, why hadn't she stayed with him? Listened? The swirling darkness beckoned her once more; she fought against it, concentrating on Jamie's soft litany.

"Ye were convenient for Muira, too. Fer us. I'll not deny it. We shouldn't have used ye so. It's just that we owed Muira. Please, try and understand.

"We were scattered after the massacre. She found us. She gave us a goal, a purpose, something besides scrabbling from one day to the next without pride or future or past. But she got lost somewhere. I knew it and I didna stop her and that's somethin' I'll have to live with fer the rest of me days."

The blackness receded enough for her to struggle upright in Jamie's great arms. She didn't care about his guilt. She'd had a bellyful of guilt. She only wanted Raine. "Where is she?"

"I dunno. Back to the castle I'd guess. She whipped those horses something fierce." He shook his great shaggy head sadly. "Best rest, Miss Favor. It's all over now."

"No. It's not." She pulled away from him, wincing as she rose. A sea of darkness lapped at her vision. She fought and won the battle against drowning in it. "I have to get to Raine, Jamie. You have to take me to Wanton's Blush."

"Now, Miss Favor. What good will that do?" Jamie said mournfully.

She reached out her hand and braced it on the newel post at the bottom of the stairs. She could not lose him to Muira's mad obsession. Nor to anything else.

"Didn't you hear her, Jamie? And you, who know her so well, didn't you realize what she plans?"

He reached up to steady her by the elbow. She shook off his hand. "What's that, Miss Favor?"

"She plans to kill all three—the valet, priest, and Raine—and by doing so clear the way for my marriage to Carr."

Jamie stared at her, his muteness testifying to his agreement. "But ye'll never agree to it. She must know that."

"It doesn't matter. She's mad!" Favor said, seizing Jamie's hand and tugging. "Now drive me to Wanton's Blush, Jamie Craigg. Drive like the devil himself is chasing you."

Wanton's Blush stood preternaturally dark in the deepening dusk. Few lights brightened the narrow embrasures of her central façade; and her two ells, completely dark, seemed to fold in toward the gloomy courtyard like the wings of some huge, sentient night bird. Jamie drew the lathered horses up before the enormous front doors. Favor jumped from the carriage before the poor beasts had stopped.

"Miss Favor!" Jamie called. "I'll wait without for ye!"

She didn't reply. She wrenched one massive door open, darting past the flummoxed footman and up the central stairs, heading for the abandoned east rooms.

At the top she turned and flew down the corridor to

a small passageway leading to the sea-facing rooms. Raine's lair was near the north tower. If he was here that was the place she'd most likely find him. *If* he was, indeed, still here. The thought that he'd left eased a small part of Favor's panic.

Still, Muira would be hunting—a mad, obsessed woman thwarted in her designs—and as knowledgeable about Wanton's Blush as Muira was, she would soon figure out Raine's whereabouts.

Favor slowed her pace, adjusting her eyes to the gloom. Near the center of the hallway she saw a sliver of light from under a door. It was the chapel where most of Janet McClairen's things had been abandoned.

The thought invoked an image of Raine looking at the detritus that had once been his mother's treasured items. She hadn't understood his pensive mood when she'd come upon him there. He'd accepted her intrusion with relief. Raine, too, had dealt with his share of ghosts.

She opened the door and stepped inside, looking about. An ornate silver candelabra stood on the floor, the lights from a dozen tapers glinting from its polished surface. Otherwise, the room looked empty. She frowned, moved forward, and heard the door bang shut behind her.

She swung around. Ronald Merrick, Earl of Carr, stood behind her. He was dressed like a prince, gleaming from head to foot. At his side he wore a sword in a jewel-encrusted scabbard, on his head a snowy bagwig secured with a diamond clasp. The deep cuffs and buttons of his coat shimmered with crystals and metallic threads. Even the buckles of his shoes glittered.

"You've done something to your hair," he said mildly. "Begad, I rather like it. Pretty."

She didn't know what to say, how to respond. His eyes were odd though his face was composed.

"I knew you'd come, Janet. You always liked your pretty things, though"—he cast a sad look around—"they're not very pretty anymore."

"I'm not Janet, sir."

"Of course you're not. You're Favor Donne, or should I say McClairen? Did you think I didn't know? Of course I knew. Although, I will admit, I only recently found out. Rankle told me, just before he succumbed. Chicken bone, I believe."

Dear God, he'd killed that little valet.

"Don't worry, m'dear, though I will probably have to have a little talk with your brother when . . . *if* he returns. But that has naught to do with you and me. I don't care if you are a McClairen. It doesn't matter who you are because . . ."—he moved toward her—". . . because I also know that you carry the spirit of my dear Janet."

She released her breath slowly, holding very still as he picked up a strand of her hair and coiled it nonchalantly around his finger. "Really quite lovely. I declare myself utterly taken with the hue."

Her smile was tremulous.

"It really is too bad you have to die."

She jerked back, unprepared for the sudden death

sentence and he smiled, clucking softly as one would to a frightened mare. "There now, Janet. You are somewhere in there listening, aren't you, Janet? Because everything I have to say would, I'm afraid, simply be wasted on Miss Donne."

He was going to kill her anyway. It made no sense. "Why?" she pleaded in a hoarse little voice.

"Because I can't have you hounding me through London. You're a Scottish nobody, both in this body and in your last. You aren't"—he twirled his hand, searching for the right words—"rich enough, or well-connected enough, or *special* enough to be my wife. And Janet, you were ever too proud to be anything less.

"Perhaps Miss Donne, too, suffers from this elevated sense of herself because I certainly gave her— you?—every chance to become my mistress, but she— you?—tiresomely insisted on matrimony."

"I'm not Janet," she protested weakly, uncertain whether she should reveal Muira's plot, fearful that doing so would incite him to a murderous rage.

"Of course not." He patted her cheek as one would a child, his gaze slowly warming as he studied her features. "Do you know, Janet, I actually considered for a moment acquiescing to your wishes? I'd almost decided to marry you with—of course—the caveat that I could rid myself of you when I found it expedient to do so.

"But then old farmer George died and the ban on my matrimonial aspirations lifted. There are countless heiresses in London, m'dear. Countless rich, *well-connected* heiresses. You, I'm afraid, never stood a chance."

"Why did you propose to me, then?" she asked. "Why did you send for the priest?"

"I didn't. I simply told your aunt I did." He *tched* softly. "I thought if I proposed, the old hag that guards you would finally allow us a moment alone. So I proposed. In fact, I believe dear Fia even overheard me. Then I told your aunt I'd sent for the priest. I even had a few servants look for a carriage.

"It would have worked, too. I would have insisted we spend an hour or so alone. But then I took sick. I can't begin to describe to you my frustration," he said confidingly. "Happily all has come to rights, however, for here we are."

Her eyes darted about the room, looking for a likely weapon, finding nothing. "I'll just come back," she whispered desperately. "As many times as you kill me, I'll come back."

"Ho-ho!" he chuckled, bussing her under the chin. "I knew I could draw you out. Threats now, Janet? I would have thought you'd learned the error of that particular behavior on those cliffs." He opened his palm in the direction of the windows and she saw that in spite of his jocular tone, she had, indeed, enraged him.

His pupils were pinpoints of black in his dazzling blue eyes. A tiny tic twitched at the corner of his mouth. "Do your damnedest, Janet. Come back as many times as you like, I'll simply kill you again."

She'd made a grave error. She backed up until she

banged into a wall of boxes and crates. She edged along the mass, hands behind her, groping for some weapon. Carr advanced.

"But you know something, Janet? I've been reading about haunts and ghoulies and such. It's fascinating. You ghosts seem a peculiarly hearth-loving mob. Unless you find a human vessel to house you, and that little endeavor took you how long this time? A dozen years?"

He was only a few feet away and she'd worked her way into a corner with nothing to show for it. "The point I'm trying to make, Janet"—he spoke through his teeth now, the soft, urbane tones coming from the choleric face frightening her far more than his words— "is that I don't think you—or your clan—*can* leave here. Let's find out, shall we?"

He seized her around the throat. She flailed frantically in his grip but her heavy skirts smothered her struggles. She clawed at his wrists, tearing violently but his fingers dug deep.

"You would kill your own son's wife?" she choked out.

He laughed, entertained by what he clearly imagined was a paltry diversionary tactic, his grip loosening just enough for her to gulp another lungful of air.

"I swear 'tis true!" she gasped, working at his implacable hold on her throat. "I am married to your son Raine."

"Raine?" He chuckled, his handsome face made even handsomer by his amusement. But his clasp on her throat did not tighten. Instead, it loosened slightly.

He didn't seem to care how deeply she scored his arms and hands with her nails. Like a cat with a mouse, he was playing with her, curious to see what she would say next.

"Yes. He's here. And he'll kill you if you hurt me," she said, and as she spoke she realized it was the truth. She did not for one minute doubt Raine would avenge her with all the formidable power he possessed. Because he loved her.

Stunned at learning his identity, bewildered and uncomprehending, she'd ascribed to him fantastic and horrendous motives. Now she saw that everything he'd done he'd done to protect her. Including marrying her. If only she'd listened to her heart.

Carr had tired of his play. His hands were tightening incrementally, torturously, slowly squeezing the life from her. Light-spattered darkness careened about the perimeter of her vision. Her limbs felt weightless. Her lungs burned.

"So Raine will kill me if I hurt you?" he said, chuckling as he studied her face.

"Yes, I will."

She had to be imagining Raine's voice. But Carr's body had gone as still as a hound on point, his head snapping up. His hands dropped from her throat and she crumpled to the ground, gasping for breath as he wheeled to face his son.

Raine strode from the shadowed doorway. In his hand he held a primed pistol, pointed at Carr. His shirt was open, his long hair in disarray, his boots splattered with mud. Compared to Carr's exquisite figure he looked coarse, rough, and incredibly beautiful. Gabriel come to challenge Lucifer.

"Well, blast me if it isn't my large middle child," Carr murmured, his eyes hooded. "And tell me, is the rest true, also? Are you wed to her?" He flung his hand down toward Favor. She skittered back. He did not notice.

"Yes," Raine said. His gaze was watchful, his jaw tense with barely contained fury.

"Rather incestuous, or did you not know she also carries your mother's soul?"

Raine snickered. "You've grown foolish, old man. We duped you, made you believe my mother had returned in order to keep you occupied while I searched the castle for McClairen's Trust."

We? Dear God, he must have heard her talking and deduced Muira's plan. Now he was drawing Carr's attention away from her. Carr stared, fury born of shock simmering in his expression. His lips twitched, his eyes flickered. A palsy began in his right hand.

"No," Carr said. "I don't believe it." He jerked his head around, impaled Favor with a killing glare. "You're Janet. You knew about the Part of No—" His voice trailed off, his gaze flew back, returned to Raine. "You told her what to say."

Raine grinned, a one-sided smile. Janet's smile. The same smile Muira had made her practice so many hours. Why had she never seen it?

The light of fanaticism faded from Carr's eyes, replaced by cold, killing enmity. He would hate above all things being made a fool of and Raine knew it. He deliberately goaded him.

"I should like to kill you," Carr said.

"Please, do try," Raine returned seriously, uncocking the pistol and tossing it away. It skittered across the room and lodged against a chest twenty feet away from where Favor cowered.

With a roar, Carr drew his sword and charged. Raine grabbed a crate lid, flinging it up in front of his face just as Carr's sword slammed into it, biting deep into the wood. Raine wrenched back, hurling away the lid and the sword buried in it and, for that moment, exposed his torso.

Favor saw the short, lethal blade flash from beneath the cuff of Carr's coat and slip into his hand.

"He's got a dagger!" Her warning came too late. Raine twisted as Carr lunged forward, the knife plunging inches into Raine's ribs. He gasped, staggering back, but Carr, well versed in the foulest forms of fighting, followed him. He released the blade, leaving it impaled in Raine's body and battered at his son's face.

He was going to kill Raine.

Favor scrambled along the wall to where the pistol lay. She lifted it as Raine jerked the dagger from his side. Slick with blood, it fell to the ground. Favor pulled back the hammer, pointed the pistol with shaking hands, and pulled the trigger.

Nothing happened.

Sobbing, she banged the cursed instrument against

the floor. An explosion ripped through the air, echoing in the chamber as the pistol fired, catching Carr by surprise. He turned his head toward the sound. It was all the advantage Raine needed.

His fist met Carr's jaw with a sickening crunching sound. His other fist drove deep into Carr's gut, felling him to his knees. He clasped his hands together and raised them overhead, swinging them in a telling blow on the back of Carr's neck. Carr fell flat on his face.

"Get up!" Raine demanded, standing over his fallen sire. Blood soaked the right side of his shirt and oozed from a gash over his cheek.

"I said, get up!" He reached down and grabbed the back of Carr's coat with one hand. Beads and crystals popped, skittering about the floor. He hauled Carr half up with one hand, with the other striking him back-handed across the face. Again and again he beat Carr, his lips peeled back in a feral grimace, his breath a harsh rasp punctuated by the sound of his fists meeting Carr's face.

Dear God, thought Favor. Carr had killed the mother. Now the son would kill the father. Merrick blood running true. No! She knew Raine. No matter how evil Carr was, Raine could never endure commit- ting the sin of patricide.

"Raine!" she cried, struggling upright and stum- bling across the room. "No!"

He looked up, his face savage, and she flung her arms around his neck, pressing herself to him. "No, Raine! For my love, please, I beg you stop!"

A heartbeat. Another. She felt Carr fall to her feet

and then Raine seized her in a tight embrace, his arms trembling.

"He's nothing to us. Nothing," she whispered fervently. "Let him go, Raine."

"He killed my mother! He's killed and wounded and . . . Dear God, Favor, he's a plague that needs to be wiped out!"

"But not by you. Not by me. Look at him, Raine. He'll not be going anywhere. Jamie's outside now. We'll give him to Jamie and let the McClairen decide his fate."

"No!" Raine shook his head violently. "You don't know him! He'll get away!"

"No, he won't," Favor said, pleading. Her hand moved down Raine's body, grew sticky with blood. He was wounded. Bleeding copiously. Carr wasn't worth debating while Raine bled to death. "Let *it* go. As you asked me, so I beg you. I love you. Be *mine*."

"I've nothing to give you," he said harshly. "Nothing but the assurance that this . . . creature will never be able to harm you again. Let me give you that, Favor," he pleaded in a hoarse voice. "Let me do that, at least, for you."

Her hands crept up and cupped his wounded face in tender palms. "You've already given me more than I dreamed the world contained," she returned, her voice aching with love. "All I want is within your ability to give. Your heart."

" 'Tis already yours."

"Then don't take it away from me. Let him live."

He did not hesitate this time; his capitulation came

with his kiss, tender, yearning, and reverent. He lifted her in his arms and buried his face against her throat.

"No," she protested. "Your side."

" 'Tis no great matter," he murmured.

Below, Carr stirred. Favor turned in Raine's embrace as Carr fumbled to hands and knees, his handsome face battered beyond recognition, his clothes torn and stained with blood.

"You haven't any more guts now than you did as a child," he muttered, his voice thick and muddled. "You haven't inherited anything from me, not guts, not brains, not looks. Nothing of value. Nothing! You never found the Trust, did you?"

"No. I found something infinitely more precious."

At that Carr's face snapped up, a questioning greedy gleam lit his swelling eyes. "What?" he demanded on a choked cough. "What did you find?"

"You'll never know," Raine answered, turning toward Favor. Gently he set her on her feet. Carr's gaze followed Raine's. "I'll kill you if you say a word to her," Raine promised. "If you so much—"

A figure from a child's night terror burst from the portal behind the nave, brandishing a pair of torches. Her face was livid, her mouth a gaping hole, her eyes pinpoints of madness.

"Traitorous bitch!" Muira shrieked. "You've destroyed it all, all my work and planning but you'll not reap the rewards of your treachery! If the McClairens cannot have Maiden's Blush, no one can!"

And she flung the torch into the tinderbox of rotting detritus that was all that was left of Janet McClairen.

Chapter 31

The flames leapt from rotting wood to paper boxes, traveling at breakneck haste. Cloth and books, *papier-mâché* and curtains, linens and leather fed its rapacious hunger. It danced in brilliant waves, bubbled and flowed, enveloping in an instant anything in its path.

A sudden move caught Favor's attention. As she watched, Carr rose and stumbled through the door into the outer hall. "No!" Muira screamed, seeing her quarry escape.

Raine grabbed Favor's arm, yanking her toward the door but her feet caught in her voluminous skirts. She would have fallen had not Raine caught her up in his arms and dashed toward the hall. But the delay cost them dearly.

Muira was quicker.

She darted across the room, waving her second torch in the air, shedding a cloud of living embers in her wake. She halted in the doorway beside the huge ancient armoire teetering under the weight of half-packed crates and boxes. Madly, she feinted at them with her torch, using it like an épée.

Raine reached out to seize her and caught instead the burning end of the torch. With a hiss of pain, he jerked his hand back. Favor darted forward to deal with the madwoman but Raine caught her around the waist and yanked her back just as Muira swung the flaming brand, missing Favor's face by inches. He pushed Favor behind him, scanning the narrowing tunnel of darkness behind the madwoman. Already, Favor could feel the heat from the growing inferno at her back.

"Let her go!" Raine demanded hoarsely.

"Nay! Nay!" Muira shrieked, dancing from side to side. "You'll next have yer pleasure of her in hell, Raine Merrick!" Her expression grew sly; her gaze darted to the side. She touched her torch to the wardrobe's rotting contents, setting it ablaze.

"No!" Raine shouted. Before he could act she grabbed the door of the wobbling armoire and pulled. She jumped back into the open hallway just as it crashed to the floor, choking the entrance with its flaming contents.

In the black corridor, they could see her dart down the hall, touching her torch to anything in her path. And then she stumbled. The torch fell against her skirts, catching fire to them. She shrieked not with pain but with horrific laughter. She spun her way down the hall, a burning effigy, and in seconds was lost to view.

"God have mercy," Favor whispered.

"Hurry!" Raine shouted.

Favor looked behind them. The exit by the altar was unreachable. A wall of liquid flames undulated over the wall behind them, searing the back of her neck and shoulders. They'd only one chance. She hurled herself at the mound of burning crates, grabbing hold of any unlit portion and jerking it away from the doorway. Raine was already working feverishly, hurling crates and trunks away heedless of burning his hands and arms.

Frantically and silently they worked, side by side. Smoke, a churning black miasma, rose toward the high ceiling, already billowing as it sought another egress. In minutes it would envelop them. Already her lungs burned with the noxious fumes and her eyes streamed.

Outside in the hall, the fire had taken hold. It skittered along the floorboards, tasted the walls with hungry licks. It bloomed in orange brilliance at rotted wooden door frames and raced toward the main part of the castle.

Raine seized the edge of the toppled wardrobe and with one enormous grunt shoved it away from the door. Favor darted through the small opening he'd made, reaching back and grasping Raine's wrist.

"Go!" he shouted, trying to pull free. " 'Tis too small. Go! I'll be right behind you!"

She let go, but she didn't leave. She hurled her small

body against the mammoth piece of furniture and pushed with all her strength.

"GO!" he shouted.

"Not"—she gritted her teeth—"without"—she closed her eyes and offered a prayer—"you!" She rammed her shoulder against the monolithic piece.

"Damn you, Favor McClairen!" she heard Raine roar, and then the wardrobe slithered a few blessed inches. He swung himself up and over the armoire, through an opening just wide enough to allow him through, turned, seized her hand, and pulled her to him.

Down the blazing hallway they ran, the snapping and crackling of the flames following them like manic laughter. They burst through the tower doorway into complete blackness, clattering and half-falling down the narrow spiraling steps to the main floor. Muira had done her job well; Wanton's Blush was an inferno.

The castle was burning, set ablaze by a madwoman. Carr crept step by painful step along the hall, heading for his library.

His eyes were swollen nearly shut. A red haze obscured vision that kept fading and then resolving itself. His nose was broken and his head echoed with dull noise. Pain lanced his side with each breath he took. He ignored the pain just as he ignored the deeper agony of being duped by his son—with the aid of that little Scottish heathen.

He'd no time for that now. Already the air in the

stairwell behind him shimmered with heat, the vanguard of the blaze that followed.

The few guests left emerged wild-eyed from the rooms where they'd been carousing, befuddled and stupid as lemmings on a cliff. Wild-eyed and uncertain, they stood frozen, mouthing inanities and pleas for help. Carr ignored them. A few of his footmen screamed for water. Fools! No water could save Wanton's Blush now.

He made it to the door of his library, and with swollen hands fumbled for the key in his pocket and fit it in the lock. A roar like hell's hound boomed above him. Suddenly the ceiling a few yards behind him collapsed. Fire rose like Atlas unchained and surged from the burning timbers, pounced upward, gorging itself on rich tapestries and gilt-framed masterpieces.

Carr ground his teeth in impotent fury and pushed the library door open. He'd little time. Less than little. He lumbered across the room toward the ornately carved mantel and, gritting his teeth in agony, fit his fingernails beneath a tile and pried it up. He shoved his hand down into the revealed compartment and fished until his hand closed on a packet. He removed it, stuffing the bundle beneath his shirt.

He looked at the door leading to the hall. Tendrils of smoke crept beneath it in gentle exploration, insidiously delicate. He turned and hobbled quickly to his adjoining bedchamber, bent on retrieving at least the gold he kept in the trunk beneath Janet's portrait. The thought of Janet brought a snarl to his lips, twisting the cut lips painfully. He reached for the handle and thrust the door open.

The sight that met his gaze sent him reeling backward, gasping and clutching at his chest.

Janet stood beneath her portrait.

She was silhouetted by the fire he insisted always be kept burning in the hearth of his private chambers, posed in profile, her hands folded at her waist. Her chin was tilted up at an angle as though she were studying the picture; a small smile curved her soft lips.

"No!" he whispered.

"Leave here, Ronald." Her voice seemed to come from within his own head, echoing and dim, soft and implacable. She did not turn to face him. Her figure wavered slightly. "Leave here *now*."

She'd come to save him.

Ronald Merrick, Earl of Carr, obeyed the haunt's advice.

"It's barred from outside!" Favor shouted, clawing at Raine's arm as he banged his shoulders again and again into the small door at the foot of the tower stairway. It was pitch black; only a sullen sliver of light beneath the door gave any illumination. "We have to go back up—"

"No! We'll die up there!"

He'd been working to open the door for ten minutes, though it felt like hours. The stone tower had as yet stood proof against the blaze's fury but soon the fire would find entry and they would be burned alive at the tower's base.

"Favor," he said urgently, "I need something with which to pry the hinges off. See what you can do, I'll keep battering at this."

Nodding, Favor scrambled back up the stairs, her hands feeling about for anything to use as a pry bar, her feet sliding over the width of the steps for anything that might be lying there. Halfway to the second story she almost impaled herself on a sharp edge protruding from the wall. She groped until she caught hold of a curved piece of metal. It was an old iron banister some worthy McClairen had fitted along the steep staircase and promptly left to erode. Double blessings on his head.

Favor wrapped her fingers around the cold metal and twisted. The railing moved and she heard plaster pieces falling. She leaned back against the central core of the spiral staircase, braced her foot against the wall and heaved back with all her might. With a distinct snap, a heavy section of metal came loose in her hands.

Panting and triumphant, she clambered down to Raine. Patting her way down his arm, she found his hand and slapped the three-foot section of metal in his palm.

"Now, please, get us out of here," she said.

"Yes, Milady." His tone told her he was smiling. She heard him feeling for the hinge, the scrape of metal against metal as he fit the end beneath the hinge, and then a grunt as he shoved.

The metal snapped.

For a second neither spoke.

"We're going to die here, aren't we?" she asked quietly.

In answer she heard his shoulder strike the door with a loud *boom*, the sound reverberating through the small enclosure.

"Please, Raine," she said. "If we have to die here, I don't want to die without feeling your arms around me once more."

Boom!

"I love you, Raine. I want you to know that."

"God!" His roar was part fury, part supplication.

"Please—"

Strong arms caught her up in a fervent embrace. Lips salty with blood and sweat touched hers in a kiss so tender that tears sprang to her eyes.

"I love you, Favor McClairen Merrick. I would have done everything in my power to make you happy. I swear I would."

"Where would we have gone?" she asked, an unnatural calm overtaking her. How could she feel so content in such a hell? A benefit of loving, she imagined.

"America?" he said, sounding as if he, too, struggled to reconcile himself to this fate but fared far worse than she. "Perhaps . . . India. Yes. I think India."

"It's warm there, is it not?" she asked wistfully. "I never realized how much I like to be warm until I'd returned here."

"I promise, you would have never been cold again," he swore in a rough voice.

"I should have dressed in silk saris and lain beneath white canopies and fed you pomegranates."

"No, sweet one," he replied in a hushed voice. "I would have fed *you* pomegranates and kissed the juice from your lips."

"Then I should have been the first woman on earth to have grown fat on pomegranates," she said, smiling softly.

He did not reply and she felt a shiver pass through him, heard the hiss of a breath drawn in pain. She hurried on, determined to take him away from this black place and, for a brief moment, to the brilliant future they would never know.

She touched his mouth, trying to soothe him. "And how many children would we have had?"

"Dozens." His voice was hushed. "All with shining hair and fierce dark brows and . . . Oh, God, I cannot do this. *I will not do this!*" He pounded his fist against the door.

Silently, it swung open.

She stared as Raine grabbed her hand and pulled her out after him. They were in the front hall, leading to the main staircase. Part of the ceiling had fallen in midway. Flames shot from the hole above and curtained one wall in a sheet of rippling fire.

A footman carrying an empty sack ran far ahead of them and disappeared into the dining room. A scullery maid emerged shrieking from a doorway, beating at the fire climbing up her skirts but refusing to drop the silver tray she carried. She wheeled back into the room from whence she came and was lost to sight.

They stopped. They needed only to make it past the blazing mound of plaster and wood that the ceiling had dumped in the corridor. The heat was intense, scorching their cheeks and singeing their hair. They were so close; they'd need only to turn the corner to be at the front door. But the pile was deep and the flames engulfing it were high.

Abruptly, Raine spun her around. He clutched handfuls of her satin gown and with a mighty jerk, tore the heavy skirts off her. He scooped her up, tossing her over his shoulder and with a muttered oath, ran straight over the pile of burning debris. On the far side he dropped her, slapping his smoldering boots before motioning her ahead. She took hold of his hand. A few more yards. They turned the corner leading to the front entrance.

There, impossibly, set on the floor directly in front of the door to the outside, stood a life-sized portrait of Janet McClairen. Some hand must have set it there, barring that portal. Yet who? It was afire, the painted canvas curling at the corners, little yellow flames lapping from the edges in toward the painted visage, burning away the beautiful one-sided smile, the haughty nose, and the gorgeous too-knowing eyes. As they watched, thunderstruck, Janet's face disappeared exposing the backing and secured to it a large leather satchel. Then the backing, too, caught fire and the pocket dropped from where it had once been lodged.

"Raine . . . ?"

He knelt and quickly retrieved the heavy leather bundle, untying the thong and lifting the flap. A fierce Celtic lion the size of a man's hand glared up at him with marble-sized ruby cabochon eyes.

"McClairen's Trust," Raine murmured.

"Do you think that . . . that someone put it here just for you to find?" she asked. The flames behind them were growing nearer.

Someone had. Raine gazed at the empty picture frame, a scowl hardening his features and then, just as the fire had burned away Janet's lovely visage, the frown disappeared from his face replaced by tenderness and warmth and fierce certainty. He retied the bundle and thrust it inside his shirt.

"Raine?" Favor asked again.

"Aye," he said. "I do. My mother, Favor. She gave it to us as a wedding present and that belief I will carry to my grave."

He held out his hand. She took it.

Together they walked out of the burning castle and down the granite steps and past the huddled, whimpering queues of guests and servants.

And they did not look back.

You met Ashley Merrick in

The
Passionate One.

You got to know his brother, Raine Merrick, in

The
Reckless One.

Now turn the page for an introduction to their younger sister, Fia Merrick. She is . . .

The
Ravishing One.

The third novel in Connie Brockway's breathtakingly romantic McClairen's Isle trilogy will be available from Dell in August 2000.

The Ravishing One

Thomas pushed the door open without knocking.

Though only midafternoon, a half-dozen men crowded Fia's boudoir to offer their opinions on her toilette for the coming evening. They flanked her ornate rosewood dressing table, their primped and carefully painted faces reflected in the huge velvet-draped mirror sitting atop its lacquered surface. One sat on a tufted stool by her feet; another knelt beside her and peered into a silver dish containing several beauty marks. The others stood close. Jonathan was among their number.

His presence alarmed Thomas and disappointed him. He turned his head from his friend, concentrating on the object of Jonathan's attention and that of every other man in the room: Fia, Lady MacFarlane.

In the midst of this coterie of gentlemen, like a rose in a field of bracken, she reclined on a small gilt chair, glorious and feminine and deadly in her fashionable dishabille. Her black tresses spilled in glossy, artful disarray over her spare, smooth white shoulders, naked above the filigreed lace that edged the deep bodice of her dressing gown. Sheer shell-pink silk flowed along the curves of her body and pooled about her feet. When she was a child, her beauty had been disconcerting; now that she was a woman, it was devastating. An untried boy would never be able to resist such as she—especially if she'd targeted him.

She'd not remarked his entrance, Thomas noted bitterly. Why would she? What could one man more in her chambers mean to her? What had the absence of one boy meant? Nothing.

He approached her directly, boldly cutting through the ranks of admirers until he stood within a few feet of her. The men turned their heads, looking irritated at finding a new contender for Fia's attention. But when they saw what he carried, their irritation gave way to alarm.

Thomas lifted the blood-smeared épée like a talisman and pitched it into the air, seizing the middle of the bare blade in his equally bare fist, feeling the bloodied edge cut into his palm. The men's mutters faded, the room grew still with hushed expectancy, and Fia, who'd been speaking to the poor sot kneeling beside her, froze too.

Slowly she turned her head, her eyes still downcast, as if to first assess his presence with other senses besides sight. Her lashes swept across the creamy curve of her high cheekbones. She was unearthly beautiful.

He waited for her to look up. She would acknowledge him, damn her, before he spoke. Her brow knotted, then smoothed and slowly, with what seemed to him trepidation, her gaze rose to his. By God! Her eyes were just as startling a blue as he'd remembered. Mayhap more so.

"Lord Donne." Her voice was slight, breathless. She looked frightened, cornered, but she hadn't yet dropped her gaze to the épée he clenched.

"Lady MacFarlane."

"I say, Lady MacFarlane, who is this fellow?" a swarthy youngster asked.

"Lord Donne is a . . . very old . . . friend of the family's." Her lips curled with sarcasm. Her eyes remained locked with his.

"Thomas?" Jonathan spoke from his side. His voice held one note of confusion, another of concern.

For an instant Thomas was locked in her gaze's sapphire embrace, until the pain of the blade cutting his palm recalled him to his purpose. He didn't want to be here. He'd thought himself done with the Merricks years before and he resented her having drawn him back into their poisonous web. He also resented the regret that rose within him as he registered the fine lines at the corners of her magnificent eyes, the shadow of a downward pull at the corners of her still, full mouth. He steeled himself against any compassion these subtle signs of weariness awoke.

She played havoc with men's hearts and lives. Now she must pay the price of her sport.

"I've brought you a memento," Thomas said.

Twin lines of consternation appeared between the dark wings of her brows. "A memento?"

"Of a particularly successful seduction."

"Thomas . . ." Jonathan laid a cautioning hand on his forearm. Thomas ignored the friend who'd fallen under her thrall—a fitting term, for Fia was certainly a siren, or a witch, or some other black-hearted sorceress. He could think of her as nothing less, for couldn't he himself feel the draw of her, the potent attraction she wielded with such blithe disregard?

"Here." He dropped the bloodied blade on her lap. "You can add this to your collection."

Instinctively, she recoiled from the sword. A dark red stain instantly marked the pale fabric of her gown. He waited, the pulse beating thick and urgent in his veins. He could not see her expression. Her face remained bowed over the blade, her hands arrested in the air above it, her tumbled locks masking her face.

"What is this?" she asked in a low, hoarse voice.

"By God, Thomas, you go too far!"

"Do I?" His gaze slew to Jonathan, white-faced and trembling by his side. "And here I'd thought *she'd* gone too far, for 'twas for her sake the boy offered himself up to be used as a demonstration of Tunbridge's art. For her—"

"What boy?" she interrupted, her head snapping up.

"Are there so many, then?" His smile felt like a rictus.

"*What boy?*"

"I'd best describe him lest you never knew his name," he said, failing to achieve the cavalier tone he attempted. "A boy of eighteen years but who looked younger. Fair-haired and fair-skinned—"

"Oh, no. Not Pip," she murmured. Her eyes were tragic, and for a moment his resolve wavered. But then, he remembered, she had an audience to woo.

"I see you do recall him. He'll be so gratified. Phillip Constable. Pip. Not rich Pip, not powerful Pip, but as capable of love as any grown man. Indeed"—his gaze swept through the group of posers like the blade he'd so recently discarded—"more so. But then, the young love so ardently, so wholeheartedly, don't they? So very, very foolishly."

"Yes," she said, lifting her head to a defiant angle, "or so I've been told. Where is he now? What happened?"

He tallied the brightness of her eyes, the adamantine quality of her expression. She waited, seemingly remorseless, demanding, regal, and haughty.

"Your name was being besmirched," he said. "Pip would have none of it. The young fool challenged Tunbridge to a duel. Tunbridge accepted. They fought. Young Pip, as you can see"—he jerked his chin in the direction of the bloodstained épée—"lost."

She shuddered slightly. "Is he dead?" she asked.

"Not yet. The blade pierced the meat of his breast but no vital organs." The tension in her eased. She wasn't going to get off so comfortably. "If he's very lucky, no infection will set in and he'll live to learn a lesson from his ill-advised gallantry. *If* he's lucky."

"Perhaps we all will," she said softly before raising accusing eyes. "And what of you? Apparently you have some feelings for . . . this boy. Could you not have stopped it?"

"I knew nothing of the duel." How dare she place the onus of Pip's fate on him! And why should he feel the need to defend himself to her? Guilt made his voice harsh. "Only happenstance led me in their direction. I heard the clash of steel and followed the sound. It did not go on very long. Pip is not much of a swordsman."

And having been stung by her inference that he had let the boy challenge so superior an opponent, he repaid her in kind—by attacking. "When did *you* first come upon him? Pip, that is. You could have circumvented this, then, by simply *letting the lad be*. He couldn't have presented much of a challenge. Not for you."

"No," she said tautly. "No challenge at all."

" 'Sblood, man," Jonathan burst out. "Continue and I'll be forced to call you out myself!"

Fia put her hand down on the chair's arm and pushed herself upright. The sword clattered to the floor.

The sharp sound shattered the paralysis that held the other men in its grip. The swarthy young man Thomas had noted earlier pushed the others aside and moved to confront Thomas. With one fluid movement he struck Thomas across the cheek.

"Name the place, sir!" the dark youngster ground out.

"No."

"Coward!" another man spat out in disgust.

The dark youth's jaw bulged in frustration. He raised his hand to deliver a backhanded blow to Thomas's other cheek, but before he could do so Thomas caught his wrist in midair.

"Don't do it, son," he said coldly. "She's not worth a broken jaw, let alone your life." To emphasize his point, he tightened his grip until he felt bones grind together. The youngster's brows snapped together in startled pain. Helplessly he tried to yank free, but Thomas's grip had been honed holding his own weight one-handed from a yardarm fifty feet above deck while he secured a sail with the other.

"I will not tolerate your insult to this lady!" the young man panted, his fear causing his voice to break.

"Thomas, desist!" Jonathan commanded as harsh exclamations erupted around them. Faces grew livid. Hands clenched.

"Stop it!" Fia's voice rose above the ensuing clamor. "Let him go!"

Thomas turned on her with a snarl. "Don't fret, Madame. Your *snowy* conscience will not be marred on my account." He looked back at the youngster twisting angrily in his grip. "You can call me out as many times as you like. *Sir*." His gaze swept over the shocked, angry faces of the others. "Any one of you can, but you won't find any satisfaction. Not now, not ever. Enough blood has been spilled because of her and her own.

And from the look of you pitiful fools"—he included Jonathan in his scathing scrutiny—"more will be. But not mine. Never mine."

With a muttered oath, Thomas released the youngster's wrist. He snatched it to his chest, backing away.

Thomas waited, so focused on what he was sure would be the pup's fool bid at recompense that he didn't hear or see Fia move. He just suddenly felt her close by. His head swung around. She stood less than an arm's span away, small and delicate and vibrant, Queen Mab by daylight, shimmering in silk and sunlight, her blue eyes brilliant and fierce.

"If *anyone* calls you out, Lord Donne, 'twill be me," she promised in her low, vibrant voice.

"And that," he returned in a matching tone as he turned his back on her and her coterie of sycophants and panderers and strode away, "is one challenge I might accept."

He paced across the chamber through the door and down the hallway. And so did not hear her whisper in a voice so low even those nearby did not make out her words, "*En garde!*"